Along Comes a Legend

by
Tammy L. Boulds

PublishAmerica
Baltimore

First printing

ISBN: 1-4137-0144-2
PUBLISHED BY PUBLISHAMERICA, LLLP
www.publishamerica.com
Baltimore

Printed in the United States of America

To my mom and dad, for always having faith in me.
I love you both very much.

Chapter One
New Mexico Territory

It was going to be a very long day. The air was close and thunder could be heard in the distance. Charlie McCuan was sitting in the saddle, eyes alert, following the movement of the cattle and ranch hands. The cattle were becoming restless, no doubt about it, they were in for some rough weather.

Charlie had worked on the Circle Bar M ranch for a very long time. Being the oldest of four, there had always been a lot of responsibility. Charlie was lost deep in thought, until a loud voice yelled in the distance.

Gimpy Jones was the ranch foreman of the Circle Bar M. He reported everything back to James McCuan, the owner and just as luck would have it, Charlie's father. Charlie absolutely hated him!

Gimpy's horse skidded to a halt, throwing dust and dirt up in Charlie's face. "Are you goin' to do a lick of work today?" Gimpy asked.

Charlie looked up, with eyes the color of night, and stared at him. "Why don't you get the hell off my back."

"You know your pa won't like you slackin' off'n your work, and you know we gots to move all these here cattle afore this storm breaks," Gimpy yelled.

Charlie would like to tell Gimpy what to do with the cattle, but decided not to. Life was hard enough without stirring up more trouble. Jamming the floppy hat down tight, Charlie slapped the reins against the horse's rump, racing back toward the cattle.

They were moving the cattle as fast as they could, but the storm seemed to be catching up. The cattle had become spooked and wild eyed, which made the men nervous. They all knew there was nothing worse than a bunch of out of control cattle. Everything was moving at a pretty good speed, until a bolt of lightning came out of the sky and hit the ground.

After the lightning struck the ground, Charlie didn't have time to think, the cattle started running and the ranch hands were chasing after them, trying to head them off. In a matter of a few seconds, all hell had broken loose.

One of the ranch hands, Jigger O'Reilly, was standing in the stirrups. He was shouting something and pointing in the direction the cattle were running, but the noise from the cattle and storm was too loud.

Looking in the direction that Jigger was pointing. "Oh my God," Charlie whispered. Standing in the path of the stampeding cattle, were a man and a small child. After a little hesitation, Charlie spurred the horse into a ground-eating run, praying that they would reach the man and child before it was too late.

Garrett Steele saw the cattle moving closer, but there was no place for him and his little sister Maddie to go. They were standing in the middle of an open range. Maddie started crying and Garrett really couldn't blame her, he felt like crying to. "Don't cry Maddie, we'll be alright," he said, but he didn't know for sure what to do. He was looking around for a place to hide, when he saw a horse and a rider moving very fast toward them. "Please God," he prayed, "let him reach us in time."

Charlie was bearing down on the man and child fast, but the storm had picked up speed, as well as the cattle. Leaning low in the saddle, Charlie shouted, "Grab my arm and swing up behind me."

Garrett picked Maddie up and was waiting. Charlie was almost to them. He braced his feet waiting for the impact. They were running all out and Charlie had his arm extended. Garrett grabbed hold of Charlie's arm as the horse flew by. He landed firmly on the rump of the big muscled horse, with his sister in front of him.

"Hold on, we're goin' to get the hell out'a here," shouted Charlie. The horse never slowed down until they were well out of danger.

A safe distance away, the horse came to a slow stop, he was breathing hard. Garrett slid to the ground taking Maddie with him. Looking up into the darkest eyes he had ever seen, he extended his hand. "Thanks mister, I don't know what my sister and I would have done without you."

Charlie just sat there looking down, sort of thunderstruck, because you see, Charlie was short for Charlene and she was staring down at the most handsome man she had ever seen. Now just where in the hell had that come from, she thought, shaking her head completely disgusted with herself.

"Well, are you going to answer me or not?" Garrett asked.

She looked him straight in the eye, the prettiest gray eyes she had ever seen. "Mister, you don't have the sense God gave a goose. Don't you know, you just don't stand there when there's a bunch of spooked cattle runnin' right at you," she said.

By this time, the rain was coming down in buckets, but the cattle had moved on past them. Garrett stared at Charlie with his mouth hanging wide open. "You're not a man, you're a girl."

Leave it to a man Charlie thought. "Well I'm glad to find out that you're not blind and stupid. You're just plain stupid."

That was about all Garrett could take; his nerves were worn to a frazzle. He moved so suddenly that Charlie never even saw him move, but she found herself standing nose to chest with him when he jerked her off her horse. "I've had about all that smart mouth I can take," Garrett growled. Maddie, who had been quiet all this time, started crying for him. "Now see what you've done, you've made my little sister cry." He released his hold on Charlie who was still staring at the buttons on his broad chest and moved to scoop Maddie up in his strong arms, holding her tight. "It will be all right sweetheart, we're safe now," Garrett crooned.

The ranch foreman, Gimpy Jones, had circled back around to see if Charlie was ok, but the ground was getting muddy and his horse was beginning to struggle. He slapped the ends of the reins hard against the tired animal. Sometimes Gimpy could be very cruel to animals and humans alike. He jerked his horse to a halt, the tired animal screaming in pain. Looking down at Charlie. "Get your lazy ass back on that horse missy, afore I tell your pa." Then turning to Garrett, who was standing still holding Maddie tight against his chest, he spat on the ground next to Garrett's boot. "What in the hell are you doin' out here in the middle of nowhere mister?" he asked.

Before Garrett could answer, Charlie stomped over to stand nose to nose with Gimpy, he was really short, which was a real sore spot to him. "You know what you can do with your orders don't you Gimp. You can shove 'em straight up your —" she stopped before she could finish, Garrett had interrupted.

Garrett started moving closer to the quarreling pair, when he heard the argument starting to heat up. "Now listen, there is no need for everyone to get upset. I'm sure this can all be worked out, and besides, all this yelling is going to upset my sister again," he said.

"Mister, since you don't have no dog in this fight, just mind your own damn business," Charlie said, looking up at him. Her eyes were shooting fire and Garrett could hardly look away. The rain had finally slowed to a drizzle, but they were all soaked to the bone and Charlie was in no mood to argue with either one of them. She started walking toward her horse when strong hands spun her around and she came face to face with a very angry ranch foreman. She closed her eyes, knowing what would happen next. But suddenly the rough hands were jerked loose from her arms, she slowly opened her eyes just in time to see Gimpy flying backwards, hitting the ground with a splat, right in the middle of a great big mud hole.

"Don't you ever let me see you strike a lady," Garrett said, in a low, threatening voice. He was shaking with anger, as he watched Gimpy climb to his feet. He scooped Maddie up, holding her tight, and slowly walked away in the direction from which they had came.

Charlie was stunned. First of all, he had stood up for her, but what was truly amazing was that he had called her a lady. Her mother had always said miracles happen every day, if you believe. The only problem was she didn't believe anymore, until now. She climbed back on her horse, moving off in the same direction that the man and child had taken only minutes before.

Chapter Two

Hearing a horse behind him, Garrett turned to see Charlie trotting toward him. He stopped, waiting for her to catch up.

Charlie stopped her horse beside Garrett and Maddie. She looked down at the little girl for the first time. She was squeezing Garrett's hand so tight, her pudgy little fingers had turned white. She had coal black hair and brilliant green eyes, not like Garrett's eyes, which looked like an overcast winter day. She had a round face and very fair skin, but with a healthy appearance. Charlie touched her own face with work-roughened hands, sometimes wishing her life was different than it was now. But it wasn't and probably never would be.

Maddie whispered into Garrett's ear. "Is this lady going to help us with our wagon?"

"I don't know yet sweetheart, maybe," Garrett said, looking at Maddie, then glancing up at the girl sitting astride the horse. A slow smile spread across his face. If she was to clean up a little and maybe wear something a little more feminine, she might actually be kind of attractive. The longer he thought about the idea, the more absurd it sounded. Hell! Her hat was jammed on so tight that you couldn't even see what color her hair was. Just where had that notion come from, he had absolutely no idea, but he had to get that wild idea out of his head. Besides, never in a million years would he be attracted to a female like that. Trying to get his thoughts under control, he snorted loudly, thinking he had been without a woman for too long.

Charlie was brought back from her daydreaming by a loud snort. She turned her attention back to the man standing in front of her. He was just about the best looking man she had ever seen, but the only men she had to compare to were the ranch hands that worked for her father. But whom was she kidding, anyone looked good compared to them. They all worked hard because her pa demanded it and they usually smelled bad to, but sometimes so did she. But this man was different, he looked good and smelled kind of nice to, probably better than she did right now.

She pulled her hat down lower over her eyes to study him a little closer, without getting caught. She let her eyes roam over him. He was tall, around six feet. He had broad shoulders and long muscular legs. His hair wasn't quite as dark as his sisters; it looked more like the cinnamon that Mrs. Pruitt sprinkled on her apple pies. She also noticed that his hair was shorter than most men; it hung just below his collar. But what drew her attention most was his smooth deep voice. It was hard to explain, but it made her feel calm and excited all at the same time. She had never experienced any of these feelings before. One thing was for sure, standing around daydreaming about long legs and smooth voices wasn't going to get much work done.

Garrett cleared his throat for the second time before he got Charlie's attention. "Do you think you can help fix our wagon? We broke an axle in a hole and I can't fix it by myself."

"Where did you leave your wagon at?" Charlie asked as she slid off her horse.

He knew he was staring, but he couldn't help it. The rain had soaked her clothes and they were sticking to her body like a second skin. She had a mind-boggling figure. She was about average height–maybe five-foot-four, but that was *all* that was average. She had more curves than the map of the mountains he had studied and they were in all the right places. It just didn't add up, he usually liked very slender builds, almost on the verge of being skinny, but this lady was anything but skinny. She had a fantastic shape. She seemed to be casting a spell over him. The front of his jeans were becoming a little snug, he was having some pretty erotic thoughts about what he would like to do to that well-endowed body.

The smile quickly vanished from his face when he realized Charlie was shouting.

"If you don't stop starin' at me like that, I'm goin' to shoot you." He watched her lift Maddie up in the saddle and swing up behind her. She wheeled her horse around and rode off heading in the direction of the wagon.

Garrett walked along thinking about Charlie. No woman had ever affected him like this. He just couldn't afford to lose his concentration, not now. He had too much riding on the outcome of this trip. He had to get his mind on business. But that was easier said than done. The only thing he had on his mind right now was the way Charlie's nice round bottom looked in the saddle as she rode away. He knew he was in trouble—serious trouble.

Chapter Three

When they reached the place where Garrett had left the wagon, the sun had come out and it was starting to get very hot. Charlie and Maddie were warm, but Garrett was just about to melt. He had walked all the way back to the wagon. The only good thing about the heat was that it dried out their clothes. When Garrett stopped beside Charlie's horse, he heard Maddie laughing about something. It had been a very long time since she had laughed about anything and he loved the sound of it.

"What are you laughing about Maddie?" asked Garrett, grinning.

"Charlie said you looked like you had been drug through a knothole backwards," she giggled.

He cut his eyes around at Charlie. Her eyes were shining with mischief and she was trying hard not to laugh. "Well, you can tell Charlie, that she looks like she has been wallowing with hogs," Garrett said. He turned around just in time to see the hurt flash across her face and then it quickly disappeared. Garrett wished he hadn't made that last remark, but the damage was already done. He would try to make up for it. He extended his hand, trying to make amends. "It just occurred to me, I don't know your name. I'm Garrett Steele and this is my sister Madeleine Steele, but she prefers Maddie."

Charlie wiped her hand on the leg of her pants before shaking his hand. "I'm Charlie, just plain Charlie. Glad to meet you Steele." The moment their hands touched, there was an odd sensation that passed between them. Charlie jerked her hand away, rubbing it on her shirt.

Garrett couldn't understand what the hell was wrong with him. He had known lots of women in his twenty-eight years, but none of them had ever affected him this way, especially one dressed like a man.

Maddie broke the tension between them. "Are you going to help us fix our wagon? I'm getting kind of tired," she said, yawning.

After what seemed like hours, but only about forty-five minutes, Garrett and Charlie had the wagon fixed and ready to go. Garrett was looking around for Maddie and on the verge of panicking, when Charlie pointed to the back of the wagon. His chest got a little tight. Maddie was curled up on the supplies, sound asleep.

"Have you been taking care of her long?" Charlie asked.

"About three years, ever since our parents died. We only have each other now," Garrett replied softly.

"She's a very beautiful child Steele. How old is she?" Charlie asked, her voice just barely above a whisper.

"Please call me Garrett. Maddie just turned nine, she was only six when our parents died."

Charlie was quiet for a minute. She looked at the sleeping child and smiled, thinking about her mother, who had died six years earlier. Her mother, Audree McCuan, was always laughing She missed her mother so much it hurt. She loved her brothers and sister, but she loved her mother in a special way. She had always made Charlie feel good about herself. Charlie had never been real pretty and she was a little on the plump side, but her mother always saw the best in her. If her mother had still been alive, her life would be so very different.

Garrett cleared his throat. "Excuse me, Miss Charlie, but Maddie and I need to be moving on. So if you will give me directions to the Circle Bar M, we'll be on our way."

Charlie looked up slow, her dark eyes shining. "What kind of business do you have at the Circle Bar M?"

"I need to speak to the owner about a very important matter," Garrett replied.

Charlie didn't hear him; she was lost deep in thought. Just what the hell kind of trouble was her pa cooking up this time— you could bet it wasn't good. She turned her attention to Garrett as he was talking to her. "What was that you were saying, Steele?"

"If you don't know the way, maybe you could tell me how to reach the nearest ranch, maybe, they can give me directions to the Circle Bar M."

"What's this important matter you need to take up with the owner?" Charlie asked between clenched lips.

"My business is with the owner of the ranch, not you," Garrett said. He was becoming annoyed; this woman could irritate the hell out of him pretty quick. "Do you know the way or am I just wasting my time?"

Charlie tilted her hat back. "Oh! I know the way all right, you see my pa, James McCuan, owns the Circle Bar M," she spat. She stomped over to her horse, swinging into the saddle. "If you're sure you have business with my pa, just follow me."

Garrett stood there for a moment watching the little wildcat ride off. A small smile appeared on his face, life certainly was not going to be boring over the next few weeks. He climbed up on the wagon seat, turning to check on Maddie. When he found her still asleep, he picked up the reins and released the brake on the wagon, setting the horses in motion. The wagon followed slowly along in the direction Charlie had gone.

Chapter Four

The wagon rolled along slowly. Garrett's thoughts were on the horse and rider in front of him. He just couldn't understand how someone like that could stir his interest and make him so angry, all at the same time. It just didn't make any sense — none at all. They hit a rut in the field, causing the wagon to pitch hard to one side. Garrett, who had been thinking about Charlie, had to work to keep the horses from bolting. Just as he got everything under control, Maddie, who had been thrown against the side of the wagon, started crying for Garrett. Sometimes he wondered if she was ever going to get over waking up scared. She had been like this ever since their parents had died three years earlier. He knew exactly what he had to do.

He pulled the team to a stop, wrapping the reins around the brake handle. He turned in the wagon seat. "Come here, sweet Maddie, let me hold you for a minute. I'm right here and I promise never to leave you," he said softly.

Maddie scrambled up on her knees, crawling over the supplies in the back of the wagon. She held her arms out for Garrett to lift her over the seat. He sat her down on his lap and hugged her close.

"Please, Garrett, you have to promise me, cross your heart and hope to die, that you'll never, ever, leave me all alone," Maddie whispered, wrapping her chubby, little arms around his neck.

Garrett buried his face in her baby fine hair, squeezing her tight. "I will always take care of you, and I promise, cross my heart and hope to die, that I will never leave you," he murmured against her hair.

Charlie stopped her horse, realizing the wagon wasn't following her, and turned to look back. She saw Garrett hugging his sister close. Her lungs almost squeezed shut when she witnessed the embrace they shared. It reminded her of the hugs her mother had given her and her brothers and sister. Charlie jerked her attention back to the present, it didn't pay to let her mind wander and her life was never going to be the same anyway. She wheeled her horse around and started for the stopped wagon.

Garrett could hear the hoof beats coming closer, the rain had dulled the sound, but he knew she was almost there. He loosened his hold on his sister, "Are you feeling any better now?" Maddie nodded her head against his chest. "Do you think it will be all right for us to start moving again?" he asked quietly.

"If I can sit up here, so I can be close to you. Besides, I can see better from up here anyway." She smiled up at him with tears shining in her eyes.

He knew at that particular moment that there was nothing he wouldn't do for that little girl. "If you promise to hold on tight, you can ride beside me." He felt her squeeze his thigh and he picked up the reins, waiting for the whirlwind, that was about the only word that could describe her, to reach the wagon. He didn't have to wait very long.

The horse slid to a practiced halt in the wet grass, sending clumps of mud flying into the air next to the wagon. "Steele, do you think you might be able to pick up the pace just a little. We have a pretty good distance still yet to cover and you're not movin' the fastest to begin with. But with you startin' and stoppin' every whipstitch, we'll be out here all damn night," Charlie complained.

At first Garrett just stared at her. He had never heard a lady talk like this before, not that he considered himself refined. But this lady, she could fire those words so fast, he couldn't keep up. And the bad thing was, he couldn't wait to hear her voice again, which was only a very short time.

"Is there something wrong with your mind or are you one of them slow-witted fellers? Now, I would have pegged you for one of them there dandies maybe, but not slow-witted," Charlie drawled.

Garrett looked at her and burst out laughing. He just never knew what was going to come out of her mouth next. And he loved it!

"My sister woke up scared, Miss Charlie and I had to stop and try to calm her down. She's better now. And just for the record," he said with a grin, "I'm not slow-witted, nor am I a dandy."

Charlie pushed her hat back on her head. "If you don't have no problems with your mind, then it shouldn't be too hard for you to understand. We've got to get movin' and another thing, my name is Charlie, just plain old Charlie, not Miss Charlie, or anything else. Got that?" She turned her horse toward the ranch, but she was already dreading going home. Her pa would be all bent out of shape because Gimpy had probably ridden straight to the ranch, just to tell him what had happened, and as the hands were always saying, she had stepped in it with both feet this time.

Garrett slapped the reins across the muscled backs of the horses and the wagon lurched forward. "When we get to the ranch, I need to speak to your father immediately, it can't wait. And I'm sure he will feel the same way. Did you hear what I said Miss Charlie?" Garrett yelled after her. He felt a slight tug on his pants. He looked down at this sister.

"She told you not to call her that Garrett. Why are you being mean to her, don't you like her?" Maddie asked very seriously.

Garrett was looking straight ahead, watching the horse and rider. "I like her just fine, it just seems that I can't help myself. I catch myself trying to aggravate her on purpose," he said. He knew that she didn't hear that last remark; she was too far ahead of them.

As Charlie urged her horse forward, she thought to herself, if you knew my pa, Garrett Steele, you wouldn't be in such a hurry to meet him. They were moving in the direction of the ranch once again. The closer they got, the more nervous Charlie became. Sweat started popping out on her forehead; she hated going home. If it wasn't for her brothers and sister, she would never go home again. She would just keep right on riding, never once looking back.

She swiped her shirtsleeve over her heated face. "If only my mother was still alive," she whispered. When her mother was alive, she believed in miracles, but not now.

Chapter Five

The Circle Bar M Ranch was located about twenty miles outside Broken Tongue, New Mexico. It was a large two-story log house with a wrap around porch to help keep the house cool in the hot New Mexico sun. Flowers were growing in abundance next to the steps of the house, front and back, and they were well cared for. Several large barns and corrals surrounded the main house. Horses and cattle were plentiful, so were cowboys, some young and some old. From all appearances the ranch was very well maintained and prosperous.

The atmosphere at the ranch was always a little tense. Everyone always walked around on pins and needles. The ranch hands knew what to expect, as well as those that lived in the main house. Each day everyone held his or her breath, waiting and wondering, when the next violent eruption would take place. And the cause was always the same, James McCuan, the owner of the Circle Bar M. He ruled with an iron fist, had a nasty temper and was just mean. And today was no exception.

James McCuan was not a large man, but what he lacked in size, he sure made up for it with his ugly temperament. Those that he associated with usually give him plenty of room, not wanting to make him mad. And he almost always gets his way. He had reached the boiling point today. The hands were late getting back with the cattle and some horses had broken down a gate. The men were chasing them right now. He was just totally and royally pissed off!

He was just lighting up a cigar when he heard pounding hoof beats coming closer to the house. Grumbling loudly, he swung his booted feet off of the desk and stood. With his boot heels ringing loudly on the polished wooden floor, he made his way to the front door. Just as he opened the door, Gimpy Jones swung down out of the saddle, before the horse had come to a complete stop.

"Where in the hell have you been?" James shouted.

Pushing his hat up on his forehead. "Maybe you should ask that no account daughter of yours," Gimpy said. If he had a hold of her right now, he would probably choke her. She was always making him look like a fool, but today had been even worse. One of these days he was going to get even.

James didn't like waiting for answers. "You're the one standing in front of me, not my daughter. Now I'm going to ask you one more time," he shouted. He looked down at the ranch foreman's pants, noticing the dried mud clinging to his pants and boots. He knew without asking, that Charlie was probably the one responsible. "I'm not going to wait much longer, then I'm going to beat an answer out of you," he said angrily.

Gimpy eyed the boss, sometimes he would like to knock the shit right out of him. "The boys just got all the cattle moved into the south pasture, they'll be along any minute. We ran into a storm, about an hour ago. The cattle got spooked and we had a hell of a time. We would have been done in plenty of time if Charlie had let me push 'em a little harder," he growled.

James was chewing on the end of his cigar. "Is she with the cattle?" he asked through gritted teeth. He was going to have to take that girl in hand.

"Hell, I don't have any idea where the pain in the ass is at," Gimpy replied. "The last time I saw her, she was goin' off with some man and kid. It was right after the storm broke. The cattle 'bout near ran that feller down, but she managed to tote 'em out of the way."

The dull thud of hoof beats drew both men's attention. The Circle Bar M hands were just riding through the gate. James was searching the riders, looking for his daughter, and he was getting angrier by the minute, because it appeared she wasn't with them. "If she isn't back by dark, I want you to take a few men back out and look for her. And when you find her, bring her back. I don't care if you have to hog-tie her, just bring her back." He turned, entering the house, heading straight for the kitchen.

In the kitchen, Mrs. Pruitt, the housekeeper, heard the front door slam. She had heard the men shouting in front of the house and knew that James was angry. Sometimes she wondered why she had stayed so long, but she couldn't leave the children. They were like her own. "You had better go to your room Taylor. I hear your father coming and he sounds like he's angry again." She helped the little girl untie the apron that was wrapped around her narrow body, she was such a sweet child. She would never let any harm come to this child, or any of the others.

"Do ya think Pa is mad at Charlie again?" Taylor asked nervously. She was already beginning to shake with fear. She knew her pa and Charlie got into some awful arguments. Most of the time Charlie would take the blame for everything. Pa would get so mad that he would hit her. Austin and Tristen, their twin brothers, would say if they were a little older that they'd wallop Pa for hitting Charlie. But they just weren't big enough yet.

"You know it doesn't take much to make your father mad. You go to your room and everything will be alright, I promise," Mrs. Pruitt said softly. Today was going to be different. James was not going to strike his oldest daughter. She had been silent to long – things were going to change today. She turned as the thud of boots come closer.

He was furious. If Charlie had run off with some man, he would kill both of them. Besides, who would have her. She wasn't pretty and she was short and fat. He worked her like a mule, but she still didn't lose any weight. He just couldn't understand what any man would see in her.

"Where the hell is the kids at?" he shouted, as he stepped into the kitchen.

"Taylor is in her room and the boys are down at the barn helping Jack clean stalls," Mrs. Pruitt said, wiping her hands slowly. She always made sure Jack, one of the oldest hands on the ranch, was always close to the boys. He would watch over them, make sure they were well away from their father most of the day.

"It's a good thing they're working and not laying around reading them damn books. They waste too much time daydreaming about all those places they read about." James was pacing back and forth across the kitchen floor.

"Education is not a waste of time. Audree would have wanted them all to learn," Mrs. Pruitt said. She studied him a little longer. "Is Charlie down at the barn with the men? I just saw them ride by," she asked.

A string of curses left his lips; he was really mad. "Gimpy said she took off with some man about an hour ago. They were moving cattle and came across this fellow. And she just up and left with him. I've sent some men out to look for her. I'll tell you one thing, she'll be sorry when they find her and bring her back. I'll make sure she never does a thing like this again."

"Send word down to Gimpy that I'll be in my office when they get back. I'm going to knock some sense into that girl tonight. She will learn to listen to me," he said with a sneer. He turned to leave the kitchen.

"Mr. McCuan, you will not hurt that girl. I should have said something a long time ago. I'm going to protect these children, if it's the last thing I do. I love them!" She moved closer, raising her head to look him straight in the eye. "You have four beautiful children and I'm not going to let you hurt any of them again." She held her ground waiting for the explosion.

He stopped dead in his tracks, spinning around to face his housekeeper. His eyes were bulging and the veins in his neck looked ready to burst. He stormed back to stand in front of her. "What did you just say to me?" he asked, shaking with uncontrolled anger. "I'll have you know, those are my kids and I'll treat them any damn way I want to. They're all lazy, just like their mother. She was worthless to. I wanted all boys, she only gave me two boys and they're both book worms," he shouted.

Something inside Mrs. Pruitt snapped. "Let me tell you something," she said, pointing her finger at him. "The only worthless person on this ranch...is you! You stomp, curse, and yell at everyone. All the neighbors are afraid of you, your own children are terrified of you." She stepped back, watching him closely.

"Get your bags packed you old bitch and leave. I never wanted you here," he said through gritted teeth.

"I am not leaving. Audree asked me to look after her children, and that's exactly what I'm going to do." She knew she had pushed him into a corner, she only hoped she hadn't pushed him too far.

He stood facing her, fist clenched at his side. "I'm telling you one last time, then I'm going to kick you off this ranch. Get the hell off my property," he shouted. He glanced out the kitchen windows. When he noticed Jack and the twins walking toward the house, he realized their voices had probably carried down to the barn, they had been shouting pretty loud. Hearing movement from the direction of the small bedrooms, Taylor, he thought. "Just stay the hell away from me," he said, before turning and walking away.

There was a knock at the back door. When Mrs. Pruitt finally started breathing again, she walked to the door on trembling legs. Opening the door, she found Jack and both boys waiting.

"Are you all right?" Jack asked quietly. He gathered her close, wanting to take away part of her fear.

Tristen and Austin, the twins, pushed past both of them, stepping into the kitchen, their faces ghostly white. "You scared us to death," they both said at the same time. Just then Taylor, who had been standing in the hallway, come running in, grabbing Mrs. Pruitt around the waist. Her tears soaking the front of Mrs. Pruitt's apron.

Laying her hand on the back on the little girl's head. "I'm fine. For a while there, I wasn't so sure. But he's gone now. Children did you hear what I told your father? I'm not going to let him hurt you ever again."

Taylor looked up with tears on her cheeks. "He doesn't really hurt us, he only yells at us. It's Charlie that he's mean to," she said, starting to cry harder.

"I'm going to take care of Charlie to, we all will. Charlie has taken care of all of us for too long. She takes the punishment for everything that goes wrong. But that's going to stop," Mrs. Pruitt said. She looked around the kitchen, wondering if everyone agreed with her.

They were all standing with their heads down, thinking about what Mrs. Pruitt had just said. A shout from the front part of the house startled them. It was Gimpy's voice. Charlie was home. They hurried through the house, trying to beat James, but they were all too late. He was already waiting on the front porch. And he was furious!

Chapter Six

Charlie was riding slightly ahead of the wagon, but the closer they got to the ranch, the slower she moved. She could see the gate in the distance and was already starting to worry. Pulling back gently on the reins, her horse come to a stop. The wagon wasn't to far behind, but she decided to wait for it to catch up.

"Mr. Steele, you're about to meet the owner of the Circle Bar M," Charlie said as the wagon rolled to a stop beside her.

"Is it just through that gate?"

"Yes, you'll be able to see the house before too much longer." Charlie sat wondering if all the hands were back yet. She knew Gimpy would already be there. He had probably been back for some time, telling her pa just what had happened. And probably adding a little bit. Looking over at Garrett. "Are you ready to meet James McCuan, Mr. Steele?"

Garrett noticed that her face had gotten very pale. "The faster we get there, the sooner I'll be able to take care of my business with your father. I'm sure we can come to some kind of understanding. Actually, I'm kind of looking forward to meeting him."

Charlie sat stunned, her mouth hanging down to the saddle horn. "Trust me, meeting my pa is nothin' to look forward to. You should be dreadin' it. And if you think you can reason with him, you've got another think comin'. Your best bet would be to keep that wagon of yours rollin' right on past the gate, and never slow down."

"You act like your father is some sort of monster."

Charlie shifted in the saddle, slowly starting toward the gate. "He is," she said quietly. She rode away from the wagon, her horse slowly carrying her toward home.

Garrett simply stared at her for a moment, not quite comprehending what she had said. The reins were hanging loosely from his long, lean fingers. "Well, sweet Maddie, we're almost home." He looked down at the little girl sitting beside him, she had been very quiet for the past hour.

Maddie was tired. They had been traveling for several weeks to get here. But it didn't matter, because she loved Garrett with all her heart. "I like it here, Garrett. Will we really be able to live here now? You remember what you told me when we started this trip. You said, 'no matter where we live as long as we're together, that's all that matters'. But I hope we can stay here." The pair in the wagon became quiet, waiting for their journey to end.

As Charlie rode through the gate, she squinted, looking for her pa around the house. She didn't have to look very hard. It seemed the whole ranch was at a stand still, they were waiting for her to come home. She could hear the crunch of wagon wheels behind her. Did Garrett know what kind of place he was about to enter? He just didn't understand, nobody could, unless they lived there.

Her stomach was becoming queasy. She spotted her pa standing in the shade of the front porch. He was waiting for her. She thought about stopping and waiting for Garrett and Maddie to catch up, then decided against it. That would only prolong the inevitable. Her horse came to a stop about fifteen feet from where her pa was waiting. When she stepped down out of the saddle, she had to hold on to the saddle horn for support. With her knees trembling, she turned toward the porch, but her pa was already stomping down the steps. She was in for it now!

"Just where in the hell have you been, missy? And don't you be tellin' me no damn lies. Gimpy said you took off with some man. But I know that can't be right, no man would have you," James shouted at the top of his lungs.

Charlie knew better than to interrupt or even look at him, it would just make matters worse. She was gripping her horse's reins tightly in her hand, but when her pa yelled, it spooked her horse.

"Can't you even take proper care of your horse. I guess I'm going to have to sell that one too," he shouted. He was absolutely furious!

She could feel the tears starting to gather in her eyes. Every time she got attached to a horse, her pa would sell it. Over the past few years, she had learned to act like it didn't matter. Because, if her pa didn't think she cared, he would let the animal stay longer. She had even quit naming them. She usually just called them horse.

Not wanting her pa to see the tears in her eyes, she tugged her filthy hat down a little bit lower over her eyes.

"Are you too stupid to answer me? I'm not going to wait very much longer for an answer. What were you doing out there with that man?"

"Nothing Pa, I was just helping him fix his wagon, that's all. It took almost an hour to get it fixed. The axle broke when they hit a hole. I started for home right away," she whispered.

Suddenly her hat was knocked to the ground, rough fingers jerking her head up. Her pa was standing directly in front of her, the anger burning brightly in his eyes. He was going to kill her.

Mrs. Pruitt hurried down the steps, trying to get between them. Austin and Tristen were hot on her heels. Taylor, who had been standing very close to the boys, started to cry. Charlie could hear everything that was going on around her, but there was nothing she could do to protect herself.

"James McCuan, if you harm a single hair on that child's head, I swear I'll shoot you," screamed Mrs. Pruitt.

The twins came to a skidding halt when their Pa turned toward them. "If you two don't get your ass back on that porch, you'll be next." Their faces turned deathly white. They wanted no part of their pa's temper.

Turning to Mrs. Pruitt. "Look you old bitch, if you don't get your nose out of my business, I'm going to take care of you permanently. And that goes for all the rest of you sonofabitches," he said. He looked around at all the ranch hands. "Everybody get back to work. Now!" he shouted.

Turning his attention back to Charlie, he slapped her across the face. "Now that I have your attention," he sneered. "What was you doing out there with that man?" he asked, slapping her again, but even harder this time.

Charlie couldn't think straight, the first blow had stunned her, but the second blow had just about knocked her senseless. She thought she could hear Mrs. Pruitt and the children crying, but her ears were ringing so loudly, she couldn't be positive.

With all the commotion going on, nobody saw the wagon pull into the yard and stop. And they certainly didn't see the very angry man jump from the seat. He hit the ground running and he had steam coming from his ears.

Garrett couldn't believe his eyes. There was a man beating on Charlie, right in the front yard, and nobody was even trying to stop him. He could hear the blows and see her head snapping back from the impact. The bastard was going to kill her. The closer he got, the faster he ran. He tackled the man that was beating on Charlie, but unfortunately all three of them tumbled to the ground.

"Charlie, get out of here!" Garrett yelled, dodging a blow.

She tried to stand up, but she was too dizzy, she couldn't quite get her bearings. Strong arms wrapped around her, dragging her out of the way. She managed to look up, seeing Jack, the ranchhand, smiling down at her. "It will be OK, Charlie," murmured Jack. Before she had time to think, Mrs. Pruitt and the children had surrounded her.

"Oh Lord! Look what he's done to her this time," cried Mrs. Pruitt.

Taylor was sniffling, trying to hold back the tears, but the boys seemed to be watching something in the front yard. Charlie turned her head just in time to see Garrett Steele punch her pa right in the nose, it made an awful crunching sound. Her head was starting to spin, but her last thought before she passed out was, two miracles in one day, then her eyes fluttered closed.

Garrett was mad. "I should beat you until you can't walk. The next time you feel like hitting someone, just come look me up. I'll be glad to oblige you," he said, breathlessly. He threw two more quick punches, both of them finding their target.

"Mister ... just who the hell ... do you think you are?" James said between punches.

"I'm the man ... that's going to kick your ass ... all over this yard .... You don't treat a woman like that."

"Woman ... that ain't no woman ... that's my no account daughter ... and I'll treat her any damn way I want to," James said, trying to regain his balance.

Garrett was so stunned, he stopped fighting. "I'm assuming that you are James McCuan ... owner of the Circle Bar M ... Is that right?"

"You are assumin' right," James said, eyeing him warily. He wiped the blood from his nose and mouth. He was beginning to feel like he had been run over by a wagon.

"I've traveled a very long way to discuss some important business with you." Garrett extended his hand. "My name is Garrett Steele. My sister and I are the ones that Charlie helped." Garrett watched James through narrowed eyes, he understood now what Charlie had been afraid of. McCuan was a monster.

James looked down at the hand Garrett had offered, which he promptly ignored. "I don't care what your name is. It don't mean nothing to me. Tell me what business you have with me, then I want you on your way." When Garrett didn't answer immediately, James became aggravated. "I'm not going to stand here all day jawing with you, besides, I want you off of my property."

A slow smile spread across Garrett's face. "You should care what my name is, you see, my father's name is Benjamin Joseph Steele, your stepbrother. And it seems that half of this ranch belongs to my sister and I." Garrett had enjoyed that last part.

It got very quiet, for once even James was speechless. He just stood there looking at Garrett, not believing what he had just been told. This couldn't be his stepbrother's kid, or could it?

"I'm going to be living here now. And I will see to it that you do not harm your daughter ever again. I've been told that a lot of people are afraid of you.

But I just want you to know…that…I'm not one of them." He turned away, walking in the direction of the porch, never looking back.

Chapter Seven

Garrett's emotions were running wild. He was torn between beating the hell out of James McCuan and checking on Charlie. The decision wasn't hard, he had to see if she was all right. When he saw James hitting her, something inside him had snapped. He couldn't control the rage inside of him.

He had calmed down just a little, until he reached the porch and saw Charlie's battered face. She looked so helpless lying there. She had several bruises starting to show on her cheek. Her lip was split and swollen and her left eye was starting to swell. His temper flared all over again.

"I don't know who you are. But we're sure beholden to you mister," said an older gentleman.

That brought Garrett's thoughts back to the present. He extended his hand toward the older gentleman. "My name is Garrett Steele and you don't owe me anything. I should have killed that bastard for what he did to Charlie." Hearing a small sniffle, he turned his head to the side, noticing a small girl standing between two boys. The boys were mirror images of each other, the little girl looked like a miniature version of Charlie.

"My name is Jack Winsloe, and this is Beatrice Pruitt," the older man said, as he continued to shake Garrett's hand.

For the first time, he noticed the older lady standing back on the porch. She was crying, obviously very upset. "Nice to meet you ma'am," Garrett said, tipping his hat toward her.

Jack gestured to the children. "This is Austin and Tristen, they're twins in case you couldn't tell. And this little scrap is Taylor," he said.

Mrs. Pruitt was the first one to move. "You men can talk later, right now we need to get Charlie inside. I need to get her cleaned up and see how badly she's hurt."

Jack and the boys moved next to her, but before they could lift her, Garrett scooped her up in his arms, holding her snug against his chest.

As Garrett entered the door, he suddenly realized he had forgotten all about Maddie. Spinning around as quickly as he could, he looked in the direction of the wagon. He saw that Maddie had climbed out and was standing beside the horses. He could see the fear on her young face.

"Please, my sister Maddie, she's out by the wagon. I'll take Charlie inside, but I'd be much obliged if someone would please see to her," he said. This was the first time since their parents had died that he had left her alone. He was feeling a little guilty, but he had to make sure Charlie was going to be all right.

"Follow me, I'll show you where to take her," Mrs. Pruitt said, hurrying through the house.

As he followed Mrs. Pruitt into the house, he could hear Jack's calm voice talking to the children.

"Boys, take Mr. Steele's wagon and team down to the barn. Make sure you rub them horses down good, and don't forget to give them some grain." Taking Taylor by the hand, Jack smiled down at her. "Come on Taylor, lets go see about Maddie. She looks like she could use a friend about now."

Maddie was standing perfectly still. She saw Garrett lift Charlie and take her in the house. She saw Garrett stop before entering the house, he seemed to be talking to the older man. After Garrett was gone, the man and three children stepped down off the porch. They were walking straight toward her. She was so scared, she couldn't breathe. She saw the little girl holding the man's hand and he was smiling at her. That was when she noticed they were all smiling. She knew Garrett wouldn't let anything happen to her, so he must trust them.

Taylor released Jack's hand, walking over to Maddie. "Hi, my name is Taylor, and these are my brothers, Tristen and Austin. And this is Jack. Don't be afraid, he's real nice," Taylor said, pointing at Jack.

Maddie looked at Taylor. "My name is Maddie. Where did my brother go? I like to stay close to him," she whispered.

Stepping closer, Jack took both little girls by the hand. "Come with us Maddie, we'll take you to see your brother." Before walking away, he turned to the twins. "Boys, go ahead and see to the wagon and team. Be sure to park the wagon under the shed, and it might be a good idea to pull a tarp up over the supplies in back." Jack and the girls started toward the house. The boys were leading the horses down to the barn. They didn't know that they were being watched.

Gimpy had helped James after Steele had gotten done with him. While they were all fussing over that bitch Charlie, he had taken the boss to his small house, next to the bunkhouse. They had a perfect view of the main house.

James McCuan was livid! He had never been this mad in his entire life.

And for the first time in his life, he didn't know what to do about it. He never thought he would hear from his stepbrother ever again. What was he going to do? His mind started slowing down, first of all he had to get rid of Garrett Steele. When Steele was out of the picture, then he would deal with that no account daughter of his, and that damned housekeeper. He should have gotten rid of that pesky housekeeper a long time ago.

Gimpy turned away from the window. "What was that Steele feller talking about boss? He said he owned half the ranch."

James didn't bother to look at Gimpy. "When I think you need to know what's going on, I'll be sure and tell you. But I do need to know if you're going to remain loyal to me. If you do, I'll make it worth your while."

"And if I don't," Gimpy replied warily.

"That's simple. I'll just kill you, no questions asked." James finally turned, looking at his ranch foreman. "Tell me right here and now if I can count on you."

"I've got one question. Will we be gettin' even with Steele and that damn daughter of yours?" He looked at James, who simply nodded. "Then you can count on me boss, I've got a bone to pick with both of 'em."

Both men sat down at the battered table, they had a lot of planning to do. They were going to go over every detail.

Chapter Eight

Garrett followed Mrs. Pruitt, while carrying his delicate burden, through the house. As they walked through the living room, he noticed a staircase leading upstairs. The house was very large and well cared for, no dust or dirt in sight. Glancing down at Charlie, he could see that the bruises were getting larger and darker. He would make sure her father never got close to her again.

"It's right in her, just on the other side of the kitchen. There's some small rooms just off the kitchen," Mrs. Pruitt said.

They walked through the kitchen and entered a hallway. Mrs. Pruitt stopped at the first door on the right and held it open for Garrett to carry Charlie through. "Please be careful with her. I feel so bad for not trying to stop James. I just hope she isn't hurt too bad. Just lay her there on the bed, I need to get some warm water and salve, then I'll be right back." She hurried down the short hallway leading back to the kitchen.

Garrett crossed the room slowly, then gently laid Charlie on the bed. Her hat had come off in all the confusion, but he just noticed it was missing. He carefully brushed her hair back from her bruised face, letting his knuckles lightly skim across her cheek. Her face was going to be swollen and discolored for a while. Taking her small hand in his much larger one, he examined her fingers. Her fingernails were either broken or had been bitten off. He continued to search her hand, turning it over to trace the palm with his thumb, finding several large blisters and even larger calluses. Her hands were rough and scratched from hard work, but the skin on her face was smooth and baby soft. In fact, he had noticed while carrying her through the house that her whole body was soft, it felt wonderful against him.

Mrs. Pruitt called from the kitchen. "Mr. Steele, I'll be there in just a few more minutes. I have the water heating on the stove. If you don't mind, just stay there with her."

It was a good thing Mrs. Pruitt called out, Garrett thought to himself. His imagination was starting to run wild, he felt like a schoolboy with his first crush. He could hear Mrs. Pruitt rattling around in the kitchen, that should keep his mind from wandering, but it didn't. He just couldn't manage to keep his mind from straying. It was a strange feeling. No woman had never affected him this way.

Garrett sat down on the edge of the bed, carefully leaning forward. "I promise, cross my heart and hope to die, that I'll never let anyone hurt you like this again," he whispered. He bent closer, kissing her soft lips.

As soon as their lips touched, Charlie's eyelids fluttered, but remained closed. Garrett pulled back, a look of astonishment on his face, something had just happened between them. He just wasn't sure what it was. He was sitting on the edge of the bed, still holding Charlie's hand, when Mrs. Pruitt hurried through the bedroom door.

Mrs. Pruitt saw the strange look on his face, but brushed it aside. She knew he was just concerned about Charlie's welfare. After setting the warm water and towels down, she turned to Garrett. "If you don't mind, I need to get her cleaned up. There's coffee on the stove in the kitchen, the cups are by the sink. Just make yourself at home. When I'm done, I'll let you know." She turned her back, starting the task of undressing Charlie.

He just stood there looking at Charlie. When Mrs. Pruitt's capable hands started undressing her, the words finally started sinking in. She would have to undress her to get her cleaned up. Jerking his head up, he spun toward the door. "If you need me, I'll be right outside. I'm going to check on my sister." He closed the door softly. His mind still on the undressing part. Hearing footsteps from the kitchen, he tensed and waited, if it was McCuan, he might just finish what he had started in the yard.

"Girls, come on in the kitchen, and I'll fix you a nice big glass of cool milk."

"No, Mr. Jack. I have to find my brother. He'll be afraid without me. We take care of each other."

Garrett smiled when he heard his sister's argument. It was Maddie that was afraid to be alone, not him. He stepped into the kitchen. "Come here, sweet Maddie and let me give you a big hug." He knelt down on the floor, holding his arms wide.

"Garrett, I was so afraid!" shouted Maddie. She squealed, running into Garrett's outstretched arms. "I thought you had left me behind. But I knew you promised never to leave me. Then Mr. Jack and Taylor came to get me. They said you was just taking care of Charlie." She was hugging his neck so tight, he could hardly breathe.

"I told you I would never, ever, leave you. I'm going to take care of you, I promise," he said, standing and lifting her in his muscular arms.

Jack cleared his throat. "The boys are seeing to your team. Then they're going to park your wagon under the shed and cover it with a tarp."

After giving Maddie one last squeeze, Garrett sat her on her feet. "Why don't you go play with Taylor. Just stay pretty close." He watched both girls skip out of the kitchen, they were going to play in the living room. He turned to Jack, who was pouring two cups of coffee. "Where is that snake McCuan?" he asked.

Setting both cups of hot coffee down on the table, Jack took a seat to Garrett's right. "I saw Gimpy, that's the foreman here, helping him up. Then they went down to Gimpy's place. It's down by the bunkhouse." Sipping his coffee, he looked over the rim. "You do know the old man is going to be pissed to high heaven at you, don't you? He ain't somebody you want to tangle with."

Garrett lifted the coffee cup. "I really don't care how pissed he is. I can take care of myself, actually I wish he would start something. The next time I get my hands on him, he'll wish he had never been born." He paused before continuing. "And by the way, I have met your foreman, knocked his ass in a mud hole."

Jack laughed for a minute, wishing he had seen Gimpy lying in a mud hole. "What was your father to McCuan?" he asked. "If you don't want to tell me that's OK. But you see, me and Bea, we've always tried to look after the children, they're just like our own. And like you, Charlie always said she could take care of herself. I promise you one thing after today, McCuan won't get near her. I'll see to it."

Leaning back in his chair, Garrett smiled, although it didn't quite reach his eyes. "You'll have to stand in line to get a piece of McCuan, if he goes after Charlie again. He won't get off so easy next time. And I sure hope there is a next time." He sat his chair down on all four legs. "I don't mind answering your questions, because I've got a few of my own I want you to answer."

Garrett paused for a few minutes, deep in thought. "My father and McCuan are stepbrothers," he said. Toying with the cup on the table, Garrett spoke softly. "McCuan's father, his name was Alex, married my father's mother, her name was Anna. My father was about four years old when they married, James was about two. Alex wanted to adopt my father and give him the McCuan name. But Benjamin, that's my father, was the last of the Steeles, and Grandmother wanted him to pass on the family name. As time passed, no more children were born. They just had the two, my father and McCuan. As James and my father got older, James started arguing with Grandfather, and it was always about money. One day, Grandfather ordered him away, telling him never to return. About six months after he left, he wrote my father, asking for money, at first he wouldn't send him any. Finally my mother, her name

was Diane, begged Father to send James money. Father finally agreed."
Garrett suddenly pushed his chair back, standing up, too nervous to sit.
Pacing the length of the kitchen floor, he started talking again. "Father didn't
send much at first, just enough to keep James happy. Then James telegraphed,
informing my father that he had found a ranch he wanted to buy. My father
agreed to the amount, about twenty-five thousand, with one exception. Father
wanted to be a full partner in the ranch, James agreed to those terms. Before
Father would transfer the funds, he made James sign an agreement.
According to my attorney, James has tried to buy back Father's portion of the
ranch, but he refused to sell." He stopped pacing, dropping back down in the
chair across from Jack. "After our parents died, I was talking to my attorney,
he knew I was looking for a fresh place to start a new life with Maddie. That's
when he informed me of my father's share of this ranch. So Maddie and I
packed up, left Arizona and here we are. And we're going to stay. I owe it to
Maddie," he said quietly.

Jack was looking at Garrett as if he was stunned, then his face split in to
a wide grin. He extended his hand. "Well boy, welcome to the Circle Bar M.
I'm gonna tell you right now, you'd better watch your back. The boss don't
take kindly to strangers, especially ones that own part of his ranch."

"You don't have to worry about me. I'm a retired U.S. Marshall," Garrett
said, shaking Jack's hand.

Jack looked at him in disbelief. "Just how old are you boy?" he asked.

"I'm twenty-eight, going on sixty. I had to retire to take care of Maddie.
She came along a little late. I was already grown when she was born."

"She'll do fine here. Taylor needed someone to play with anyway. And
Bea, she'll be like an old mother hen to that youngin'."

"Who are you callin' an old mother hen anyway, you old coot?" Mrs.
Pruitt was standing with her hands on her hips, glaring at Jack, trying not to
laugh.

Both men had been so preoccupied, they didn't hear her in the hallway.
Jack spun around, his face turning beet red. Garrett burst out laughing, the
look on Jack's face was hilarious.

Then remembering Charlie, Garrett sobered quickly. "How's Charlie? Is
she going to be all right?" he asked.

Mrs. Pruitt looked at him with tears of happiness shining in her eyes.
"She's going to be just fine, this time. Her face is going to be pretty swollen
and bruised for a little while, but thank the Lord, he didn't hurt her too bad,"
she said, wiping the tears from her eyes. "And guess what, she's asking to see

you Mr. Steele." .

Jack was the first one to move. "I'm going down to the barn to check on the boys. I'll also tell them the good news about Charlie." He grabbed his hat, heading for the back door. "Bea, the girls are in the living room playing, so keep an eye on them. You know what I mean. We're not quite sure where the boss is at." After Mrs. Pruitt nodded her understanding, Jack closed the back door, heading for the barn.

"I'll take care of those little girls, don't you worry for one minute that I won't," she said. "Mr. Steele, you'd better get on back there before Charlie drops off to sleep."

Garrett had been standing glued to one spot. Actually he was shocked that she had asked for him. When Mrs. Pruitt spoke to him, it prompted him to action. "I'm going right now. Just call me if you need me. As I was telling Jack, Maddie and I are here to stay, and things are going to be very different here from now on." He walked past Mrs. Pruitt, then turned around. "Please call me Garrett," he said, before turning away.

Just as he reached the bedroom door, the front door slammed. He heard the sound of heavy boots, pounding on the wooden floor. Well the mystery was over, they all knew exactly where James McCuan was at, he had just walked in the front door. He really needed to talk to him, but decided it could wait. Charlie was more important right now, and she was waiting for him, just on the other side of the bedroom door. McCuan could wait.

Chapter Nine

James walked across the yard, in deep thought. He had never wanted to hear his stepbrothers name again. He had worked too hard to make this ranch what it was today. Benjamin, his stepbrother, had furnished most of the money to buy this place, but he was the one that had worked night and day for the last twenty three years to make this place what it was today. And if that no account wife of his had given him all sons, it would have been even better. His temper was starting to boil again.

As he neared the front steps, he looked around. His so-called family, was probably all inside. He grinned, thinking about the way Charlie's face had looked when he had gotten done with her this afternoon. He had gotten some pretty good wallops in. As he stepped up on the bottom step, he felt a twinge in his ribs. He grimaced, holding them tight. Steele had gotten several good punches in. But it wouldn't happen again. He had to find out how much Steele knew about the money. Then he and Gimpy would set their plan in motion.

Twisting the doorknob, he stormed into the house. He had to get to his office. Pausing outside his office door, he heard a voice in the living room. It was probably Taylor, but he didn't bother to look. Before entering his domain, he also heard Mrs. Pruitt talking to someone. She was going to be the next to leave, even before he got rid of his oldest daughter. He needed time to think, but first he had to have a drink. He entered his office, closing the door behind him.

Taylor and Maddie were in the living room playing with dolls when James had stomped in. Taylor held her finger to her lips to shush Maddie. Both girls were very quiet.

"As soon as my Pa goes in his office, we'd better go find Mrs. Pruitt. Just be real still and don't make a sound," Taylor whispered.

Maddie was sitting very close to Taylor. They were listening for the office door to close. She wondered if Mr. McCuan would treat them like he did Charlie. "Do you think he would hit us like he did Charlie?" Maddie asked.

"Yes, I think he would. He don't like girls much. I'm afraid of him. Was you afraid of your pa, or was he mean to you?"

Maddie was quiet for a moment, then answered softly. "No, I wasn't afraid of my father. He was very nice and wasn't mean at all. My mother was nice to. I loved them both very much and I miss them so bad, sometimes it hurts." She wiped at the tears rolling down her cheeks with pudgy fingers.

"What I can remember of my ma, she seemed nice. She never yelled or got mad, not that I can remember anyway. And she always smelled so good. I miss her to, we all do, but I think it's been hardest for Charlie. Pa is real mean to her."

Both little girls were quiet, waiting and listening for any sign of James. About five minutes passed before they moved. They scampered down the hall in search of Mrs. Pruitt.

Mrs. Pruitt was busy in the kitchen. She was making snacks, she knew everybody would be starving. She held her breath when she heard James come in, but soon relaxed when his office door closed. She smiled to herself when she heard a slight noise in the hallway. "You girls come on in here and have some milk and cookies." She waited, knowing they would answer soon.

"How did you know it was us? We were real quiet," Taylor said.

Mrs. Pruitt smiled, she knew as soon as James returned, Taylor would come to her. She was scared to death of her pa, but she had good reason to be. She turned to Maddie. "Have you and Taylor been having a good time?" she asked, offering her a cookie from the plate.

Maddie nodded her head, she was very shy around strangers. "Do you know where my brother is at? He said he wouldn't go very far," she said, reaching for a cookie.

"He went to see Charlie. Don't worry, he should be out in a few minutes. Charlie's room is just down the hall."

"I really like her. She helped us fix our wagon and she made my brother very angry. It was funny when he got mad," Maddie said with a giggle.

Just then the back door opened, Tristen and Austin came in from outside. "Jack will be here in just a few minutes," Tristen said. Both boys were looking toward Charlie's room. They started talking at the same time. "Are you sure she's gong to be OK?" When both boys realized they had asked the same question, they both repeated it. Each one trying to talk louder than the other one.

Mrs. Pruitt finally got both of them to listen. "Yes boys, she's going to be just fine. She's going to have a lot of bruises, but other than that, she's fine." She sounded so relieved.

There was a soft knock at the back door before Jack entered. "Is everything all right in here? I heard some loud voices just a minute ago," he said, stepping into the kitchen.

36

"Everything is just fine. When James came in, he went straight to his office," Mrs. Pruitt said, motioning for everyone to have a seat at the table. "I've got some snacks fixed, find a seat and we'll all have a quick bite to eat." Mrs. Pruitt busied herself pouring milk and coffee while everyone settled around the large kitchen table. After prayers were spoken, they all began to eat.

"Is Garrett still in there with Charlie?" Jack asked between bites. "When he's through I need to have a long talk with him."

"He'll be out shortly. Right now let the children eat, you two can talk business later. Besides, I want the children away from here when James comes out of his office later," whispered Mrs. Pruitt.

"I've got a feelin' that things are going to be different around here. When push comes to shove, Garrett will shove back," Jack said. He was watching the hallway, looking for any sign of Garrett.

"I think it's about damn time," Tristen said.

Sometimes the sentences that one twin started, the other one would finish. "That somebody stood up to pa," Austin finished.

Jack and Mrs. Pruitt jerked their attention to the boys. They were startled, that was the first time the twins had ever cursed. Jack was the first to recover. "Boys, I know you're getting older, but you have to watch your language in front of ladies. That's a part of being a gentleman."

The twins looked at each other and shrugged. Then Austin turned to Jack. "We know that, but there ain't no ladies here, it's just Mrs. Pruitt and the girls."

Jack was stunned. He just sat there for a minute, finally he turned to Mrs. Pruitt. They both burst out laughing, and it wasn't long before the whole table had erupted into laughter.

James was sitting at his desk. He had calmed down a little, he had had a couple of shots of whiskey that had helped to settle his nerves. When he heard the laughter coming from the kitchen, he got upset all over again.

You better laugh now, because in a few weeks none of you will have anything to laugh about, he thought. He couldn't hardly wait. Garrett Steele would wish he had never come to the Circle Bar M. He leaned back in his chair, relaxing. Yes sir, things were going to get mighty interesting over the next few weeks.

Chapter Ten

Garrett raised his hand to knock on Charlie's bedroom door, he paused. He had to get his emotions under control. It just didn't make any sense; no woman had never affected him this way before. There wasn't any specific reason, it seemed like he was somehow drawn to her. This was never going to work, if he and Maddie planned on living here, and they did, he had to get her out of his system. Hell! She didn't even really look like a lady, not with those baggy pants and shirt she wore. But he couldn't stop wondering what she would look like with the mud cleaned off and clothes that actually fit. Who was he kidding, with that round little body, she would look great.

The picture his mind had conjured up was more than the lower part of his body could stand, the front of his jeans were becoming a little too snug. He snorted, disgusted with himself. This is just great, he thought, I'm going to have to walk around the next few months hard as a rock. It wouldn't be to bad if he could hide it, maybe he just needed to buy some bigger pants. That would probably work. He stood there for a few more minutes, trying to get his body to cooperate, then knocked softly, waiting for a reply. He didn't have to wait long.

"Come in," Charlie said. Her voice was slightly muffled through the wooden door.

Garrett opened the door, stepping inside. He never looked at her until he had closed the door. When he finally saw her, all his good intentions flew right out the window. He definitely had to get some bigger pants and fast.

When Charlie looked at Garrett, she felt something very strange. It was as if she had known him all her life. There was also a longing that she couldn't explain. She felt drawn to him, but she'd only met him that very afternoon. He was so handsome, it almost took her breath away. And here she sat in her nightgown, all scraped and bruised, not that it mattered anyway. He would never notice someone like me, she thought. Why did she have to be ugly, and heavy to boot. Her mother had been beautiful and small, actually delicate was a better word to describe her.

She had dreamed of getting married and having a family of her own, but that's just what it was, a dream. How many times had her pa told her that no man would ever want her. She lowered her head, but not before a tear escaped the corner of her eye, rolling down her bruised and swollen cheek.

Garrett had been staring. He knew it was rude, but he couldn't help it. She was sitting in the middle of her bed, with pillows propped behind her back. Her skin had been bathed. He noticed that her face and hands were darker than the skin on her neck and upper arms. Her hair was short, but it had been brushed until it was shiny, and it was the color of expensive whiskey. He let his gaze roam over her luscious body. She had a very simple nightgown on. But it wasn't the gown that held his interest, it was what was beneath it that had his full attention. She was absolutely beautiful!

She wasn't very tall, but what she lacked in height, she made up for it with curves. The quilt that covered her was pooled in her lap. He could see the outline of her shapely legs, and what fine legs they were, but it was her breasts that held his attention. The floppy shirt she had been wearing disguised her womanly shape, but her gown lay soft against her. Her breathing had increased, which made her breasts swell. With each deep breath she took, her nipples strained against the material of her gown. He knew he should get the hell out of there, but he just stood there. The longer he watched her, the more he wanted her. He could feel his body reacting, this was not a good time. He was in serious trouble.

Garrett brought his gaze back to her face, just in time to see a tear slip down her battered cheek. That single tear almost brought him to his knees. He knew at that point, no matter what, he would do whatever he had to. He would protect her.

"Are you in a lot of pain? Maybe I should get Mrs. Pruitt," Garrett said. The mattress dipped under his weight as he sat down on the edge. He gently touched the side of her face with the palm of his hand.

Charlie was shocked with the sensation. "No it's not too bad. I want to thank you. My pa can sometimes be pretty mean." She lowered her eyes, trying to hide her fear.

"Look at me Charlie. I'm going to promise you, cross my heart and hope to die," he said, making the motion with his finger over his heart. "That he will never do this to you again. We have a lot to talk about in a couple of days, when you feel like it. Right now I want you to take it easy and rest. I'll handle everything here at the ranch."

Her eyes were large with fear. "You don't understand. I have to look after my brothers and sister. I have to keep Pa away from them, they depend on me," she whispered.

"You lie back and relax. I'm going to look after your brothers and sister also. I won't let anybody harm them."

"This is comin' from a greenhorn that was standing in the middle of a cattle stampede. That's comfortin', real comfortin'," she said, rolling her eyes toward the ceiling.

Garrett laughed. "Well at least now I know your feeling better. I know you must be exhausted. You better get some sleep, you don't want to have bags under those beautiful eyes, do you?" Garrett asked. Standing up. "I'll leave you alone now and let you rest, and don't worry about a thing. I'll take care of it," he promised. Bending over, he placed a light kiss on her forehead, the only place that wasn't bruised on her face.

"I'm not tired," she said, yawning, "And I'm tellin' you right now, don't be makin' fun of me. There ain't nothin' about me beautiful," she protested.

As he looked down at her, he shook his head. "I'm not making fun of you. You are very beautiful," he said. But is was too late, she had already dropped off to sleep. He turned away from the bed, grinning as he walked toward the door. It certainly was a good thing that she had fallen asleep, because if she hadn't, she might have gotten an eye full. Looking down he laughed, he sure was going to have to buy some bigger pants.

Charlie was playing possum. She had heard every word. She knew he wasn't telling the truth, but it didn't hurt to dream. When the door closed behind him, she relaxed, letting sleep overcome her. Her last thoughts were of Garrett. What if he really thought she was beautiful, then she had the most wonderful dream.

Chapter Eleven

Garrett couldn't keep the smile off his face. He whistled a tune as he walked toward the kitchen, things were probably going to get very interesting in the next few weeks. He only hoped he could stand it. As he neared the kitchen, he could hear Maddie laughing, along with Charlie's brothers and sister. It was the best sound he had heard in a long time. He stopped for a moment, trying to clear his head. So much had happened in the last few weeks, actually the last few days. It seemed like it wasn't just Maddie that needed a change, it had helped him tremendously as well. After meeting Charlie he knew his life would never be the same.

A look of worry appeared on his handsome face. What if she doesn't feel the same attraction that I do, he thought? The worry didn't last long, he had seen the look of longing on her face when he had touched her. This strange attraction was obviously mutual, he hoped. He didn't have time to ponder long, he needed to see about Maddie. Then he could discuss business with McCuan, in that particular order. Taking a deep breath he stepped into the kitchen.

"Garrett, I'm so glad to see you," Maddie said, jumping up from the kitchen chair. She ran into his waiting arms, squeezing him tight.

Garrett barely had time to open his arms before the excited little girl came barreling at him. "Sweet Maddie, it hasn't been that long, just a short time. Have you been good for Mrs. Pruitt?"

Nodding her head, she finally let go of his neck, looking at him. "I know it wasn't that long silly. But I know how scared you get when I'm not here to keep you company. And I've been very good. Taylor and me have been playing with her dolls, and it was really fun."

He moved the hair from around her face, tucking it behind her small ear. "If you're not to far away from me I don't mind it. I want you to have friends. But always remember, I'll always be here for you." He looked past Maddie, focusing on the end of the table, where Jack and Mrs. Pruitt sat smiling. Taylor and the twins were sitting at the other end. "It looks like we have both found some very good friends," he said, hugging his sister close.

Walking toward the kitchen table, he stopped, leaned forward, setting Maddie back in her chair. She looked up at him with a smile. "I really like it here Garrett." Not being able to sit still any longer than necessary. "Taylor, would you like to go play some more?" she asked.

Taylor looked at Mrs. Pruitt. "Is it all right for us to play some more?" Her eyes were hopeful.

"Yes dear, just stay close, and holler if you need me," Mrs. Pruitt said, shaking her head at the girls. She turned her attention back to Garrett. "Are you hungry Garrett? Just sit down here and I'll fix you a snack." She walked by Tristen and Austin. "Have you boys got all your chores done for the evening? If you haven't, you better go right now and finish them. I don't want you down at the barn after dark," she said.

"Do we have to?" both boys asked in unison. "We really wanted to see Charlie first, make sure she's OK," Tristen said. He was usually the one that done all the talking.

Before Mrs. Pruitt could answer, Garrett spoke up. "Boys she's fine. She has several bruises and some swelling, but she'll be all right. Besides, she's asleep right now, and she needs to rest."

Heading toward the back door, they stopped, grabbing their hats from the rack before leaving the house. Mrs. Pruitt chuckled when she saw them with their heads together, probably discussing everything that had happened today. Carrying a large plate of snacks over to the table, she set them down in front of Garrett. After refilling both men's coffee cups, she sat down beside Jack, listening.

Slowly taking a sip of hot coffee, Jack eyed Garrett over the rim of his cup. "How do you plan on handling James?" he asked warily. "I don't mean to repeat myself, but you do know it's not going to be easy," he said.

Garrett laid his fork down beside his plate, before wiping his mouth on his napkin. "I've been giving it some thought, and after finally meeting him," he paused. "I've decided not to pull any punches with him. I'm going to tell him how I plan to move in and do my part. Because after seeing Maddie laughing again, I truly believe this place is right for both of us. It seemed we both needed a change," he said quietly.

Mrs. Pruitt had been quiet, listening to every word Garrett had spoken. Reaching across the table, she patted Garrett's hand. "Jack and I want you to know that whatever you decide to do, we'll stand behind you all the way."

Garrett looked up, a smile showing in his eyes and his heart. "I'm glad to hear you both say that. And while we're talking, there's one more thing I want to say. I'm going to make a promise of my own. As long as I'm around and able to draw a breath, I swear James McCuan will not hurt any of the children again." The smile had vanished from his face, a look of pure hatred had taken its place.

With tears shining in her eyes and her lips trembling, Mrs. Pruitt looked at Jack, then Garrett, before speaking in a quivering voice. "James has never been very good to any of the children, but he has been down right wicked to Charlie. That girl hasn't got a mean bone in her body, and he's just plain cruel to her. It makes me sick to think of the way she's been treated by her own father," she said. She turned to Jack, seeking comfort in his arms.

Jack wrapped both arms around Mrs. Pruitt, holding her close. "Bea, things are going to be different around here from now on. Garrett and I will see to it. I'm just plum ashamed of myself for not standing up for that girl sooner."

Garrett sat quietly, watching and listening. From all the information he had gathered so far, Charlie had been treated pretty rough. But that was going to come to a stop. The images he had of Charlie suddenly changed, he couldn't stop thinking about the way her legs had looked with those quilts wrapped around them. She had looked so helpless with all those bruises on her lovely face. But the fight wasn't out of her. If he had provoked her the least little bit, she would have tried to climb out of bed and defend herself, that thought brought a smile to his lips. He sure wished she had gotten out of bed, that way he could have gotten a better look at her fantastic body. What the hell was he thinking? One thing was for sure, he was going to have to ask Jack where the nearest cold pond or creek was, because he sure needed one.

Garrett's attention was brought back to the present when Jack cleared his throat. "Have you figured out an exact plan yet?" Jack asked.

Garrett realized Jack was looking at him a little strange. He decided he better get his mind on real business and off of monkey business. Choosing his words carefully, he finally answered. "First of all, I need to talk to James. After that I'll have a better idea on how to handle things, maybe. I have an attorney back in Tucson, Arizona that is working on a new contract for James and I both to sign. Right now I think the less I tell McCuan the better off I'll be."

Mrs. Pruitt and Jack both nodded their heads in agreement. "I'm telling you right now, don't trust him no farther than you can throw him. He's a mean sonofabitch, just don't turn your back on him or that damn foreman of his," Jack said, his voice low.

"They're like two peas in a pod. One would lie and the other one would swear to it. Gimpy would do anything that James asked him to," Mrs. Pruitt said.

"I've handled his kind before. They're not used to people fighting back and when that happens it rattles them – shakes them up. And I plan on shaking him up plenty. I'm going to make this a good home for Maddie and the other children, but especially for Charlie. She needs some of the burden lifted from her shoulders, and that's exactly what I'm going to do," he said. He became quiet, planning his next words. "It's hard to explain, and to be honest, I feel like a fool sitting here talking about it. But just looking at her makes me want to protect her. It's the damnedest feeling I've ever had. I just can't explain it," he said, looking down at the floor, waiting for the outburst he was sure would happen, but nothing happened. He looked up slowly to find Jack and Mrs. Pruitt, both grinning from ear to ear.

"That's the best news we've heard in a long time," Jack said with a huge smile.

Mrs. Pruitt was so happy, she grabbed Garrett's hand again, squeezing it tight. "Jack and I have prayed for a long time that someone would come along and sweep Charlie off her feet. But I'm going to warn you, she's not the meek and helpless female type. Now I'm not saying she couldn't stand a little spit and polish. Maybe kind of smooth the rough edges down just a little. But she's a good girl and she's always had to work so hard."

"Now slow down. I didn't say anything about sweeping her off her feet. I just said I wanted to protect her, maybe even make her life a little easier, that's all," Garrett said, eyeing the pair as if they had the plague. That wasn't all he wanted to do to her, he would very much like to get his hands on her. This wasn't good, he had to get out of this kitchen before he embarrassed himself.

Standing. "I thought I heard McCuan come in a little while ago. Do you know where I can find him now? There's no need to put this little meeting off any longer," he said.

Jack stood, nodding toward the hallway. "He'll be in his office. It's just down the hallway, first door on the right, the only door on the right," Jack said grinning. "I'll be in here or close by if you need me," he added.

"Thanks for the offer, but I'll be OK. Just do me a favor and watch Maddie for me," he said, walking down the hallway, already planning his next move. But first he had to talk to the owner of the Circle Bar M...well actually...the co-owner. He was beginning to enjoy this.

Chapter Twelve

James was sitting behind his desk with his feet propped up. He had been drinking steadily for the past hour. He was in a foul mood, a very foul mood. The whiskey he was drinking was causing him to become slow and unsteady, but his mind was still racing.

Taking a long drag from the cigar he held in his unsteady fingers, he slowly exhaled, sending the smoke rising to the ceiling. If worse come to worse, he thought, he would take care of Steele and his sister, permanently. He would fight tooth and nail to keep his ranch. First he was going to try to buy back Steele's portion of the ranch, if that didn't work, he would just have to persuade Steele in other ways. But one thing was for sure, he wasn't going to let him have any part of this ranch.

Just as he lifted his whiskey glass back to this lips, a knock sounded at his office door. He lowered the glass back down to the desk. He sat quietly waiting. If it was that damn pesky housekeeper of his, maybe she'd take the hint and go away. But after a few minutes, another knock came, a little louder and longer than the one before.

"Who the hell is it?" he growled.

There was no answer, but the door opened slowly. Before the door was opened completely, an unfamiliar voice said, "Garrett Steele…your partner." The door opened allowing Garrett to enter the room. "I need to speak with you, and I really don't want to wait. We need to iron out a few details," he said, moving farther into the office. "My sister and I will need a place to stay, two rooms will do nicely, but they need to be close together." Garrett was really starting to enjoy this. He decided to give McCuan a little more to think about. "And another thing, after we get settled in, I would like to look at the books, start familiarizing myself with the day to day operation," he added with a grin.

James shot up from his desk, so fast he turned the heavy chair over. "Now you just wait a damn minute there boy. You and that sister of yours can sleep in the barn for all I care, besides you won't be staying that long anyhow. And…you're not going to touch my books, or have anything to do with the operations of this ranch," he shouted, staggering around the corner of his desk.

Garrett smiled, but it was the kind of smile that was very deceiving. "I'm

45

not going anywhere, this is going to be our home, and there is not a thing you can do about it. My father invested a large sum of money in this ranch. And as far as I can tell, it was a very good investment," he said, looking around at all the expensive furnishings inside James' office. "As I said before, I want to become familiar with ranch work, top to bottom. And besides, I'm really beginning to like it here already."

"The only thing you're going to be familiar with, is the toe of my boot, I'm going to kick the living dog shit out of you. Then I'm going to send you, and that sister of yours, back to where you came from," James said. The effects of the whiskey had quickly worn off. "Nobody, and I do mean nobody, is going to take my ranch or any part of it away from me," he shouted.

Garrett moved closer to the older man, forcing James to look up. "That's where you're wrong McCuan. My attorney has informed me that my father's name is already on the deed to…your ranch. It seems my father didn't trust you. He wanted his name on all the ownership documents before you actually were able to purchase it," Garrett said, watching the anger simmering on James' face.

"Speaking of your father," James spat, "Whatever happened to that sissy? Why isn't he here taking care of his own business? Or wouldn't that bitch mother of yours let him out of her sight?" James didn't have time to blink, Garrett snatched him up by the collar of his shirt, lifting him off the ground.

"Don't you ever talk about my parents that way again, or I'll do more than just beat the shit out of you, I'll kill you. Do you understand?" Garrett hissed. When James didn't answer, Garrett started shaking him, trying to scare James. "All you need to know is, that you're going to be dealing with me from now on, not my father, and I'm warning you, I'm not like my father. In fact, I've been told that I can be one mean sonofabitch." Releasing James, Garrett backed away, stopping a few feet away. "That's not a threat, it's a promise," he whispered in a low, deadly voice.

For the first time, in a very long time, James was afraid. He saw something in Garrett's eyes that made him uneasy. He turned away from Garrett, swallowing hard, not wanting the younger man to see the effects of his statement.

After taking a few steadying breaths, and another shot of whiskey, he turned around to face Garrett again. "What's it going to take to buy you out? Just name your price and we'll go from there. I'm sure we can come to some sort of profitable agreement," James said, the whiskey already giving him a little false courage.

"I'm not interested in selling out to you or anybody else. I told you, I want to make a home for my sister and me. We won't take up much room, besides, the house is big enough for all of us. Later on, when things settle down a little, I plan on building a small house, just big enough for the two of us to live in, and we'll be out of your hair," Garrett said, preparing to leave. "McCuan, I have proof of legal ownership, and Maddie really likes it here, and, I always wanted to be a rancher," he said.

James was fuming, but not wanting to antagonize Garrett further, he tried to control his temper. He almost had a stroke in the process. "You might have some sort of claim or you might not. You haven't shown me any evidence to back up what you've been saying. If you have, I would like to see it now."

Garrett snorted loudly. "Do you think I'm crazy?" he asked. "If I brought the documents out here with me, I would never make it off this ranch alive. We'll handle this my way. You give me the name of your attorney and the address where he can be reached and I'll forward the information to my attorney. We're going to settle this through legal channels. Believe me, I've dealt with your kind before, and I can tell you right now, I don't trust you."

"I'm going to ride in and wire my attorney first thing in the morning, smart ass. I'll be sure and tell you when I hear back from him, until then, keep your nose out of my business."

"I suggest you do talk to your attorney, but you better make it fast, because like you, I'm not a very patient man either." Garrett turned, walking to the door. He stopped, twisting around quickly to face James. "Oh yeah, I forgot to tell you. I'm going to take two rooms upstairs, for my sister and me." He knew that would enrage the older man. And he was right.

"Didn't that no-account housekeeper of mine tell you that no females is allowed in the main bedroom upstairs. Why do you think them good for nothing daughters of mine sleep back there by the kitchen," James sneered.

Garrett was furious, he was shaking all over with anger. "There are a lot of things around here that's going to change, and that's one of them. Starting tomorrow, your daughters will also be sleeping upstairs in comfortable surroundings, not in the kitchen. You will learn to treat them with respect, especially Charlie, or you will answer to me. And for the record, the only good for nothing around here, is you!" Garrett said, taking pleasure in the sudden anger that appeared on James' face. He turned, not waiting for an answer, slamming the door loudly behind him.

James was suddenly nervous again. The boy had a legitimate claim against his ranch. What was he going to do? He really needed to talk to his attorney, but it would have to wait until morning.

Grabbing the bottle of whiskey, he poured another glass. If he had to resort to other means, it certainly wouldn't bother him, he'd done it before, and would probably have to do it again. This was a harsh land, sometimes calling for very harsh actions in order to survive. But he would do whatever he had to.

Deciding to go back to Gimpy's, he picked up the bottle from his desk. When he left the house, he noticed a light burning in Gimpy's window, it seemed to be calling him. Besides, he knew if he could count on anybody it would be his foreman. They had a lot more plans to talk about, over a few more drinks of course. He decided not to worry anymore, until he had a chance to wire his attorney. And he would do that first thing in the morning. Right now he had to get down to Gimp's place.

He tried to whistle a tune while he staggered down toward the foreman's place, but his mouth was too sore from the pounding he had taken from Steele. Touching his mouth gingerly, he thought, I owe you for this one Steele, and I'll be paying you back real soon. He would make him sorry he ever came to the Circle Bar M.

Chapter Thirteen

The following morning breakfast was in full swing. Everybody was seated around the table. The twins were sitting together, both little girls were sitting side by side, and the adults were scattered among the children. The kitchen was buzzing with happiness and laughter. The steaming bowls of food were being passed around the table. All activity suddenly stopped when a door closed down the small hallway, light footsteps could be heard on the wooden floor, coming toward the kitchen. All eyes turned, watching the hallway, waiting for Charlie.

Charlie thought she heard laughter coming from the kitchen. She rolled over and sat up, shaking her head to clear her fuzzy thoughts, she must be delirious. She slipped out of bed, groaning loudly, her body was stiff as a board. Suddenly, she remembered everything that had happened yesterday, she felt nauseous. Her father was going to kill her. Laughter, she did hear laughter, her head snapped up, jerking toward the sound that she was unfamiliar with. It was coming from the kitchen!

She gathered her clothes, dressing as quickly as possible. She had avoided looking in the small mirror above her dresser, but she had to find out how bad she looked. After glancing in the mirror, she felt like crying, her face was a mess. She wondered if Garrett Steele was still around or if her father had run him off.

Before leaving the room, she decided to take one more quick look in the mirror. She stopped in front of her dresser, noticing that her reflection hadn't changed in the last five minutes. It was still the same old Charlie looking back, actually looking a little worse than usual. She splashed some cool water on her battered face, hoping to take some of the swelling down. It felt like the whole right side of her face was on fire. She raised her hand, touching the side of her face, it hurt like a sonofagun. But she would survive, she always did. Picking up her hat, she walked to the bedroom door. This was one of those times she wished she was pretty, not beautiful, just pretty. Turning the knob, she slowly made her way to the kitchen, and the sound of laughter. It had been a very long time since any of them had had anything to laugh about. She couldn't keep the smile from finding its way to her lips and she was still smiling when she stepped into the kitchen.

Garrett was the first to notice her and he jumped quickly to his feet. The noise in the kitchen had stopped, all eyes were on Charlie. She was absolutely beautiful, he thought. She was dressed in clean pants and a floppy shirt, and her short hair had a brilliant, glossy shine. Although her face was badly bruised and swollen, it didn't alter the fact that she was breathtaking. He suddenly realized all attention was focused on her and she was a little uncomfortable. He quickly recovered from the shock of seeing her.

"Please come over here and have a seat. Are you sure you need to be up moving around," he asked, concern showing on his handsome face.

Charlie had been pretending to look at everybody around the table, trying not to look at Garrett, but that was impossible. She couldn't seem to keep her eyes off of him. Well one good thing, she thought, her pa had neither ran him off or killed him, and she truly was thankful for that. Pa! She had completely forgotten about her pa. She looked around frantically, searching for him. But when she saw no sign of him, she visibly relaxed.

"You don't have to worry. I told you last night that I would protect you and I mean it," Garrett said softly. "Your father and I had a long talk last night, things are going to be different from now on."

"I'm sorry, I don't remember much about last night. When I first woke up this mornin', I thought I'd been kicked by a cow, that has happened before. Then it all came back to me, what happened yesterday I mean," she said, shuddering slightly. Her face was completely without color.

Taking her by the elbow, Garrett helped her to the table. Mrs. Pruitt was waiting with a steaming, hot cup of coffee and a plate of mouth-watering food. "Just sit down right there and take it easy. We've been very worried about you," Mrs. Pruitt said. After making sure Charlie was all settled in, Mrs. Pruitt scurried back to the stove for more hot coffee.

The room was very quiet, but it didn't last long. It seemed everybody started talking at once. The twins were talking a mile a minute, Taylor and Maddie was trying to talk louder than the twins, which was impossible, even Jack was trying to get a word in every now and then. Charlie looked over at Garrett and Mrs. Pruitt, both of them were grinning like idiots. She suddenly realized how things had already changed. She almost felt like crying, but instead, she started to laugh and it felt good.

Garrett was standing by the sink with Mrs. Pruitt when Charlie started laughing. He studied her very closely, noticing how her whole face seemed to light up when she laughed. At that point, he knew he wanted her like no other woman. He was lost deep in thought, dreaming about a short, sassy woman, when he felt a little action below his belt, this was not a good time for that to happen. He turned toward the sink, away from everybody, pretending to look out the kitchen window.

Mrs. Pruitt was watching the sparks fly between Charlie and Garrett. They just didn't know it yet. She looked at Jack, smiling when she noticed his expression. They both had waited a long time for some young man to come into Charlie's life. They were hoping that man was Garrett.

Charlie answered all sorts of questions as she finished her breakfast. Finally one by one the crowd left the kitchen. Tristen and Austin went with Jack to the barn, they had to finish their morning chores. Taylor and Maddie went with Mrs. Pruitt to gather eggs at the hen house. That left Charlie and Garrett alone together.

"I want to thank you," Charlie said softly. She was still sitting at the kitchen table, her hands folded in her lap.

"You don't have to thank me. I really meant what I said before. Things are going to be different from now on. I don't want you to worry about your father any longer. I'll take care of him. I'm not afraid of him."

"If you're not afraid of him, you must be stupid. He's a very dangerous man. You have to watch that damn foreman of his to. He's my pa's puppet and he's lower than a snake's belly. He'll do whatever my pa tells him to do. I'm tellin' you right now, don't turn your back on either one of 'em."

Garrett bristled at the insult. "I've been taking care of myself for a very long time, and just for your information, I'm not stupid." This woman could get under his skin faster than a tick.

Charlie snorted with laughter, "It looked like you were really handling things yesterday…greenhorn. You bout near got yourself and your sister killed. Who ever heard of walking around in the middle of an open pasture."

Garrett refused to be baited further. "I'm not going to argue with you. You know what I think. I think you argue with me because you're scared of me. That's what I think. You feel the same attraction that I do, don't you wildcat?" He watched her closely, wanting to see her reaction.

For once Charlie was speechless, almost. "Afraid of you. Ha! That'll be the day. I'll have you know that I'm not afraid of nothin', especially not—"

She never had the opportunity to finish her sentence. Garrett grabbed her, pulling her delectable body up against him, covering her mouth with his. He released her after what seemed like hours, but actually was only seconds, at that point, amazingly she was speechless. She stared after him as he walked out the door, he was saying something about moving her furniture upstairs. She shook her head, knowing that would never work, her pa would have a fit.

51

While everybody was eating breakfast, there was some activity going on at the barn. James and Gimpy was saddling up, getting ready for the ride into town. "When we get to town, I want you to start sending telegrams to all those people we discussed last night. I want to find out anything I can about that sonofabitch up at the house," James said, mounting his horse.

"If I don't get answers back right away. How many do you want me to send?" Gimpy asked. He was busy trying to strike a match against his saddle.

"As many as it takes. I want him gone from here as soon as possible. And I aim to do whatever it takes to get the job done. Now quit foolin' around with that match and follow me," he said. He gouged his horse with sharp spurs causing the animal to twist and turn before heading in the right direction. "Now remember, I'm going to stop at the telegraph office with you. I need to send a wire to my attorney. Then I'm going on over to the saloon," James said. He looked at Gimpy, making sure he understood.

"Yeah boss, I remember."

Both men rode by the house very slowly. They could hear the noise and laughter coming from the kitchen. Neither man turned their heads in the direction of the house. Once they reached the gate, they urged their horses to a faster pace. They were both in a hurry to reach town. The sooner they got there, the sooner they could be rid of Steele, once and for all.

Chapter Fourteen

Charlie was nervous! It had been two days since her pa had been home and that was completely unlike him. He was up to something, and that worm Gimpy, was right along with him. She just wished they would come home, then the waiting and wondering would be over. Garrett had told her not to worry about something that hadn't happened, but she couldn't help it. She had to admit, things had been pretty calm the past couple of days. Everyday had been very busy, they had gotten a lot of work done, but there was still a lot more left.

She was sitting quietly on her horse, thinking about the changes that Garrett's presence had brought about. The atmosphere at the ranch had changed considerably over the past two days. Everybody seemed more at ease. The men had been working side by side with Garrett. They all had been working close to the ranch.

Garrett was a natural rancher. He wanted to learn all he could about ranching. Jack and the twins were helping him tremendously. And so far, Garrett was adapting to the work, like a duck takes to water. He really enjoyed being on the ranch.

There was something else Charlie liked about having Garrett on the ranch. She liked to watch him, hoping not to get caught of course. He was one with his horse. She would never get tired of watching those impossibly wide shoulders, but that wasn't all she liked to watch. She just didn't know how to explain the effect he had upon her. At that moment Garrett turned in the saddle, looking directly at her, their eyes seemed to bond together, but the spell was broken quickly. Austin let the gate swing back, smacking Garrett's horse on the rump. The horse bolted, jumping and twisting all at the same time. Garrett, who had been daydreaming about Charlie's fantastic body, went flying, landing hard.

Garrett was stunned, one minute he was looking into the prettiest dark eyes he had ever seen, and the next he was lying flat of his back, feeling like a damn fool kid. What made it worse, Jack and the twins saw it all happen, and of course, don't forget Charlie. He was never going to live this down. Turning his head slightly to one side, he noticed Charlie had dismounted and was walking toward him. He could hear Jack and the boys snickering behind his back. He was in for it now.

The more Charlie thought about the situation, the funnier it became. When she saw Garrett leave the saddle, it had scared her. She climbed down off her horse, trying to get to Garrett as fast as possible. But when she saw Garrett roll to his knees, his face covered with dust, she started to laugh. It didn't take her long to reach his side, still snickering, quietly. Everything was OK until she looked at Jack and the boys, after that she just couldn't help herself. She started laughing harder, unfortunately, Garrett didn't think it was funny.

"Just what the hell do you think you're laughing at?" Garrett growled. He was standing now, slapping the dust from his clothes and searching for his hat, which didn't escape harms way, his horse had stepped right in the middle of the crown, smashing it flat.

Charlie wiped the tears from the corner of her eyes. "Well, I haven't quite figured it out, but when I do, I'll be sure and let you know. In the mean time greenhorn, you might have to try that trick again, that way I can make up my mind for sure." She erupted into another round of laughter, bending over slightly, her hands resting on her knees.

By this time, all the commotion had brought some of the ranch hands, and of course Mrs. Pruitt, closer. They were all within hearing distance of the pair. Mrs. Pruitt walked closer to Jack. "What in the blue blazes is goin' on out here?" she asked.

Jack looked at her and grinned. "Those two have been proddin' each other for the past couple of days. You might want to step back, I think the fireworks are about to start," he said.

Mrs. Pruitt turned a worried eye toward the pair. "You don't think he'll hurt her do you? I know sometimes she can be trying, but she don't mean a thing by it. She's had to be rough to survive." She started over to stop them but Jack stopped her.

"Come back here Bea. He's not goin' to hurt her. Why he wouldn't harm a hair on her head. He just hasn't figured out what's goin' on yet, that's all." He couldn't keep the smile off his weathered face as the pair squared off, getting ready to do battle.

"Just what hasn't he figured out yet?" Mrs. Pruitt asked warily.

"That's as plain as the nose on your face. He's crazy in love with her, he just can't help but fight it. A man always does," Jack said, wrapping his arms around Mrs. Pruitt. She snuggled deeper into Jack's warm embrace, loving the feel of his arms around her. When they turned their attention back to

54

Garrett and Charlie, they found the younger couple standing nose to nose. This was going to be something to watch.

"I have never in my life been around such a smart ass woman," Garrett shouted.

"Well, I sure can't help it if you're used to hangin' around dumb women, that's your own fault," she yelled right back.

Garrett stared at her for a minute, then exploded. "That's not what I meant and you know it. I was talking about that sharp tongue of yours, not your intelligence."

Charlie raised her hat, scratching her head. She seemed to be thinking. "Just because I don't use five dollar words, don't mean I'm stupid. I'm just as smart as the next guy," she ground out. She was starting to get riled.

God! She was amazing, just barely reaching his shoulder, but what she lacked in height, she sure made up for it, with wit and a few other assets. Here she was, standing toe to toe arguing with him. He had to be close to a foot taller and probably about eighty pounds heavier. What in the world was he going to do with this little wildcat? He knew what he would like to do with her.

Garrett was brought back from daydreaming with fingers snapping in his face. He looked down, only to find Charlie glaring up at him. "Did you say something to me?"

"I sure did. Do you have trouble hearin'?" she asked. "I know I don't have real good manners, but even I know it ain't polite to ignore people, like you was doin' to me. Do you know what I'm talkin' about greenhorn?"

Garrett let her finish her little tirade before answering. He just couldn't stay mad very long. She could sure irritate the hell out of him, faster than any female he had ever come into contact with. "First of all," he began, "I wasn't ignoring you. It must have appeared that way, but I wasn't. Actually, I was daydreaming, and if you wouldn't mind repeating the question, I'll be glad to give you an answer," he said.

"That's the point I'm tryin' to get across to you greenhorn. You have to keep your mind on your business out here, if you don't, you might end up gettin' hurt. Accidents can happen real fast and some of them are deadly," she said very serious.

"Are you afraid that I'm going to get hurt? If you are, you must care about me to be afraid for me." Garrett was trying to find out if she felt the same way about him.

Charlie stood with her head hanging down for some time. When she lifted her head, she had sparks shooting from her eyes. "I think you're just making fun of me. Don't you think I know that I'm not the kind of woman a man like you would want, but still yet that don't give you the right to be makin' fun of me. You know what I ought to do. I ought to just punch you in the nose and give you something to think about." And the funny thing is, that's just what she did, then stomped off to the house.

Garrett stood holding his nose. This was not going to be easy. One minute they had been arguing, the next he was almost ready to tell her that he loved her, then the little wildcat had punched him in the nose. He noticed that Mrs. Pruitt had followed Charlie into the house. He walked slowly over to Jack, still holding his nose.

"Did you see that?" he asked. "She punched me right in the damn nose."

Jack couldn't hardly keep a straight face. "I sure did, looked like she walloped you pretty good, but if you're just playing with her, you deserved it. That girl has had a hard life. You got to understand, her pa has always run her down. Always told her she was good for nothin' and ugly to boot. And you know what's sad?" he asked. "She believes it."

When the back door slammed shut, both men turned, watching the two women enter the house. "I wish he was here right now. Believe me, I'd do more than punch him in the nose. I'd kick his ass all over again," Garrett said. He was staring at the back door, still holding his sore nose, wondering how to make it up to Charlie.

Mrs. Pruitt followed Charlie into the kitchen. "Are you all right Charlie?" she asked softly. She stepped closer, engulfing Charlie in a motherly embrace.

"I'm fine," Charlie said, wiping tears from her face, "You know me, I'm as tough as nails."

"Come here child and let me hold you. It's been a long time since I've done that." Mrs. Pruitt didn't have to wait long before Charlie turned, walking straight into her outstretched arms. "Do you want to talk about anything? You know sometimes that can make a world of difference in the way you feel."

"Oh, Mrs. Pruitt, I don't know where to begin. I've never in my life felt like this. The only thing I know for sure right now is that I miss mama," Charlie said, hugging Mrs. Pruitt tight. How she wished she was beautiful, and delicate, maybe that would make a difference. Her looks had never really bothered her before, until now. She was just going to have to make the best of the situation.

"I know you miss your mama, because I miss her to. I loved her like she was my own daughter. She was a special person, just like you." Mrs. Pruitt was squeezing her tight, her voice trembling. "I know things have been mighty rough, and I'm sorry for not taking better care of you, but it's going to be different now that Garrett is here."

Suddenly Charlie stood up straight, her eyes red from crying. "You've always taken good care of all of us. I love you just like you were my mama, never forget that. If you hadn't been here, I don't know what would have happened to us, even before mama died." Charlie pulled away from the older woman's embrace, twisting her hands as she walked back and forth across the kitchen floor. She stopped in front of Mrs. Pruitt, crying again.

"What's wrong? Don't you believe Garrett will change things? Maybe if you tell me what's troubling you, I can help fix it." Mrs. Pruitt had a pretty good idea what was bothering Charlie, but she was waiting for Charlie to admit it.

Charlie didn't quite know how to answer. She finally decided to blurt it out. "Garrett, that's the problem. I don't know what in the hell is wrong with me." She was trying to hide her emotions under a tough exterior. "Sometimes he makes me so mad, I could just punch him in the nose, and other times I want to—"

Mrs. Pruitt finished Charlie's sentence. "Kiss him silly," she said smiling.

Charlie jerked her head up so fast that she bit her tongue. "How did you know?" she asked, her face turning bright red under her sun-darkened skin. "I mean why would you say a thing like that?" she asked.

"Because I've got eyes. Garrett is a very handsome man, there would be something wrong with you if you didn't notice."

"That's the whole problem. He's just about the best lookin' man I've ever seen. And he's got the widest shoulders that I've ever seen on any man. Not that I've looked at a lot," she stammered. She lowered her head, her face was starting to heat up again.

Mrs. Pruitt was confused. "You mean it causes some sort of problem because he's so handsome. I've never heard of such."

Charlie couldn't hold back the tears any longer. "It's causing a big problem. Somebody like that would never look at me. I'm as big as a cow and ugly as a wore out old boot, look at me," she cried, holding her arms out.

"You're not heavy, and you're not ugly, in fact, you are a very lovely woman, not just on the outside but on the inside to. Where did you get the notion that you are big and ugly?" Mrs. Pruitt asked.

"Pa, he always said no man would ever want me. He always told me that I'd better learn to work and take care of myself. Because I'd always have to."

Mrs. Pruitt gathered Charlie into her arms. "Let me tell you something young lady. Your pa is wrong! Any man would be lucky to have you. You know what else I think…. I think Garrett is attracted to you. He gets a special glow in his eyes every time he looks at you." She rubbed small circles on Charlie's back as she talked. "I'm going to give you one more piece of advice."

"What's that," Charlie asked, looking a little skeptical.

"You've got to stop punching him in the nose. He might get the idea that you don't like him." Both women erupted into fits of laughter.

Chapter Fifteen

James was sitting in the corner of the Spotted Horse Saloon. He was very nervous and edgy. He rode into town two days ago, Gimpy had come with him. They were trying to find out any information about Steele. So far, they had sent several telegrams to different locations, but had come up empty handed. The waiting was beginning to drive James crazy. He wanted to get back to the ranch, but they were still waiting for replies on two telegrams.

Slowly lifting the glass to his lips, James swallowed the amber liquid, welcoming the taste of good whiskey. The first thing he was going to take care of, he decided, was that damn housekeeper. He had put up with her for the past eighteen years, and he was going to enjoy tossing her out on her ear. The next thing he was going to deal with, was that pig-headed daughter of his. When he got done with her this time, she would never cross him again. Hell! He might even make her sleep in the barn, he thought.

James motioned for the bartender to fill his glass, one more time. He tossed a coin down on the table, waiting for another full glass. After the bartender, Sam, refilled his glass, he lifted it off the table. Before reaching his lips, he slammed the glass back down, hard, sloshing amber liquid over the rim of the glass. Just thinking about Garrett Steele made his blood boil. He was really going to enjoy chopping that sonofabitch down to size. He had worked his ass off making the Circle Bar M one of the most prosperous ranches in New Mexico, and nobody was going to take it away from him. He would do whatever he had to, but he would keep his ranch safe.

He had often wondered in the past two days why in the hell his father had to marry that bitch, Anna Steele. Things had been good between him and his father before his father had married Anna. And what had made a bad situation even worse was, his stepbrother Benjamin, Garrett's father. Benjamin had always been a thorn in James' side. Shortly after Anna and Benjamin entered their lives, things had changed forever.

Everybody thought Benjamin could do no wrong. He was a very intelligent person, and things just seemed to fall in place for him. It wasn't long before James' own father, Alex McCuan, started to turn against James. It seemed like he was always taking Ben's side.

James reached for the glass of whiskey on the table, lifting it all the way to his lips. A sudden smile curved his mouth. He was really going to enjoy the next few weeks, after he got done with that sniveling coward...Steele...absolutely nobody would mess with him. He leaned back in his chair, after finishing off his drink. The saloon doors suddenly swung open and Gimpy came hurrying through them, looking for the boss.

Gimpy spotted James. He raced over to stand directly if front of him. "You're never goin' to guess what happened," Gimpy said.

James pushed his hat back on his forehead, studying Gimpy very closely before answering. "You best be tellin' me before I have to guess."

"I was just makin' my last stop over at the telegraph office, you know to see if any more answers had come in, and just as soon as I walked in, Jeb told me I had a message. Well, it seems our friend Steele used to be a U.S. Marshall down in Arizona Territory. But he just up and quit about three years ago," he said. He pulled out a chair while motioning for the bartender to bring over another glass, and bottle of whiskey.

"Is that all you have to tell me?"

"Hell no! I just need to wet my whistle, this is kind of a long story and it's been real hot outside."

James grabbed Gimpy by the shirt collar, pulling him over the table. "If you don't hurry the hell up, you're not goin' to be needing anything to drink for a long time," James growled.

Gimpy sat back down. After straightening his collar, he put the cork back in the bottle. "It seems about three years ago Steele's parents were killed in a stage holdup. There were four men responsible. They robbed the stage, killin' the driver and all the passengers. When Steele found out about it, he sort of went crazy. He vowed to hunt down the men and bring 'em back to stand trial. And remember, he was still a marshal then. Anyways, it didn't take long to track the men down. The thing is, only two made it back alive, the other two was grave yard dead."

James was becoming more interested. "I'm sure there is a point to this story, and if there is, I'd appreciate it if you would get to it."

"I'm gettin' to it boss, just give me time," he said. He took a long drink from his glass, emptying it, before finishing his story. "Just so happens them four men were cousins, two sets of brothers. One brother from each family was killed, and the other two were sent to prison for life. After the trial was over, Steele just up and turned in his badge. He had to take care of his little sister. About eight months ago, he sold out and moved on. He lived down around the Tucson area. But do you know what the best part is?" Gimpy asked.

"Hell no! You stupid idiot. I've been waiting for the last thirty minutes for you to tell me. And I'm starting to get pissed off." James was bellowing at the top of his lungs. The few people in the saloon turned to stare at the two men in the corner.

Looking at James with an evil grin, Gimpy calmly answered. "One of those men, the ones that robbed the stage, has a couple of brothers that are looking for Steele. It seems they want to settle a score with Steele."

Sitting back, taking a long slow drink, James studied the man in front of him. "How do you know this information is correct?" he asked.

"I have a cousin that lives down around Tucson, and he heard the information first hand. The brothers were there asking questions one night about six months ago, and they've been seen around there pretty often ever since. Rowdy, that's my cousin, even knows their names, Brett and Chad Gilkey. Oh, and there is one part I forgot to tell you. According to Rowdy, Steele is really one mean sonofabitch. He's deadly with a gun. Rowdy said they call him Cold Steele, because he's ruthless. He has no mercy when it comes to outlaws."

"I think I have the solution to our problems Gimpy. Do you think your cousin could track the Gilkey brothers down? If he can, I'll make it worth his time and effort." James leaned back, a pleasant smile on his face. "If he can find them, tell him to wire me here, and wait for my reply." He stood up from the table, walking away. He stopped, turning back around. "I'm going to start for home tonight. You stay here and wait for an answer of some kind. When you find out something, come back to the ranch. Then, we'll plan our next move." James reached into his pants pocket, grabbing a handful of coins. He tossed them on the table in front of Gimpy. "That should cover expenses, if there's any left over, you can keep it for your own entertainment."

Gimpy scooped the money off the table. He watched his boss leave the saloon.

"Don't worry none boss, I'm sure I can find something to keep me entertained." First thing he had to do was, send a telegram to his cousin Rowdy, then he was going over to the Rusted Bucket for a look at the new girl.

Later that night, back at the ranch, everyone gathered in the kitchen for a late supper. Everybody was tense, all eyes were on Garrett and Charlie. They were sitting on opposite sides of the table and so far had completely avoided all contact with each other. They were both polite to everyone, except each other.

Jack looked up, grinning at the sight of Garrett's swollen nose. Charlie sure had smacked him a good one. When those two finally figured out what was wrong with them, it sure was going to be funny. Jack took a bite of mashed potatoes and just happened to look over at Charlie. If looks could kill a feller, Garrett sure would be dead about now.

When supper was over, Mrs. Pruitt told the twins, Tristen and Austin, to take Taylor and Maddie to the living room and read them a story before bed. She was clearing off the table when Garrett stood, heading for the door. "You have not been excused, so just sit yourself back down," Mrs. Pruitt said. Garrett stopped dead in his tracks, looking back at Mrs. Pruitt then over at Jack, before sitting back down.

Charlie caught herself smiling. She quickly lowered her head so Mrs. Pruitt wouldn't catch her laughing. The only problem was Jack, he was sitting right beside her.

"You can just wipe that smile off your face missy," Jack said.

Charlie raised her head to look at Jack. He had never spoken to her in that tone of voice, it startled her.

Mrs. Pruitt set four cups of fresh coffee down on the table. She sat beside Garrett at the table. She slowly stirred her coffee, finally looking up as she spoke. "Jack and I have talked this over, and at first we weren't going to interfere, but we think it's time to step in." Looking over at Garrett, Mrs. Pruitt continued. "We haven't known you very long, but in the short time that we have, we've become very attached to you. You're a very fine man."

Jack turned and looked at Charlie. "Charlie, you know that Bea and I love you like a daughter. We always have and we always will. But the thing is…you two have got to settle down and work out your differences," he said, patting her hand.

"It tears us apart each time you fight with each other. You are both adults and it's time you started acting like it," Mrs. Pruitt said quietly. Jack walked around the table, holding out his hand to Mrs. Pruitt. "Come on Bea." They walked toward the living room to join the other children. "We want you two to stay in here until you can work out some sort of arrangement with each other," Jack said. Then the older couple disappeared down the hallway.

Garrett was the first one to speak. "Look Charlie, I'm really sorry for what happened this afternoon. I wasn't making fun of you. Hell! I would smash any man's face for just thinking about making fun of you." He stood up. pacing in the kitchen, walking back and forth trying to expel some nervous energy. "I have to be honest with you. What I feel for you scares me, it scares me real bad. One minute I'm so mad I could spank your lovely bottom, the next I want to grab you and kiss you until you can't think straight. I've never felt like this before, about anyone." He stopped in front of the sink, turning to look at Charlie. He shoved his right hand through his thick hair, waiting for Charlie to say something.

Charlie was sitting with her head slightly bowed. She looked up at Garrett, tears shining in her eyes. "I've dreamed about someone like you all my life, but my father always said I would never be good enough," she said, her voice quivering. "I won't lie to you, I feel something very strong for you, but I can't explain it. It's just hard to believe that anybody would be attracted to me, especially someone like you," she paused, then rushed on, "I'm just plain fat, and ugly to boot. I don't have good manners, and I don't even know how to dress like a lady," she sniffed.

Garrett closed the space between them. He gathered Charlie into his arms, tilting her face back. "I don't ever want to hear you say those things about yourself ever again, do you hear me?" She nodded her head, tears streaming down her cheeks, but her dark eyes were shining bright. "It takes a lot more than manners and clothes to make a lady, and I happen to like you just fine the way you are," Garrett said softly. "You're soft and round, everywhere a lady is supposed to be, to tell you the truth, I don't like those ladies that look like a fence post," he said. He was rewarded with the most devastating smile he had ever seen.

Charlie stepped back out of his embrace. She held out her hand. "Truce."

"Truce. But that's not the way to seal an agreement," he said, grabbing her shoulders, pulling her close. He lowered his mouth to hers. And that was a big mistake, because he didn't want to stop at one kiss. Finally pulling away from her, he looked down at the dreamy expression Charlie had on her face. He knew he was definitely going to have to buy some bigger pants. But he would worry about that later, much later. He took her in his arms again, for just one more taste of those sweet lips.

Mrs. Pruitt had been standing in the hallway, just making sure things didn't get out of hand. But from the looks of things, everything was working out perfectly. She turned, walking back toward the living room, back to Jack, with a smile on her face.

The lights at the main house were still burning bright when a lone rider came through the gate, heading for the barn. As he rode by, he turned his head in the direction of the main house. He grinned, thinking, it wouldn't be long now, not long at all. Everything would be back to normal. He would just have to be patient for a few more days, even if it killed him.

Chapter Sixteen

The next morning Jack was walking up to the house for breakfast. He had some bad news, James was home. At least the waiting and wondering was over, everybody had been on pins and needles waiting for his return, most of all Charlie. Jack started walking faster, he needed to talk to Garrett, maybe they could come up with some kind of a plan so the women wouldn't be left alone at the ranch. Just as he was about to knock on the back door, it opened and Garrett walked out.

"I was on my way to find you," Jack said.

"Something wrong? You look pretty serious."

Jack didn't know any other way to tell Garrett, except flat out. "James is back. His horse is in the barn this morning. He must have come in late last night. I haven't seen him yet, so I guess he's down at the bunkhouse or maybe even over at Gimpy's place."

"What do you think the snake's been up to in town?" Garrett asked warily.

"My guess is he was trying to find out some information about you. He didn't have time to talk to his attorney, unless he sent him a telegram. His attorney is located over in Santa Fe, and that's a good three days ride from here," Jack said, squinting toward the barn.

Garrett stood quietly, looking out over the ranch yard. One thing he had learned in his life, never underestimate your enemy. He had learned that little lesson first hand, and right now James McCuan was his enemy. "You know we're going to have to tell Charlie and Mrs. Pruitt, they need to know. They can't be left alone, it might take us a few days to figure out our options, but until then, we need to watch every move that bastard makes. I promise you one thing, if he makes a move toward Charlie or one of the other children… I'll kill him…flat out…no questions." Garrett walked past Jack, heading for the barn. He had a specific purpose in mind.

Jack continued to stare at Garrett as he walked away. He almost shivered from the cold look that came to Garrett's stormy eyes. He sure would hate to be on the receiving end of that look. Maybe…just maybe, James had bitten off more than he could chew this time. He opened the back door and walked into the kitchen, he had a bad feeling about this.

Garrett walked through the side door of the barn. He was looking for his gear that was still stored in the barn. He needed something from his old trunk.

He was so pre-occupied that he didn't see Charlie backing out of one of the stalls with an armload of straw. He ran right into her, knocking her and the straw to the dirt floor.

Charlie was in her own little world. She was trying to get part of her chores done before breakfast, this was the last stall she had to clean today. She was upset! She had seen her pa's horse in the stable and that could only mean one thing, he was finally home, and it terrified her. With her arms loaded down with straw, she backed out of the last stall, her thoughts were a million miles away, so far away, she didn't hear the approaching footsteps, until it was too late. The force knocked her to the ground. The first thing she thought of was her pa, and she came up ready to fight. But before she could land any good solid blows, two strong arms wrapped around her, lifting her off the ground. She went crazy, kicking and biting anything she could reach, but the arms around her just squeezed tighter. She knew she was in trouble.

Garrett was trying to calm the little wildcat down, she was completely out of control.

He leaned close to her ear. "Charlie, calm down sweetheart, it's me Garrett. Please, you have to listen to me. I didn't mean to scare you." But she was still struggling against his tight hold. "You have to calm down, you're going to hurt yourself. Everything is going to be fine, I promise," he whispered in her ear.

Charlie could hear a voice, it almost sounded like Garrett's. She began to calm down, when she realized it was his voice. When he loosened his grip on her arms, she almost fell to the ground with relief, but it didn't take her long to perk up. "Geez Garrett, you scared the livin' shit right out a me. I thought you was my pa. I saw his horse in the stall this mornin' and I just knew I was in big trouble."

Garrett couldn't keep the grin off his face, most women would have been shaking and crying, but not Charlie. "I was just on my way down to get something from my gear. My mind was wandering, I didn't even see you until it was too late," Garrett said. He was still watching Charlie, trying to figure out the best way to tell her to stay close to the house. After a few minutes, he decided there was no good way. "Charlie, since your father is back. Well, Jack and I think it's a good idea if you stay close to the house, that way you'll be safe." Garrett could tell by the look on her face, she didn't like that idea one little bit.

"You can just forget that. I have work to do in case you ain't noticed. We got a ranch to run here, and it sure don't run all by its lonesome. You must be crazy thinkin' I'm going to stay up at the house with Mrs. Pruitt and the kids. I haven't done that in probably ten years. If you think you can come down here and—"

Garrett stopped her in mid sentence the only way he knew how, he kissed her, but it didn't stop there. He slowly ran his tongue along the seam of her full lips until she opened them, the tip of his tongue danced a duel with hers. When the kiss finally ended, both of them were breathing hard. Garrett pulled Charlie closer. He could feel her breasts pushed hard against his chest, and if felt good, actually it felt right. He slowly lowered his head, nibbling her neck just below her ear, her pulse was beating rapidly in the same spot. Gradually he eased his body away from her. He looked down into her beautiful face, her expression was dreamy, but her eyes remained closed. Suddenly her eyes popped open, glittering with shooting sparks.

"Just what the hell did you do that for? I was tryin' to tell you something. Until all this mess settles down you better keep your mind on business," Charlie fumed.

"I did have my mind on business until you distracted me. You practically knocked me down, then tried to seduce me," Garrett said, grinning.

"Me! I didn't knock you down, your the one that ran over me, and I don't even know what say…whatever the hell it was…means. What the hell are you doing down here anyway, besides pesterin' me?"

"First of all," Garrett replied calmly, "You will know what seduce means. I plan on teaching you the definition of that myself," he said cockily. "Do you know where Jack and the boys stored the rest of my things? I'm looking for a large black trunk." He was already busy searching for the trunk, Charlie was completely forgotten at the moment.

"Did you ever stop to think that maybe I don't want to know what that word means?" she asked. "And the trunk you're lookin' for is in the tack room."

"I guess I'll just have to take my chances, but I think you really want to know, your just afraid to admit it. Besides, I don't have time to show you right now, and it's something that can't be rushed." Garrett walked past her, opening the door to the tack room. He stepped inside, waiting for his eyes to adjust to the darkness. He spied the trunk in the corner of the room. Carefully making his way across the room, he slowly lifted the lid, digging down to the bottom, searching until he found the exact item he was looking for.

Charlie was standing just inside the door, it was dark in the tack room, because there was not a single window in the room. She could see Garrett looking through the trunk, finally it seemed he had found the object of his search. Charlie watched as Garrett stood, and lowered the trunk lid. He was carrying something in his hand. He moved toward Charlie with the grace of a cat. His movement mesmerized her. But when he reached the door, she finally identified the object in his hands, it was a gun, a colt forty-five to be exact. She jerked her head up, looking at Garrett, there was a cold look in his gray eyes. She shivered from the deadly look that had transformed his handsome features.

Slowly unrolling the well-oiled leather, Garrett fastened the gun belt around his slender hips. He fastened the wide leather belt, and tied the holster down to his hard, muscled thigh. When the gun was settled in a comfortable position, he straightened up to his full height. And for the first time he realized just how small Charlie really was, and she looked absolutely terrified. "Don't you have anything to say? If not, this could be classified as an honest to goodness miracle," Garrett teased.

After taking two or three deep breaths, Charlie looked up at Garrett. "Do you know how to use that thing greenhorn? Or is it just for looks? It never even occurred to me that someone like you would even own a gun, much less know how to use one," she snorted.

"Just for your information, I'm not a greenhorn around firearms, I'm actually very skilled with one. I've had a lot of experience." Garrett was trying to change the subject, he didn't want Charlie asking too many questions. "We had better head for the house, breakfast is probably ready, and I don't know about you, but I'm starving." Garrett bowed at the waist, his right arm slightly bent at the elbow. "If you would allow me, I would like to escort you to breakfast."

Charlie placed her hand upon Garrett's strong forearm, but it didn't stay there long before Garrett lifted it to his lips, gently kissing the back of her hand. He tucked her hand very snugly into the crook of his elbow. They walked arm in arm across the yard, both unaware that they were being watched from the corner of the bunkhouse.

James was livid, that bitch had already taken up with Steele. He should have known he couldn't trust her, she was just like her mother. He waited, watching them enter the house. Soon all the ranch hands would be up, and he could find out what had been going on the last few days.

About that time the door of the bunkhouse opened, two men walked out, stopping when they saw James standing there. The older man was Pete

Jackson, he spoke first. "Howdy boss, we sure have missed you the last couple of days. I don't know if you remember John here, he's my cousin's boy," Pete said. He was pointing to the younger boy standing next to him.

"Who the hell do you think hired the boy? Of course I remember him, I'm not ignorant. What's been going on around here the last couple of days? Is there anything I need to know about?" James asked impatiently. He was starting to pace in front of the bunkhouse. He was becoming very agitated.

Pete looked at James trying to hide his reaction. James was always short tempered, but today he seemed even worse, something was really bothering him. "Boss, I didn't mean you was ignor'nt or nothin' even like that. I was just makin' conversation with you, that's all. Ain't much been happenin' around here. We've been movin' beeves like we always do this time of year," Pete said. He noticed James was very nervous, he kept looking up at the main house every so often. "Is there anything you wanted to know about in particular?" Pete asked.

Standing there, his mind spinning fast, James seemed to be two steps ahead of Pete already. "Yeah, I need you and John here to do me a favor. When Gimpy gets back from town, tell him I'm up at the line shack in the North pasture, also tell him to bring more supplies and head on up there. I'll be back in a few days, but in the meantime, I need both of you to watch everything that goes on here. When I get back, you can fill me in." James was still watching the house, trying to get an idea of what was going on. "Do you think you can handle that?" he asked.

"Sure thing, me and John can handle it. Can't we boy?" Pete turned toward the boy, who only nodded his head.

Before walking to the barn, James shook hands with both men. Several minutes later he emerged on his horse. He tipped his hat to the men still standing in the same spot. As he rode off, heading north, his mind was still spinning rapidly. He would get even with all of them.

Chapter Seventeen

Gimpy was headed toward home. He had an answer to the telegram that he had sent to his cousin, Rowdy. The boss was going to be very pleased. Rowdy had already located the Gilkey brothers, they were in Tucson, waiting for instructions. Gimpy grinned, thinking he probably should have come home last night, but he got tied up at the Rusted Bucket. He had been having to good a time to leave. Hell! Just thinking about the way he had spent last night brought a smile to his face again, that new girl was good, damn good. He hoped this mess at the ranch was cleared up pretty quick, because he aimed to take a short vacation, he was going to the Rusted Bucket and stay a week. Stopping his horse under the shade of a large tree, he lifted his canteen to his lips, taking a long drink of the tepid water. He twisted the cap back on, lowering the canteen. He loved working out here, the pay was good, but most of all he loved working for James McCuan. They were a lot alike, both of them were ruthless. A few minutes passed before he realized it, shaking his head to clear the cobwebs, he pulled his hat down a little lower, urging his horse around, pointing him in the direction of the Circle Bar M. He had to find the boss, his cousin was waiting for an answer. He couldn't wait until that bastard…Steele…got what was coming to him.

Garrett was worried. McCuan was definitely up to something, but he couldn't figure out what it was. James had ridden out yesterday morning and none of the hands seemed to know where he had gone. Garrett had followed him, looking closely for signs. The only information Garrett had found, was, that McCuan was heading north, then, he just seemed to disappear, it was like looking for a ghost.

Tilting his head back, Garrett looked up at the sun. It was getting to be late afternoon and he needed to start back. He had promised Maddie that he wouldn't be gone long. He also needed to speak with Jack, of course that wasn't the only reason he wanted to get back. He had been awake most of the night thinking about Charlie. Oh, how he had dreamed, just thinking about it caused him to start grinning like a fool. He tried to imagine what she would look like lying in bed, next to him of course, the images he had conjured up were pure torture and she was unbelievable. Hanging his hat on the saddle horn, he ran his fingers through his thick hair. Charlie was completely unaware of the effect she had on people. His thoughts quickly turned ugly, remembering the way her father had abused her. But that was never going to happen again. He was going to take care of her from now on, she just didn't know it yet. He started off slowly, back toward home, whistling a low tune, it had been a very long time since he had felt this good.

Jack and the twins were busy repairing harness in the barn. It had been a very long day, they were all on edge. Garrett had ridden out yesterday, looking for signs of James, and so far he still hadn't returned. It was making Jack nervous, every few minutes he stopped working, looking to the north, searching for Garrett's return.

Up at the main house, the mood wasn't any better. Mrs. Pruitt was baking cookies, Charlie was helping, but not liking it. Before Garrett had left, he made Charlie promise not to go out alone, just until they found out what her pa was up to. Charlie was still kicking herself for agreeing, but she had promised Garrett, and she never went back on her word. Looking out the window for the hundredth time, Charlie was starting to get worried. Garrett had promised her he wouldn't be gone long, and it had been nearly two days.

Charlie was taking a hot batch of cookies out of the oven, when a noise in the yard drew her attention. She dropped the cookies on the table, running to the back door, jerking it open. The smile that had appeared on her face, quickly vanished, it was Gimpy coming back from town. Mrs. Pruitt opened her mouth, but before she could say anything, two little girls came skidding around the kitchen doorway.

"Is that Garrett?" Maddie asked. A worried expression hovered on her young face.

"No honey, it's just one of the hands," Mrs. Pruitt said softly.

The little girl stood wringing her hands. "Do you think something bad has happened? He promised he wouldn't be gone long, and he never breaks a promise."

Mrs. Pruitt opened her arms to both little girls. "Come here," she said, closing her arms around both girls. "Nothing bad has happened to Garrett, mark my words, he'll come riding in any minute. Now you two grab yourselves a warm cookie and go back to the living room and finish playing." Both little girls grabbed a cookie and scampered out of the kitchen.

Charlie had been standing with her back to the children, listening to Mrs. Pruitt, hoping the older lady was right. "Do you really think he's OK?"

"Yes child, I really do."

The tears that Charlie had been holding back, slowly started to roll down her cheeks. She swiped them away with the palm of her hands before turning to Mrs. Pruitt. "I've never told you this, because I was always afraid Pa would find out and send you away. I don't know what I would have done without you… I love you." She didn't try to stop the tears now, they were running in streams down her face, but she didn't care.

Mrs. Pruitt was silent for a long time, her head bowed. She finally looked up at Charlie, her eyes moist with unshed tears. "It does this old heart of mine good to hear you say those words. I have loved you since the day I wrapped you in that tiny blanket that your mother and I made for you." She looked like she wanted to say something else, but she was so choked up, no words were needed. Both women held each other and cried. Mrs. Pruitt said a silent prayer for Garrett, while trying to comfort the girl in her arms.

About an hour later, everyone was seated around the kitchen table. Charlie and Mrs. Pruitt were setting steaming bowls of food on the table. Jack was about to start carving the ham. The back door was opened, it was Garrett. The kitchen had been noisy before, but the commotion was deafening now, they all started trying to talk at once.

Maddie jumped up so fast from her chair, it flipped over backwards on the wooden floor. She never slowed down until she reached Garrett. "I was scared Garrett. You said you wouldn't be gone long," she said, grabbing him around the knees, holding him so tight he almost lost his balance.

"Come here sweet Maddie and let me hold you," he said, bending over and lifting the little girl into his strong arms. He hugged her close, burying his nose in her hair. "Remember what I've always told you, I'll never leave you, cross my heart and hope to die." He held her close, feeling her small body trembling, it broke his heart.

Maddie lifted her head from his shoulder, "I know what you've always said, but that doesn't stop me from being scared," she said. She turned her head, pointing her index finger at Charlie. "Even Charlie was starting to get scared, she acted like she missed you really bad."

All eyes turned, looking at Charlie. She could feel her neck and face starting to heat up. She glanced at Garrett, noticing the stupid grin he had on his handsome face. The embarrassment caused her temper to flare out of control. "If you ever scare us like that again, I'll…I'll."

"You'll do what?" Garrett asked. He kissed Maddie on the forehead before setting her back down on the floor. "I'm waiting for an answer,"

Garrett said. He was hoping Charlie would come over and give him a kiss, something he had been dreaming about for the past two days, and nights.

Charlie marched over to Garrett, stopping right in front of him. "Do you really want to know?" she asked sweetly.

Over the top of her head, Garrett could see Mrs. Pruitt and Jack, both of them were shaking their heads, but he wasn't about to back down now, not with those luscious lips only mere inches away from his. "Yes I—" He never finished the rest of the sentence. The pain in his nose was excruciating.

She had taken about all she could take. She had been worried sick for the past two days, then he comes waltzing in, acting like there's nothing to worry about, and she did the first thing that came to mind. She punched him right in the nose, again. Not waiting to see what happened next, she whirled around and ran outside.

After the laughter died down, Garrett pulled out a chair, sitting down wearily. "What did she do that for?" he asked, rubbing his nose. It was still a little sore from the last time she had popped him.

Jack was the first one to recover. "Boy, she's been worried sick about you the last couple of days, then you just walk in and act like everything is right as rain." Jack continued to laugh, until tears ran down his face.

"Worried or not, I'm getting tired of getting punched in the nose."

Maddie walked up beside Garrett. "Sometimes you deserve it. If I was bigger that's just what I would have done."

"Oh you would, I'd like to see you try it squirt," he said. He grabbed Maddie and began to tickle her until she begged him to stop. Garrett looked around at the other children, they were all so somber, they weren't used to this type of behavior. Maddie squirmed her way out his grasp, stepping just out of his reach. She turned around and stuck her tongue out at him.

Taylor had been sitting quietly, watching. She suddenly burst out laughing. Before she knew what was happening, Garrett grabbed her and began tickling her.

The twins, Austin and Tristen, were watching Maddie and Taylor. They looked at each other, trying to decide whether or not to join the fun, it didn't take them long. They jumped right into the middle of the action. All the children were trying to wrestle Garrett to the floor, and tickle him at the same time. The laughter was so loud, they didn't hear Charlie walk into the kitchen, but Jack and Mrs. Pruitt did.

Jack and Mrs. Pruitt had moved their chairs farther back away from the ruckus. It was fun watching the children have a good time, but it was even better to see the look of astonishment on Charlie's face.

Charlie was amazed, the children were on the floor, wrestling, and Garrett was in the middle. It looked they were trying to tickle each other. She didn't have time to think about it before somebody jerked her off balance. She landed right in the middle of the melee. It wasn't long before little fingers and some big fingers started tickling her all over. The big fingers seemed to be straying just a little, but she didn't have time to think, she had to start an attack of her own.

Before long the girls were shrieking at the top of their lungs, and the twins were begging for mercy. But Garrett and Charlie were still after them. After what seemed like hours, things started to settle down, the children were getting tired.

It's a good thing all the wrestling was just about over, because Charlie's face was flushed with excitement and Garrett was hard as a rock, it seemed he had been tickling the wrong body parts. He bent his leg at the knee, trying to hide the evidence of his arousal, but it was useless. He knew Jack had already seen his predicament, the old coot was grinning like a fool. He only hoped Mrs. Pruitt hadn't spotted the problem. After disciplining his body, he stood, offering Charlie his hand, slowly pulling her to her feet. "That was the most fun I've had in a long time," he whispered in her ear.

"Actually, I enjoyed it myself, greenhorn."

Garrett's mind kicked into fast gallop. He had to do something about his attraction to Charlie. He had been saving some news, now was the time to tell everybody. "If it's all right with everyone, I think we all need a little time away from the ranch. I would like to take a little trip to Santa Fe, you know spend a few days. I need to send some telegrams and I don't want to send them from Broken Tongue, to many big ears around." He didn't have to wait long before everybody started talking at once.

"You mean we can all go with you?" Tristen asked.

"Yes, I don't see why not. We'll take the wagon for the ladies to ride in, that way we can bring back some supplies. We can have a little vacation of sorts, go out to eat, maybe see as show while we're there." Everybody started whooping and hollering, even Mrs. Pruitt and Jack.

Charlie was stunned. She had never been to a town the size of Santa Fe. Her pa wouldn't let her or Taylor go. She suddenly realized what a fool she would look like, she didn't even own a dress, let alone know how to act in town. This wasn't going to be much fun at all. She would have to think of an excuse.

Gimpy had been riding out of the yard, right past the kitchen. He heard the raised voices. Sliding down out of the saddle, he hunkered down under the kitchen window, listening. He was quiet, trying to pick up any information to take to the boss, and it didn't take long. He swung up in the saddle, spurring his horse, heading for the line shack.

Thanks to Pete Jackson, and his nephew, he knew exactly where to find the boss. And the boss was going to be real glad to hear that Steele and all the other no accounts living in the house, were all leaving for Santa Fe. That would give them enough time to get word to the Gilkey brothers. Things were beginning to look up.

Chapter Eighteen

The trip to Santa Fe took the small caravan four days, normally it would have taken three days, but they traveled at a leisurely pace. They camped out each night and the children loved it. The boys raced around on their horses, exploring every nook and cranny. They were completely carefree. The two little girls rode in the wagon with Jack and Mrs. Pruitt, they chattered all day long, until they were totally exhausted, usually falling asleep in the back of the wagon. Charlie and Garrett rode along side by side on their mounts, sometimes laughing and sometimes talking softly to each other, a few times Garrett had held her hand. Charlie loved the feel of his work-roughened hand covering hers. Things had been just about perfect for the last three days, the little group acted as if they didn't have a worry in the world.

But today was the last day on the trail. Charlie just realized that tomorrow they would reach Santa Fe, and by evening she was starting to withdraw from the others. She sat sullenly by the fire before supper, not wanting to think about tomorrow. Hearing movement to her left, Charlie looked in that direction, but after staring into the fire, she couldn't see a thing.

Mrs. Pruitt sat down on a rock beside her, after arranging her skirts, she looked at Charlie. "Is there something on your mind, if there is, maybe I can help?' Mrs. Pruitt asked in her best motherly tone.

"There's nothin' wrong with me."

"Now I don't believe that for one minute. Something is eating at you, your whole attitude has changed from yesterday. Did Garrett do something he shouldn't have? If he did, I'll string him up by his ears." Mrs. Pruitt was really becoming fired up.

Charlie quickly answered, "He hasn't done anything to me. It's just me, I'm stupid and ignorant."

"Just what do you mean by that, you're neither of those things. Come on child, tell me what's upsetting you."

"Well...we'll reach town sometime tomorrow. But the thing is, I don't know nothin' about actin' and dressin' like a lady. Garrett said we would go out to eat and maybe see some kind of show. Well hell! I don't even know what he's talkin' about." By this time, Charlie was pacing back and forth like a caged animal. "The thing is, I'm kind of startin' to like him, and I don't want to act like a damn fool. I don't want to embarrass him or nothin'." Charlie was standing with her back to Mrs. Pruitt. But after hearing the older woman snickering, Charlie spun around just in time to see Mrs. Pruitt trying to hide her humor. "I sure am glad to be providin' you with some entertainment," Charlie snapped.

After wiping her eyes, Mrs. Pruitt began to explain. "It's not that you're providing me with entertainment, it's just that I've never seen you in such a dither about anything, except maybe the time you ripped your favorite britches, but certainly never over a man. I think it's wonderful. Look sweetheart, Garrett doesn't care about your manners or the way you dress. He fell in love with the real Charlie McCuan, and you're beautiful to him all the time."

"Do you really think so? I know I'm not much to look at, and when we get there, I'm sure there will be lots of pretty ladies in fancy dresses and fine manners. I'm just afraid that…I'm just afraid," she said quietly.

"I'll tell you what, when we get to Santa Fe, you and I'll go shopping, it will be fun. We'll find you a fine dress with all the trappings. Don't worry, I'll show you how to walk in those fancy shoes. Sweetheart, I promise when we're done, Garrett won't be able to keep his eyes off of you." Mrs. Pruitt climbed to her feet, dusting off her skirt. "Now cheer up, I've got to go finish supper, Jack and the boys are probably done cleaning those fish. Now I'm telling you again, don't worry about a thing."

After supper that night, Mrs. Pruitt and Jack were settling the children down for bed. Garrett had been waiting all evening to get Charlie alone. He needed to speak with her. He picked up his coffee cup, walking around the fire, stopping, he squatted down beside her. "I've been trying to talk to you all day, but you seemed to be avoiding me." His gray eyes were shining bright.

"I haven't been avoiding you at all. I've just been busy helpin' Mrs. Pruitt, that's all."

Garrett rose to his full height, extending his hand to her. "Well if you're not avoiding me, how about taking a short stroll with me. I promise I'll be good." He looked like a little boy that had been caught with his hand in the candy jar…guilty.

Placing her hand in his much larger one, Charlie pulled herself up off the ground. "I need to tell Mrs. Pruitt where I'm goin'." She started in the direction of the wagon until Garrett pulled her slowly into his waiting arms.

"There's no need for that, Jack knows you will be with me." He lightly brushed his lips over hers. The jolt was instant, both of them jerked apart, wondering what had happened. "Did you feel that?" he whispered against her tender lips.'

"I felt somethin', but I don't know what it was, but it felt pretty good greenhorn."

Grasping her hand tightly, Garrett led her away from the fire. As soon as they were well away from the wagon, he pulled Charlie against him. He needed to feel her body next to his. She was driving him insane. He tucked her head beneath his chin, gathering her closer, she fit perfectly. Her body had so many curves, he didn't know where to begin, she was perfect. Lifting her chin, he kissed her again, this time not as gentle. He had to taste her. His hands roamed all over her full body. He was going to explode any minute.

Charlie's head was spinning, her senses were out of control. Garrett's mouth and hands were all over her body, yet she couldn't seem to get close enough. She wanted to fell his bare skin beneath her curious hands. She ran her hands up his back, stopping to caress his broad shoulders. Her heart was hammering in her chest or maybe it was his, she couldn't tell. She arched her back, allowing him better access, as his lips skimmed over her cheek down to her neck, nipping her lightly, causing her to groan deep in her throat. He was moving farther down, leaving a trail of small kisses as he went.

Charlie's legs turned to jelly as Garrett turned his attention to her breasts. All that was keeping her upright was Garrett's strong arms. They were like bands of iron around her, she felt so safe.

Two more buttons and he would have her shirt off. She was incredible, Garrett thought, her breasts were large and plump, her hips were round and full, just right for cradling a man. He was glad that he was going to be her first lover. The other two buttons were almost undone. Garrett felt Charlie stiffen in his arms, she was trying to pull away from him. He started to mentally kick himself, he was moving too fast, he had probably scared the living hell out of her, that's when he heard it. It was Jack, he was looking for them. They sprang apart so fast Garrett lost his balance and fell. Charlie was busy stuffing her shirttail back down in her pants when Garrett fell. She looked at Garrett and laughed, it was full of joy, making Garrett smile in the darkness.

Charlie touched the side of Garrett's face one last time before turning to answer Jack. "I'm over here Jack, I'll be right there." She was gone, swallowed by the black night.

After locating his hat on the ground, Garrett sat there breathing hard, damn he wasn't going to get any sleep tonight. He was hard as a rock, first thing tomorrow he was going to stop by the mercantile, and buy some new pants, maybe it wouldn't be so painful, he hoped.

The next morning, at dawn, Jack and Garrett was feeding and grooming the animals. Jack looked over the broad back of the sorrel horse he was brushing, noticing Garrett looked like shit. He lowered his head. "Have a rough night?" he asked grinning.

"NO!," Garrett grumbled.

Jack looked down at Garrett's pants. "Your pants look a might bit wrinkled. Did you fall in the creek accidental like?" he asked in a sincere tone of voice. Jack pulled his hat down, trying to hide his amusement. "Or maybe you decided to take a midnight swim in that cold water down at the creek."

"Shut up! Just shut the hell up. I'm in no mood for foolishness this morning." Garrett stalked over to his gear, lifting his saddle off the ground. He had his horse saddled and ready to go in no time. He grabbed the saddle horn and swung into the saddle, all in one fluid motion. He needed time to think. Pulling his hat down tight, he thundered out of the small camp.

Jack continued caring for the animals, but he couldn't keep the smile off his face. The boy had it bad, he was just afraid to admit it.

Mrs. Pruitt and Charlie had just finished getting water from the creek when Garrett flew by on his horse. "Oh my, did the two of you have some sort of disagreement last night?" Mrs. Pruitt asked, amusement heavy in her voice.

Unable to answer, as the memories flooded back to her mind, Charlie shook her head. They had had a wonderful time last night. The only thing she would change next time, would be Garrett's gun belt. She would ask him to remove it, the buckle kept poking her in the stomach. Her eyes grew round and her face began to heat up when she figured out what had been poking her. "Everything was just fine," she answered. Maybe when they reached Santa Fe, she could find out just exactly what was supposed to go on between a man and a woman.

They would reach Santa Fe today. She was kind of looking forward to it now. She was hoping to spend some time alone with Garrett. When Charlie turned around, she saw that Mrs. Pruitt was gone, she was talking to Jack. They were both laughing about something. Charlie smiled, she was glad everybody was having a good time. After they reached Santa Fe, she decided she was going to do a little investigating, she would find out just what Garrett's gun belt was for. She hurried with the rest of her morning chores, because the sooner they left, the sooner they would reach town.

People stopped on the main street of Broken Tongue to get a good look at the two strangers riding into town. They looked like death on horseback. They were both short and husky, with long beards and even longer hair. But that wasn't what caught their attention, it was the twin colts strapped down low on their thighs, they looked deadly.

Stopping in front of the Spotted Horse Saloon, both men stepped down out of the stirrups with practiced ease. They entered the saloon slowly, scanning the entire building in just a few seconds. One stopped just inside the saloon doors, the other man walked to the scratched bar. He motioned to the bartender. "I'm lookin' for a man by the name of James McCuan. Can you help me?" he asked.

Sam, the bartender at the Spotted Horse, looked nervous. "That feller over there at the back table by the stairs, that's McCuan's foreman." He picked up the towel he had been using to dry the glasses, moving to the other end of the long bar.

The man at the bar crossed the room, stopping next to the stairs. "The bartender said you might be able to help me and my brother. We're lookin' for James McCuan," he said, his voice was low and gravely.

Gimpy was lost deep in thought, his mind was still on the girl over at the Rusted Bucket. He was startled when the stranger spoke to him. "Just maybe I can help you. But first tell me why you're lookin' for him?" he asked, after recovering.

"My name is Chad Gilkey, and that man over there by the door yonder is my brother Brett. We was told McCuan had an important job for us. We made real good time gettin' here." He pulled the long, filthy coat back, showing the two gleaming colts. "Me and my brother don't have a hankerin' to stand around jawin' with you all day. Our business is with McCuan."

Looking up at the man standing in front of him, and then over at the other one by the door. Gimpy smiled, an evil smile. "The boss has been waitin' on you. We wasn't sure when you'd get here. He'll be glad you made good time. Now follow me, I'll show you the way."

Sam watched all three men leave together, shaking his head. He knew there was going to be trouble. James McCuan was not to be crossed. He sure felt sorry for the person that had riled him, because he didn't stand a chance against James McCuan, or the two strangers that had just ridden into town.

Chapter Nineteen

When the small group arrived in Santa Fe later that afternoon, Charlie was overwhelmed. She was not prepared for her first look at the city, never had she seen so many people in one place. The farther they moved along the busy street, the more nervous she become, but she wasn't the only one in awe. Taylor, Maddie and the twins had a look of excitement and fear on their faces. They were talking so fast you couldn't understand a word. Charlie looked at Garrett and was amazed, he appeared right at home in the large crowd of people and traffic, it wasn't bothering him at all.

Garrett had been watching Charlie from the corner of his eye. He could tell she was becoming nervous. He guided his horse next to hers. "Where would you like to stay?" he asked softly.

Staring at him with her mouth hanging wide open, Charlie finally answered. "What in the hell are you askin' me for? You know I've never been any place like this before. Are you tryin' to embarrass me?" she snapped, fire shooting from her eyes.

"No, I'm not trying to embarrass you. I was actually trying to calm you down, that's all." Twisting in the saddle, he spoke to Jack. "Do you know of a good place to stay? I'm not to familiar with Santa Fe."

Jack had been busy trying to settle the two little girls down in the back of the wagon, finally he had them calm. "I would suggest the Hartford House, it's a few streets over at the other end of town, out of the hustle and bustle." He looked at Mrs. Pruitt. "Is that all right with you Bea?"

It took Mrs. Pruitt a few seconds to answer, she was busy looking at all the sights. "That's fine with me, it doesn't matter where we stay. I'm just looking forward to heated bath water," she said, blushing.

"Well I guess that settles it, the Hartford House it is," Garrett said. He turned to Tristen and Austin. "You boys ready? As soon as we get the ladies all settled in, you two fellows can help me with the horses, that way Jack can look after the womenfolk."

Both boys let out a loud yelp, scaring the team of horses that was hitched to the wagon, Jack had to grab the reins. "Sorry Jack," the boys mumbled at the same time. But they couldn't hardly wait to get moving again, this was their first time in a big city. Garrett gave the word, and the wagon and its passengers rolled off down the busy street, the twins following close, their excitement showing on their identical faces.

Charlie had been quiet, watching everybody around her. The ladies to be exact. They were dressed in fancy dresses with hats that matched. They strolled down the sidewalk, taking short graceful steps. Charlie looked down at her own clothing, realizing she was in trouble, deep trouble. Pulling her floppy hat down even lower, she followed the wagon through town, wishing the ground would open up and swallow her.

The Hartford House was an impressive building, it had two stories and a large dining room. The halls and lobby were decorated with a rose patterned wallpaper, and polished wooden floors. The carpet runners were plush and expensive looking. When the trail weary group entered the lobby, Jack and Garrett walked to the front desk to check in. The clerk behind the counter seemed a little reluctant to offer his services. Garrett was just about to lose his patience when the man finally acknowledged their presence.

"You can probably find cheaper accommodations at another establishment," the snippy clerk said. He made it a point to look over at Mrs. Pruitt and the children. Charlie was still standing just outside the door, she was still trying to work up the courage to walk inside.

Garrett's temper was on the rise, but before he could answer, Jack motioned for the clerk. "Come here son. I need to speak to you." The prissy little man walked closer to Jack. He was startled when Jack made a grab for his shirt collar. He tried to step away, but wasn't fast enough.

"You better not speak the thoughts out loud that just crossed your mind, if you know what's good for you. The accommodations as you called it, are just fine here. We need two sets of adjoining rooms, don't matter what floor they're on, but we'd like them as close together as possible." When he let the clerk go, Jack gave him a slight shove, making Garrett grin.

The nervous clerk handed them four keys. "Is there anything else that I can help you with?" he asked, swallowing a huge lump of fear in his throat.

Turning toward the ladies, Garrett pushed his hat back on his head. "Would you ladies like a good hot bath brought up before dinner?" he asked. A wicked gleam appeared in his eyes, as he watched the clerk behind the desk.

Mrs. Pruitt had been watching Jack and Garrett deal with the rude hotel clerk, and it didn't take her long to answer. "We would love a bath brought up to our rooms, wouldn't we girls?" Both little girls were nodding their heads up and down. "And while you're at it, bring up a bath for Tristen and Austin, I'm sure they could use one to."

The twins, Tristen and Austin, were walking out the door when they heard Mrs. Pruitt's statement. Tristen never slowed down, just went right out the front door, Austin stopped and turned around. "We don't have time to take no bath, we've got to help Garrett with the stock," he said before following Tristen out the door.

"I'd better go see what those two are up to," Garrett said shaking his head.

"Don't worry about a thing. I'll see to the womenfolk," Jack said. He had already taken Mrs. Pruitt's arm to help her climb the stairs. Taylor and Maddie were following closely behind, talking a mile a minute.

Halfway up the stairs, Mrs. Pruitt stopped and called back down to Garrett. "If you see Charlie, be sure and send her on up, on second thought, maybe you should walk up with her. It might make her feel a little better, this is a strange place to all of us."

Charlie's head was in a whirl, there were people everywhere. Sweat started popping out on her forehead, and she felt sick at her stomach. She felt like a fish out of water. Standing very still, she closed her eyes, trying to calm down. Hearing footsteps stop beside her, she slowly opened her dark eyes only to find herself staring into the most beautiful gray eyes she had ever seen, they belonged to Garrett. She was so happy to see him, that she threw her arms around his neck. "Oh Garrett, I don't think it was a good idea...me coming here I mean. I don't belong here, I just don't fit it," she rushed on.

She buried her face in the crook of his neck and began to cry. It just about ripped his heart from his chest. He gathered her close in his arms. "Sweetheart, don't cry, everything will be all right, you'll see. Let me walk you up to the room, then you can have a nice warm bath and rest a while. After that, we'll go get something to eat, then you'll feel much better." Slowly pulling her out away from his embrace, he tilted her head back and wiped the tears from her face with the pads of his thumbs. After watching her beautiful face, he lowered his head, gently kissing her tear stained lips.

The moment Garrett touched his lips to hers, Charlie didn't care where she was or what was going on around her, she felt totally safe with him. She deepened the kiss, hearing a groan, but unable to tell if it came from her or Garrett, and she really didn't care. At that particular time, she knew that she loved him, but she couldn't tell him, not yet.

Holding her body against him tight, Garrett lost control of his senses. He needed to be closer to her. He had forgotten that they were standing on a busy sidewalk, until he heard the whispers penetrating his foggy brain. "That hussy should be arrested for her behavior, and the was she's dressed is a disgrace," one female voice muttered. He heard the word 'hussy' several more times around him, and apparently he wasn't the only one that had heard it, because Charlie had gone completely stiff in his arms. Charlie backed away a few steps and ducked her head away from the prying eyes of the other women.

Something snapped inside Garrett, how dare these people pass judgment on someone they didn't even know. He pulled Charlie close to his side, wrapping an arm around her waist, holding her tight. "For your information, this is my wife. We haven't been married very long, so surely you can understand why we were kissing." He looked down at Charlie, her face had turned a pretty shade of pink.

The women all mumbled some type of apologies, then continued on their journey through town. "Come on," Garrett said, grabbing Charlie's hand, "I promised Mrs. Pruitt that I would bring you upstairs. After that, I've got to find your brothers." He didn't wait for an answer, they were already heading up the lobby stairs.

Charlie was in shock, but halfway up the stairs she regained some of her composure. "The boys ran down toward the livery stable. They were leading their horses, but left the wagon sitting out front," she said, thinking for a moment. "What in the hell do you think you was doin' tellin' them old bats we was married." They were at the top of the stairs now, but she wasn't done with him yet. "I'm not goin' in there until you give me some sort of answer." She had stopped dead in her tracks, jerking her arms away from him, folding them across her chest, waiting for an answer.

Sliding his hands down in his front pockets, he grinned. He could tell she was upset, her speech always changed. "That was the first thing I could think of. I wanted to protect you from those old biddies. They had no right to pass judgment on you," he said very softly.

She lowered her head, trying to hide her disappointment. "You don't have to lie to protect me. Believe me, I'm used to takin' care of myself, besides they probably knew you was lyin'. Nobody would have me, just look at the way I'm dressed. I don't even look like a respectable female." She turned away. "What's our room number? I suddenly feel kind of tired."

"I'm sorry if I've offended you in some way, but I do want to protect you and take care of you. I told them that because I wish it were true. I've never felt like this before about any woman but you. I don't care how you dress or act. I love everything about you." He stopped for a moment, thinking before he continued. "Maybe I was hoping that when this is all over we can be married, it you want to that is. I think you're beautiful just the way you are. I wouldn't change a thing about you."

Charlie was standing with her back to him, trying to make sense out of his declaration of love, it was too much to hope for. Warm hands lovingly caressed her arms, pulling her back against a warm, solid chest, she was in heaven. "Do you really love me?" she whispered.

"Yes."

"You know, I've always wanted a husband and a family of my own, all my life. But my pa always said nobody in their right mind would ever want me, not the way I looked or acted. He never really wanted me either, he wanted a son. I don't know if I can live up to your expectations. I'm not as well educated as you seem to be, and I don't have any idea how to dress like a lady." The words were muffled against the fabric of his shirt, her face was pressed tightly against his chest.

"Sweetheart, if it will make you happy, I'll buy you the prettiest dress in town, but you don't have to wear it for me," he said, caressing her from hip to shoulder. Looking down into her upturned face, it felt like a herd of horses were galloping in his chest. He had to kiss her one more time.

She watched as he lowered his head, he was going to kiss her. She closed her eyes, waiting, suddenly one of the hotel doors opened and Mrs. Pruitt walked out. They both sprang apart, feeling a little guilty.

"I've been wondering what was keeping the two of you." Mrs. Pruitt hurried out into the hallway. "Charlie come on inside, the bath water will be here shortly," she said, grasping Charlie's hand, pulling her inside the room, shutting the door in Garrett's face.

Garrett ran his hands through his hair, still trying to figure out what had just happened. He was trying to clear his mind. He needed to get the wagon down to the livery and check on the boys, then stop by the telegraph office. Well, maybe not in that particular order, first he would check on the boys, then he was going to stop at the mercantile and pick out a dress for Charlie, a bright yellow dress with all the trappings to go along with it. After both stops were made, then he would go by the telegraph office. As he climbed into the wagon seat, he released the brake, but his mind was still on the yellow dress that he was going to buy for Charlie, actually his mind wasn't on the dress, it was what went in the dress that held his attention. He had to hurry!

All four ladies had completed their baths. Mrs. Pruitt was helping both little girls, Maddie and Taylor get their clothing on. Charlie still had a damp towel wrapped around her curvy body. She was in quite a predicament, she had nothing but pants to wear to dinner.

"Charlie, you had better hurry up and get dressed. The men will be ready for dinner soon. Jack stopped by about thirty minutes ago asking what time we would be ready," Mrs. Pruitt said. She was braiding ribbons into Maddie's hair.

"I think I'll just stay here tonight. I don't want to wear pants, everybody will stare at me. Please don't make me go downstairs," she begged in a strangled voice.

Before Mrs. Pruitt could reply, someone knocked on their door. Cracking the door slowly, Mrs. Pruitt peaked around, to her surprise there was a small boy holding a very large box. "What do you have there young man?" she asked, opening the door wide.

"I have a deliv'ry for a Miss Mac......MacCuban," the little boy said.

"I'll take it and see that she gets it."

"I can't give it to nobody but the lady or I don't get my nick'l," the little boy said stubbornly. "The man told me to make sure the lady gets it, and that's what I aim to do."

Mrs. Pruitt was about to argue when Charlie came to the door, she had slipped her robe on. "I'm Miss McCuan, and thank you very much," she said, taking the large box from the small boy.

Handing the box over to her carefully, the little boy suddenly blurted out. "The man said you was bu-ti-ful, but I thought he was lyin'." He stood there a few more seconds before turning away from the door.

Both ladies hurried over to the bed. Charlie untied the ribbon that held the box closed. She carefully lifted the lid, inside the box was the most beautiful yellow dress she had ever seen, and there was a note. She unfolded the small piece of paper, reading every word. It was from Garrett, and it simply said, 'With all my love, Garrett'. She started to cry, realizing that he truly loved her.

Mrs. Pruitt was so happy. She took the dress from the box, holding it up. It was lovely, and evidently the way Charlie was acting, it was from Garrett. Things were working out just like her and Jack had planned.

James was getting restless. He was tired of hiding like a snake in a hole, never in his adult life had he hid from anything. But he needed to keep his wits, he had to be able to think. Just a few more weeks and all this mess would be over, then he could go back to the ranch, and settle the score for good.

Grabbing the bottle of whiskey from the shelf, he sat down at the table. After filling his glass, he slowly sipped the amber liquid. He should have taken care of his stepbrother long ago. If he had, he wouldn't be in this trouble now. Tilting the glass back, he swallowed the whole contents of the glass, letting it burn a path to his stomach. He was going crazy, it had been five days since Gimpy had gone back to town, he didn't even know how long Steele and the others would be gone to Santa Fe. He filled his glass one more time and drained it quickly. Picking up his hat, he decided to head to town.

Gimpy and the Gilkey brothers were getting close to the old line shack. They should have been here yesterday, but they decided to spend the night at the Rusted Bucket. They were all moving pretty slow this afternoon. The Gilkey brothers were usually quiet by nature, but Gimpy was usually very talkative, but not today.

"How much further?" asked Chad Gilkey.

"Just through this thicket. It's up on that little ridge. It's kind of hidden," replied Gimpy. He could find it with his eyes shut.

When they topped the little rise, Gimpy saw James saddling his horse. "There's the boss now." He spurred his horse forward, the two dangerous looking brothers following.

James stopped saddling his horse, when he heard horses thundering toward him. His hand moved down to the handle of his gun. He instantly recognized the lead horse, it was Gimpy's bay. The other two men he didn't know, but from the looks of the two strangers, maybe his wait was over.

Drawing his horse to a halt, Gimpy stepped down out of the saddle. "Boss," he said excitedly, "These here are the Gilkey brothers, all the way from Arizona. They've come to take care of your little problem."

Both brothers had dismounted and were standing in front of James. "We got here as quick as we could. I'm Chad, and this here is my brother Brett," said Chad, pointing to the man standing beside him. "Your foreman tells us that you know where Garrett Steele is at. All you have to do is point us in the right direction, and we'll take care of the rest."

"I know where he's at all right. But we haven't discussed fees yet," James said, looking at both brothers.

Brett Gilkey had been standing quietly, letting his brother Chad do all the talking. He finally spoke up. "We ain't to worried about money. Hell, we'll do it for nothin'. We aim to kill that sons-of-a-bitch one way or another."

James grinned at Gimpy. This was going to be better than he expected. He turned to the brothers. "Let's go inside and talk this over. We've got a little bit of time before Steele is back at the ranch anyway. But we'll be ready for him," he said.

After the men had taken care of their horses, they went inside the line shack.

James thought things were beginning to shape up nicely, maybe in a few more days they would be even better. He threw back his head, laughing, the sound carried through the surrounding tress and bushes, it had an evil ring.

Chapter Twenty

Garrett looked up the stairs for the fourth time. How long did it take two women and two little girls to get ready for dinner. He paced back and forth across the carpeted hallway at the bottom of the stairs. He was a nervous wreck. He had tried to imagine all afternoon what Charlie would look like in that yellow dress, but his mind just couldn't conjure up an image. When he had walked by the store and saw the dress in the window, he knew he had to buy it, and just as luck would have it, it was pretty close to Charlie's size, he hoped.

Finally stopping, resting his foot on the bottom step, he had a chance to think. After leaving the store he had gone straight to the telegraph office. He had sent several telegrams, including one to his attorney in Tucson. He had wired instructions, just in case something happened to him.

Working as an U.S. Marshall he had developed a certain type of instinct for trouble, and it was telling him to be very cautious. He wanted to make sure the ranch went to Charlie and the children, if anything should happen to him. While waiting for a reply, which didn't take long, he realized he needed to make some sort of arrangements for Maddie, maybe ask Jack and Mrs. Pruitt. It was something he would discuss with them in the next few days. After reading the message from his lawyer, his mood turned to ice. It seemed someone had been making inquiries about him in Tucson, the same person had also located the Gilkey brothers, and they had left town about four or five days ago. If he had to make a guess, he would bet that James McCuan was behind it, that's as far as his thoughts got, he was interrupted by someone clearing their throat. It was Jack.

Jack couldn't seem to take his eyes off the top of the stairs. He was spellbound. After what seemed like an eternity, he swallowed hard. "I think our wait is over. The womenfolk have finally arrived. And let me tell you, the wait was sure worth it," he said, never taking his eyes off the two beautiful ladies waiting at the top of the stairs.

Garrett tried to breathe, but was not able to. "Breathtaking," he whispered. That was all he could manage. Because standing beside Mrs. Pruitt was the most amazing…he was at a loss for words, there was only one word that came to mind…Charlie…his Charlie to be exact.

She was absolutely gorgeous, her body was molded by the contours of the dress, she was more than lovely, unbelievable was a better word. Garrett thought he was the luckiest man in the world.

Charlie was uncomfortable. It felt like she was about to smother to death. She had on at least five layers of clothing, and the shoes were pinching her feet something awful. But Mrs. Pruitt had insisted that all proper ladies wore them, this was going to be harder than it looked.

As they exited their rooms, Mrs. Pruitt had instructed her to walk slow and take small steps. But that was about all Charlie could manage in these tight shoes. They not only hurt, they were hard to walk in, she like her old boots much better.

"They're waiting for us at the bottom of the stairs," Mrs. Pruitt said. "Girls," she said to Maddie and Taylor, "Please follow us down the stairs, and we'll have a delicious dinner."

Everything was perfect, Jack and Garrett were waiting at the bottom of the stairs, their eyes were bright with appreciation. It seemed neither man could take their eyes off the women as they neared the bottom. Garrett extended his hand to Charlie. Just as she placed her hand in his, the toe of her shoe caught the hem of her dress, causing her to lose her balance. She pitched forward, hitting Garrett square in the chest, knocking both of them to the floor.

Sprawled on top of him, Charlie's face was flushed with anger, not embarrassment. "These damn shoes are too hard to walk in. I told Mrs. Pruitt that I'd rather wear my boots. But she said 'Ladies do not wear boots with their dresses', well I guess that proves I ain't no lady." She was mad, and getting more riled by the minute, as she tried to disentangle her limbs from Garrett's.

Most women would have been mortified, but not Charlie. She was trying her best to get back on her feet. The only problem was, the more she wiggled, the more aroused Garrett become. He couldn't take much more. "Would you please hold still, just stop wiggling around and I'll help you to your feet."

Jack and Mrs. Pruitt had been stunned. It was a few minutes before Jack reacted. "Here let me help you Charlie," he said, grabbing her by the hands, pulling her to her feet. By this time, some of the other hotel guests were watching the spectacle.

Garrett, after brushing the dust from his pants, turned to the clerk. "You should have someone look at the carpet on those steps, I think it might be loose. It just caused a nasty fall," he said, winking at Jack. The hotel clerk's face turned red as they walked past the desk, but he made no answer.

As the little group entered the dining room, Mrs. Pruitt turned to Jack.

"Where are the boys?" she asked.

"They stayed over at the livery stable. Dan Roberts, that's the owner, has two boys about their age. Dan and his wife invited them to stay for supper." Jack gently squeezed Mrs. Pruitt's waist. "Don't worry, I've known Dan and his wife for a long time. The boys will be just fine."

"Well, if you say so." Mrs. Pruitt called to the little girls. "Come along girls," she said, following Garrett and Charlie into the dining room.

Charlie walked beside Garrett with her hand resting on his strong forearm. They followed the waitress through a maze of tables, their table was located toward the back of the dining room. As Garrett seated her, she took a few moments to study his handsome profile, he took her breathe away. He was so handsome, and he loved her.

"Will you be comfortable here?" he asked.

As she turned her head to answer, his lips lightly brushed over hers, it was instant pleasure. He slowly pulled away, a look of pure love upon his features. "I can't wait until we can be married," taking her hand in his, "That is, if you're still willing."

She was lost in the depths of his smoky gray eyes, finally finding her voice. "I can't wait either. But…you have to know you won't be getting a fine upstanding wife in the bargain. I'm more at home in the barn than I am in a place like this. I don't want you to be ashamed of me. I just knocked you flat back there just a little bit ago." She lowered her lashes, expecting him to turn away.

"I will never be ashamed of you. As for falling down, everybody does that every now and then, don't worry about it. Besides, I fell off my horse not to long ago. I got mad at first, but I got over it pretty quick."

"It's a good thing I didn't have time to think about it a while ago, or I would've just been plum embarrassed." Then she leaned closer to Garrett, whispering into his ear. "I haven't fell on my ass like that since I was a kid."

Garrett threw back his head, roaring with laughter, she was totally unpredictable.

Jack, Mrs. Pruitt, and the girls had stopped to talk to an acquaintance of Jack's. They arrived at the table just as Garrett howled with laughter. "What's going on? Did we miss something?" Jack asked. He was busy pulling a chair out for Mrs. Pruitt.

A smile hovering on his face, Garrett looked at Jack. "I have just come to realize that Charlie is priceless. And I love every inch of her," he said taking a seat next to Charlie. He slid his hand beneath the table, caressing her thigh.

Her face was becoming warmer by the second. Garrett's hand had a strange effect on her body. It was making her hot and cold at the same time. Mrs. Pruitt was sitting directly across the table from her, Charlie was afraid Mrs. Pruitt would figure out what was going on. She wished Garrett would stop, well…not really, it felt wonderful.

Busy trying to settle Maddie and Taylor into their chairs, Mrs. Pruitt glanced at Charlie, noticing her face seemed flushed. All those layers of clothing were hot, but she would get used to it in no time. After finishing her task, she turned to Jack. "I can hardly wait to eat someone else's cooking for a change. I'm starved," then asking the little girls, "What would you two like for supper?"

Both little girls started chattering at the same time. Garrett, who had been watching his little sister, smiled. It had been a long time since Maddie had been so carefree. Taylor had done wonders, helping her come out of her shell. Turning his head ever so slightly, he studied the beautiful woman sitting by his side. She had certainly made his life a much better place. He wanted her with him each and every day of his life.

The waitress arrived, and the little group began the process of ordering supper. While waiting for their evening meal, Jack and Mrs. Pruitt entertained by telling stories about Charlie and the other children growing up on the ranch. Everyone laughed, so hard sometimes their eyes watered. Charlie's eyes would shine with mischief as they told stories of some of her escapades, other times she would duck her head and blush. When the meal finally arrived, everyone was more than ready to eat, they were all hungry. The mood around the table was still festive, all except Charlie. She had become quiet and a little reserved.

Noticing her hesitation, Garrett covered her hand with his much larger one. Feeling the turmoil in her body, he gently squeezed her hand. "What's the matter, is something bothering you?" He could see the uncertainty in her eyes, it unsettled him. What had upset her?

First looking at Mrs. Pruitt, then down at the food on the table in front of her, she looked horrified. That was when it dawned on Garrett just what the problem was. She was unsure how to act around all the people in the restaurant. "Don't worry about a thing, just have a good time. Not a single person is paying any attention to what is going on at this table. Look," he motioned with his head, "Taylor and Maddie are having a great time."

"I just don't want to embarrass you. I really have no idea how I'm supposed to be actin'," she said to no one in particular.

Before anyone could comment, Jack patted her on the shoulder. "Charlie girl, you could never embarrass any of us. We all love you girl, especially that big hombre sitting there beside you. Now get all the unpleasant thoughts out of your head, and have a good time, that's an order," he said winking.

The rest of the evening was very enjoyable. Not wanting the evening to end, they all lingered over coffee and dessert. But the girls were starting to nod off, it was time to retire for the night. When their bill was paid, both men lifted a tired little girl in their arms, carrying them through the hotel, holding each child tenderly against their chest.

Mrs. Pruitt and Charlie followed. Charlie's eyes followed Garrett as he ascended the stairs with Maddie in his arms. It brought a lump to her throat. Maybe someday he would be carrying their child to bed. He would make an excellent father. She only hoped she would be a good mother. It was probably just a silly dream anyway.

When the little girls were tucked into bed, the four adults left the room.

"Would you two mind to walk over to the livery, and bring the boys back," Jack asked.

Garrett had just been wondering how he could get Charlie alone for a few minutes. "We'd love to," he said, grabbing Charlie's hand and dragging her back down the stairs.

Watching from the top of the stairs, Jack slipped his arm around Mrs. Pruitt's waist, pulling her close. "Things couldn't be working out any better. I've waited a long time to see that girl happy."

"There was times that I cried for her, and other times that James made me so mad, I would've liked to strangle him. She has a good heart, just like Audree. And I believe that Garrett will be good for her. He won't let people run rough shod over her," Mrs. Pruitt replied, leaning back against Jack.

A shudder ran through his body, he closed his eyes briefly. When he opened them they were burning with anger. "You don't know how many times I've thought of killing that bastard myself. I've had him in my rifle sights several times, just couldn't bring myself to pull the trigger."

Mrs. Pruitt turned and stepped into Jack's embrace. She was glad that Jack hadn't killed James. "I'm glad you never killed him, they might have hanged you or sent you to prison for twenty or thirty years."

"Would you have missed me?"

"You know the answer to that. Of course I would."

"You know Charlie and Garrett probably won't be back for a while. What are we going to do with ourselves?" Jack asked with a sly grin.

Taking his hand, Mrs. Pruitt opened the hotel door next to the girls' room. "Come on in and sit down. We can enjoy a little peace and quiet, it will be relaxing." The older couple hurried through the door, both had a very pleasant smile on their faces. After the door closed, the hallway was quiet once again.

Practically dragging Charlie out the front door, Garrett slowed his pace once they were outside. They strolled along in the moon light, holding hands and giggling like two small children with a secret.

"I've got a great idea. Lets go on a picnic tomorrow. I'll rent a buggy and we can enjoy the countryside."

"A picnic." Charlie looked shocked. "That would be wonderful. I've never been on a picnic before, neither have my brothers and sister. They'll really like it."

Stopping and gathering her full, lush body into his arms, he brushed his mouth lightly across hers, slowly lifting his head. "Charlie, I was talking about just the two of us. We'll have plenty of time to take the others on a picnic, we can do that closer to home. I want to spend some time alone with you, get to know you a little better. I'm sure Jack and Mrs. Pruitt will watch the children for us," he said, kissing her a second time.

How in the world did he expect her to think, let alone answer him. Her body turned to mush and her mind went blank when he kissed her, and it was the most wonderful feeling in the world. When he finally ended the kiss, it took her several minutes for her head to clear. "Well greenhorn, I'll be glad to go with you on a picnic, but I don't know if it's a good idea for us to be going alone." She placed her hands on his muscular biceps. "Every time we're alone together we end up kissin', not that I don't like it, but I've heard some of the hands talkin', and I know what comes next," she said, her eyes getting larger with each word.

"Is that right, so tell me, what does come next?" he asked, slipping his arms around her waist, drawing her tight up against his rock hard body. He could feel those fabulous breasts, they were burning a hole right through his shirt. Lowering his hands to her hips, he explored every curve, as he nibbled her ear. "I'm waiting for an answer," he whispered.

Charlie felt like she was in another world. Garrett's hands were busy all over her body, they left a path of scorching fire. Her hands were busy also, she traced his muscular back and broad shoulders, mapping every square inch with her fingertips. She pulled back slightly, her eyes glazed from passion. "Did you say something?"

When she pulled away from him, he gained some control of his senses. He had to stop, they were almost standing in the middle of the street. "Yes I did, I'm still waiting for you to tell me what comes next, after kissing I mean."

Charlie looked him straight in the eye. "Kissin' comes first, then the men always goes to dip their worm in the nearest fishin' hole...whatever that means...that's what all the hands say anyways."

At first Garrett was stunned, she had no idea what that statement meant. He began to laugh, pulling Charlie in the direction on the livery stable. "Don't ever change Charlie, promise me. I love you just the way you are, and life will certainly never be boring around you." As the couple strolled arm in arm toward the livery stable, laughter filled the quiet streets.

Chapter Twenty-one

Early morning finally arrived, after tossing and turning most of the night, Garrett was bone tired. He had too much on his mind to sleep. What the hell was James McCuan up to? There was a lot riding on the decisions he made over the next few days, possibly weeks. He had to send a telegram to his attorney, first thing this morning, but he hadn't gotten an opportunity to speak with Jack and Mrs. Pruitt. In the back of his mind there was trouble brewing. James McCuan was not going to go down without a fight, his kind never did. Looking up at the ceiling, tucking his hands behind his head, he let his mind drift. Thoughts of a sassy female invaded his head, just thinking about Charlie brought a quick smile to his lips, and it also had an effect on other parts of his body. The smile vanished from his face, he had to get things under control, find out what those damn Gilkey brothers were up to. He had a very bad feeling. After rolling over on his side, he tried to punch the pillow beneath his head into some sort of shape, making all kinds of noise.

Jack had been awake for some time, listening to the younger man toss and turn, wondering what was bothering him. Finally he spoke, his voice just above a whisper. "Something bothering you son? If you tell me what's going on, maybe I can help."

The voice startled Garrett. He rolled to a sitting position, grabbing for his gun, all in one smooth, effortless motion. "You scared the living shit out of me," he said, sliding the revolver back inside the worn holster.

By this time Jack was sitting on the edge of the bed, looking a little peaked. "I never even seen you make a move for your gun, you're fast. You really are a marshall. I thought you was just tryin' to impress me with that tale."

"Ex-marshall, I'm retired, remember," Garrett said.

Reaching for his pants, Jack made a snorting sound. "Retired my foot, what's really going on? Tell me the truth, I think I have a right to know."

Garrett stood, buttoning his pants. He turned, walking to the window, looking out at the dark streets. "My parents died about three years ago…actually, they were killed in a stage holdup. I was away on assignment when the sheriff contacted me. I rode three horses into the ground trying to get home, but I was too late, my folks had already been buried. I went sort of crazy at first, then I realized what had to be done. First I checked on Maddie, she was staying with some friends of my parents, after that I started tracking the dirty vermin that had killed our folks."

Leaning his forehead against the glass, Garrett took a deep breath before continuing. "It didn't take long before I picked up their trail. They weren't being very cautious. I rode like the devil was chasing me, I don't even remember stopping to sleep, slept in the saddle most of the time."

Jack was listening to every word, there was a chill to Garrett's voice, at that moment he realized how dangerous the man standing in front of him really was. "If it's not too painful for you, I'd like to hear the rest of the story, but I'll understand if you can't."

When Garrett turned away from the window, his eyes were cold and harsh. "I caught up to them about two weeks after they robbed the stage. It was a short fight, but a bloody one. There was four of them all together, killed two of them and wounded the other two. I took two bullets myself, nothing real serious. It took me five days to get back to town with my prisoners, couldn't hardly stand the stench of the two that were dead, but I was determined to take all of them back in."

By this time Garrett was pacing back and forth across the room, his movements agitated. "The two outlaws that were alive, were sentenced to life in prison, should have been hanged, but the judge decided it would be harder on them to spend the rest of their lives behind bars. Those four men had two brothers, they've been looking for me for the past two and a half years. That's why Maddie and I decided to come to the Circle Bar M, but it seems they may have found me."

"Is there anything I can do to help?" Jack asked seriously.

"As a matter of fact there is. I need to know that Maddie will be taken care of if something were to happen to me. I would like you and Mrs. Pruitt to take care of her for me. You wouldn't have to worry about money, I have a trust fund set up for her in Tucson, and I'll give you the name and address of my attorney. He'll know what to do."

"You know we'll take care of that child, but we won't have to, because nothing is going to happen to you. Besides, what would we do with Charlie? That girl is head over heels in love with you. I've never seen her act like this before," Jack said, a huge grin on his face.

"These guys are dangerous. I don't plan on getting killed, but it's a possibility. I just want to make sure everything is covered, that's all."

"Why don't me and you go on downstairs and have some coffee. The boys will be up and rarin' to go before long, and I promised Bea and the girls that I'd take them shoppin' this morning. If we go now we can finish our little talk, and we won't be disturbed. We can make some final arrangements tonight after I've had time to talk things over with Bea."

Garrett had been standing very still, listening to the other man's voice, after a few minutes he realized the room was now quiet. "That's fine with me Jack. Besides, I've got an engagement myself this afternoon with a pretty little sassy female. We're going on a picnic." Then he finished stuffing his shirttails in his snug trousers, picked up his gun belt and headed for the door, grinning like a fool.

Standing there in awe, Jack shook his head and followed, wondering how someone could change so fast. One minute Garrett had seemed almost ruthless, the next he was happy as a lark. Slapping his hat down on his head, he pulled the door shut behind him.

Stampede, that's what her stomach felt like. Charlie was walking with Jack and Mrs. Pruitt, they were on their way to a dress shop. She wondered for the hundredth time why she had agreed to this little venture. She was actually going to a dress shop, which was a laugh. The closer they got, the slower she walked, this is probably what the cattle feel like when we send them to market, she thought warily.

"Charlie if you walk any slower you're going to miss your picnic with Garrett, now hurry up," Mrs. Pruitt called to her. Mrs. Pruitt was walking beside Jack, her face was, the only word to describe it was, glowing.

The reminder of the picnic didn't help her mood one bit. She must have been suffering from some kind of sunstroke to agree to something like that, but hell, that didn't hold water neither, it had been pitch black outside when Garrett had asked her. Chewing on her lower lip, her mind on the events of the previous evening, she ran into Jack, who had stopped in front of the dress shop.

"Whoa there Charlie girl. Are you daydreamin' about something? Or maybe somebody in particular," asked Jack.

After regaining her balance, Charlie looked first as Jack, then Mrs. Pruitt. "No! I didn't get much sleep last night, couldn't rest for some reason." Now that was a good answer you idiot. After giving herself a quick mental kick, she realized they could be right. It wasn't someone she was thinking about, it was something…like and earth shattering kiss. How in the hell were you supposed to think straight when someone was kissing you silly. Before she could come up with an answer, she followed Mrs. Pruitt inside the store. As she walked through the shop door, she thought, just imagine me, Charlie

McCuan, inside a dress shop, it was nothing short of a miracle, or was it.

After what seemed like days, but actually was only a few short hours, Charlie was standing in the middle of the hotel room, feeling like a complete fool. Her nerves were stretched to the limit. Mrs. Pruitt had her trussed up like a Thanksgiving turkey. She couldn't walk and it hurt to breathe. If this is what it was like to be a lady, she'd just as soon stay the way she was. "Why do I have to wear all this contraption? I like my old clothes better, they're more comfortable," Charlie said. She was busy trying to tug the bodice of her dress up, but it wouldn't budge.

Mrs. Pruitt gave her an exasperated look. "The word is lady, this is how a proper lady dresses. You need to look your best when your young man comes to get you."

"He's not my nothin'." She was still tugging at the form fitting dress.

"Stop pulling at your clothing, you'll have it all wrinkled by the time Garrett arrives to pick you up." Mrs. Pruitt was proud of Charlie, she was beautiful, just like her mother. "You know something," Mrs. Pruitt said, walking across the room to stand in front of Charlie. "You look just like your mother. She would have been so proud of you—" She couldn't finish, the emotions were too strong.

After seeing the tears in the older woman's eyes, Charlie moved forward to hug her tight. "Thank you Mrs. Pruitt, I love you. Now don't get me to cryin', seems like that's all I've done the past couple of weeks. Do you think Garrett will really like my new dress?" she asked, trying to change the subject.

Before the other woman could answer, there was a knock at the door. Mrs. Pruitt opened the door to find a very handsome man standing in the threshold. "Come on in Garrett, Charlie's ready to go." She moved out of Garrett's line of vision, allowing him a glimpse of the loveliest creature he had ever seen. She was standing in the center of the room.

Garrett was standing with his mouth hanging wide open. He couldn't find the word to describe her. "Your beautiful," he whispered, finally, as he closed the distance between them.

At that moment, Charlie felt as if she and Garrett were the only two people on earth. Did he really think she was beautiful? If only that statement was true. "You look pretty handsome yourself, greenhorn. You do know that I'm not goin' to dress like this every day, don't you. I'd never get any work done, couldn't even sit a horse with all this garb on," she said, trying not to think about all the flesh that was showing above the bodice of her dress.

99

Garrett laughed, it was funny, he had laughed more in the last few weeks, than he had in the last few years, and it felt great. "Come here," he said, wrapping his long muscular arms around her. "I don't expect you to change or dress any differently. I love you just the way you are. But you do look good enough to eat." The last part was whispered in her ear, sending tingles down her spine.

He held out his arm. "Are you ready to go? Your chariot awaits you downstairs."

As the couple made their way down the stairs, Mrs. Pruitt stood and watched them leave. Everything was working out just perfectly. She started humming a little tune as she went in search of Jack and the kids. Nothing could go wrong now.

Chapter Twenty-two

James was back in his office at the Circle Bar M, waiting for Steele's return. All the details had been worked out. The Gilkeys were staying at the line shack, Gimpy had returned to the ranch, everything seemed normal. But all hell would break loose when the travelers returned from their little trip. After Steele was eliminated, James would take his own family in hand.

He had been making some inquiries about Steele's attorney, but so far, hadn't come up with a lot of information. Everyone had a price, James was hoping that held true for Steele's attorney. He needed all the information he could get, before the Gilkeys took care of Steele, find out who would inherit after the bastard was gone. But his contacts in Tucson couldn't even come up with a name. He had to find out fast, they were running out of time.

Slamming his fists down hard on the desk, he grabbed a bottle of whiskey, then sat back down. After taking a long slow drink, he rose slowly from his chair, walking to the window. All the land as far as the eye could see, belonged to him, and he would do whatever it took to keep it that way. He was going to enjoy watching the Gilkeys in action. He might even have them take care of that good for nothing daughter of his. Just looking at her made him sick, she was just like her damn mother.

He was becoming accustomed to the peace and quiet at the ranch, it felt good to have them all out of his hair. He just might make it a permanent feeling. He was jarred back to the present with the sound of the front door, someone had entered the house.

There was a brief knock on the door before it opened, it was Gimpy. "Boss, you in here?" Poking his head around the door, he spotted James standing by the window.

Wondering how he had gotten mixed up with such a stupid bastard, James answered. "Where the hell else would I be?"

Gimpy just stared with a blank look on his face, closing the door behind him. He walked farther into the room. "I just got word from town. My contact in Santa Fe says they're still there, havin' a humdinger of a time to. They've been shoppin' and eatin' at them fancy restaurants, and stayin' at an even fancier hotel." He stopped in front of James, eyeing the bottle of whiskey, licking his lips in anticipation.

James was standing with his back to his foreman, letting all the information sink in. Imagine his little family trying to act like normal people – that was a laugh. They would never amount to anything, no matter how hard they tried. He turned to look at the man standing in his office. "Can your man be trusted?" he asked. He watched the other man licking his lips, his mouth watering for some of the whiskey sitting on the table.

"He can be trusted."

"First thing in the morning, I want you to ride back to town and send another telegram. I want to know the minute they leave town and start for home," James said. He wanted to be ready for Steele.

Gimpy was waiting, ready for a drink of smooth whiskey. "Boss, if it's all right with you, can I have a drink of whiskey? A feller gets mighty thirsty doing this here de-tective work."

"Detective work my ass, you probably spent most of your time over at the Rusted Bucket, whoring and drinking," James snorted. "Go ahead, you can have a drink, then I want you to get busy. I'm not paying you to loaf around all day."

Grabbing the bottle and filling a glass, Gimpy guzzled the smooth liquid down fast. He slammed the empty glass down hard on the table. "Thanks boss, shore appreciate it." After finishing his drink, he didn't waste any time leaving.

It wouldn't be long now, James thought, everything was falling into place. Cold Steele would be soon be Dead Steele, before too much longer. He tilted his head back, laughter ringing through the empty house. Things were getting better everyday.

The buggy was rolling along smoothly, the passengers enjoying their surroundings. The weather was beautiful, the countryside breathtaking, it was a perfect day for a picnic.

Garrett had asked the livery stable owner where the best location could be found for a picnic. Mirror Lake, that's where the owner had told him, then gave him directions. The only problem was that he was having a hard time looking at the road, instead of the beautiful woman riding in the buggy beside him. She looked exquisite, absolutely stunning. The dress he had bought, hugged and accentuated her full figure, but she had no idea the effect she was having on him. About a mile back, he had propped his booted foot on the dashboard of the buggy, trying to hide the evidence of his full arousal. The closeness they shared was making him miserable.

"Isn't this just about the prettiest sight you've ever seen?" Charlie asked.

Her face was glowing with happiness.

Looking at her profile, he answered softly. "Yes, I can honestly say it is."

Charlie turned her head, just as he finished the last word, realizing that he was talking about her. Her heart swelled within her chest, beating so rapidly she was afraid it was going to fly right out of her body. "You know what I was talking about. I've never been able to enjoy the countryside. I've always been too busy trying to get my work done. Come to think of it, I've never ridden in a buggy that I can remember. Pa never had one, we used a wagon instead." Her eyes were sparkling, they were so dark a man could get lost in their depths.

Pulling the horses to a stop, he tilted her chin up, lowering his mouth to hers. The jolt was strong, so strong it startled them both. They were dazed when they pulled apart. Garrett was the first one to recover. "I don't understand what's happening between us, but I sure know there's definitely something going on. It just seems so right, like it was our destiny to meet. I know that sounds kind of stupid, but it's how I feel."

Tears formed in Charlie's eyes, maybe there really was something special between them. If there was, it was more that she had ever hoped for. Her feelings for Garrett ran deep, so deep, it almost scared her, fearing he would reject her, just like her pa had her whole life. Laying the palm of her work roughened hand on his cheek, she spoke through the tears. "The feeling I have for you scares me to death. I'm so afraid that this is all a dream, and when I wake up you'll be gone. But I can tell you one thing, even if you leave me, I won't go back to my pa's ranch. I just can't live like that again."

Garrett hugged her close, vowing to protect her for the rest of her life. He could handle a lot of situations, but women's tears he couldn't stand. "We've got a beautiful day ahead of us, lets not spoil it with talk of your father. I will promise you one thing, I will never leave you, never." Then remembering how he always had to re-assure Maddie, he added. "Cross my heart and hope to die," he said, making the motion across his broad chest.

When they reached the lake a short time later, they discovered it lived up to its name. It looked just like a giant mirror. After searching the area around the lake, Garrett found a perfect spot, very secluded. He pulled the horse to a stop, wrapping the reins up tight. He jumped down and walked around to Charlie's side of the buggy. He laughed out loud when he saw Charlie, she was trying to climb down out of the buggy, unassisted, and it wasn't working to well.

"Damn dress," she sputtered. "They're not good for nothin' as far as I can tell. You can't even get down out of a damn buggy by yourself." She caught the hem of her dress on the corner of the seat, she was jerking it with one hand, when that didn't work, she grabbed it with both hands, tugging hard. The material come loose all at once, causing her to lose her balance, she fell right on her ruffled rump, sending dust flying around her.

Garrett saw what was about to happen, but couldn't reach her it time. There she was in the middle of a small dust storm, her skirt and petticoat hiked up around her thighs. He let his eyes wander down the length of her shapely legs, wondering what her ankles looked like, when his gaze reached her ankles, he grinned. There was his angel sitting in the dirt with a beautiful dress on, wearing her work boots, she was priceless.

Glaring at him, she tried to get up, but her skirts were too full. "I bet I never wear one of these god awful things again. If I had to run or try to mount a horse real fast, it would be might near impossible."

Wiping his eyes, Garrett held out his hand. "Take my hand and let me help you up. From now on, wait for me to help you down out of the buggy. You're always supposed to wait for assistance from the gentleman you're with." He pulled her up from the ground effortlessly, brushing the dust from the back of her dress.

"I guess you think I'm an idiot, don't you? I just don't think this is goin' to work, lets just head back to town and call it a day." She pulled away from him, trying to get back into the buggy. Strong hands wrapped around her waist, lifting her back to the ground. It startled her! "Put me down, before you hurt your back. Are you crazy or something?"

"I'm not going to hurt my back on a little thing like you," he replied. She wasn't waspish thin, but she wasn't large either, actually she just fit his hands.

"Now your makin' fun of me. I know I ain't dainty like them other ladies I saw in town. But that don't give you the right to make fun of me." She was mad enough to spit fire.

A man could only take so much nonsense, and he had reached that point. He stood in front of her, glaring at her. "I want to get one thing straight. I was not, nor will I ever make fun of you or anyone else. You got that! He had moved a little closer, his face just inches from hers. "Why is it so hard for you to believe that I love you just the way you are? I haven't known you for long, but that doesn't matter. I want to spend the rest of my life with you. Do you understand?" He calmed down when he saw the look of fear on her face. "You have to believe me. I'm not like your father," he whispered.

"I'm sorry. I always get mad when I get scared. I might always be like that, who knows," she said, shrugging her shoulders.

Reaching in the buggy, Garrett lifted out the picnic basket. He placed his other hand in the small of Charlie's back, guiding her down to the lake. At that moment, there was only one thing he was certain about, his deep love for the woman walking beside him. She held his heart in her hands.

Jack and Mrs. Pruitt were walking along the streets of Santa Fe. They had just left the livery stable. The twins had wanted to stay there and help out around the barns. Maddie and Taylor were walking a few feet ahead, peering into the glass of every shop along the street. They were chattering non-stop, laughing and pointing through the windows.

The older couple walked slowly, holding hands, watching the excited little girls. Both of them were enjoying this trip. Mrs. Pruitt spoke softly to Jack. "How do you think Charlie and Garrett are doing?"

"I'd say they're doing just fine. You worry too much, Bea."

"I can't help it. I've seen what that girl has gone through. I just don't want anything to happen and spoil her happiness, she deserves it. It seems like Garrett was a gift from heaven. For a long time, I've prayed for Charlie and the other children, hoping they'd have a better life than James provided for them. It's a terrible shame that a father would treat his own children that way."

"He's no father! He's a rotten, low down snake," Jack spat. "A real father wouldn't treat his children that way. I know I wouldn't have, if I had had any children of my own."

"You would have made a wonderful father. You've been a better father to Tristen and Austin than James ever thought about being."

Before Jack had a chance to reply, Taylor and Maddie came running back. "Can we have some candy? It looks real good from the window," Taylor said, her eyes shining as bright as the clear, blue sky.

Jack winked at Mrs. Pruitt. "Well, I don't know if you two should have any candy or not, it's not good for your teeth you know."

Maddie, trying to sway Jack's decision, started talking fast. "I'm sure they have some that's not real bad for our teeth. They have jars and jars in there on the counter. And we promise not to eat it all at once, that way it won't stick to our teeth." Both little girls were nodding their heads up and down, pleading with their eyes.

"What do you think Mrs. Pruitt? Do these two little girls need any candy?"

Jack was watching the girls closely. They were holding their breath, waiting for Mrs. Pruitt to decide their fate.

"I guess it won't hurt this one time, if they—" She never finished the rest of her sentence, both little girls were jumping up and down in front of the store. Jack and Mrs. Pruitt laughed, following them into the store, waiting for the little girls to look at all the candy.

About fifteen minutes later, the little group was leaving the store. A young boy stopped in front of Jack. "Are you Mr. Jack Winsloe?" the boy asked.

"Yes, I'm Jack Winsloe. Is there something I can do for you?" Jack replied warily.

The boy removed a folded slip of paper from his shirt pocket. "Mitch, over at the telegraph office, said to give this to you. It's a telegram from Tucson." Jack gave the boy a penny, sending him on his way.

"Garrett was waiting for an answer from his attorney. I'll bet this is it," Jack said, slipping the paper in his shirt pocket. "Come on, lets take the girls back to the hotel, and let them rest before supper. They're bound to be tired, we've been walking all morning."

They all walked in the direction of the Hartford House. The mood had changed for the two adults. Jack was worried about what was in the telegram, and Mrs. Pruitt was worried over the look that had crossed Jack's face.

"Do you think everything will be OK?" asked Mrs. Pruitt, her voice barely above a whisper.

He patted her hand, which rested on his arm. "I think everything will work out for the best, it always does, just have faith." He just had to believe in his own advice, easier said than done.

Chapter Twenty-three

Charlie and Garrett had eaten lunch by the lake and afterward splashed in the cool refreshing, shallow water by the bank, it was so peaceful and relaxing. It had been a wonderful day. Charlie lay quietly on a blanket spread beneath a large tree, thinking about the events of the day. She could stay here forever, especially if the man lying beside her was with her. Her gaze drifted to the man that had made this day possible. He was lying on his side, arm propped under his head, eyes closed. He looked like he was sound asleep. But she didn't mind, it gave her an opportunity to study him. He looked like a young boy when he was resting. The lines, caused from worry, were gone, his features relaxed. He was incredibly handsome.

Her heart done a strange flip-flop inside her chest, finally understanding this man loved her, just like she was. A frown creased the smooth lines of Charlie's face, when thoughts of her father entered her mind. She didn't want Garrett to tangle with him, he was a ruthless bastard. He would stop at nothing in order to get what he wanted, Garrett didn't stand a chance. She had to keep him safe.

Garrett had been pretending sleep, watching Charlie beneath lowered lashes. She was breathtaking! He changed positions, allowing a better view of her delectable body. It was almost more than he could stand. He wondered how feelings this deep could happen so quickly. As he continued to watch her, he saw a strange mix of emotions cross her face. "Penny for your thoughts," he said, in a deep low pitched voice.

Lost deep in thought, Charlie jumped at the sound of the deep rumbling voice, then looked in the direction from which it came. "Jeez, you scared the livin' crap right out a me. I thought you was sleepin'. Were you playin' possum?"

"No, I was not playing possum for your information. I just happened to be watching the most beautiful woman in the world." He slid closer to Charlie on the picnic blanket. "And you know what I saw?" he asked, still moving closer, not giving Charlie time to answer. "I saw you with a frown on your pretty face. Tell me what was causing it and I'll make it go away." He was sitting right beside her now, his thigh touching her skirt.

She rubbed her leg, where Garrett's thigh touched hers. "Thanks anyway, but I don't think you can take care of this problem, it's something I'll have to handle myself."

"Why do you say that? I can handle most any situation."

" It's Pa, I don't want you messin' with him, he's bad news. He's a mean sonofabitch," Charlie retorted.

"Why don't you have any faith in me? I told you that I can take care of myself, and my family." He grasped her hand tightly, not wanting to ever let go.

"Look Garrett, I know you mean well, but lets face it, you're just a green horn, plain and simple," she said, a stubborn look on her beautiful face.

Garrett, fighting an inner battle, sat for a moment thinking. After taking a deep breath, he started speaking. "There's something I need to tell you, because I want you to know everything there is about me." He paused before continuing. "I'm a greenhorn around cattle and a ranch, but not around guns. I'm a retired U.S. marshall from Tucson. I've handled men a lot more dangerous than your father." He waited for her reaction, wishing he had told her before now.

Feeling like she had been pole-axed, she sat stunned. If he would lie to her about something as important as this, he probably wouldn't hesitate to lie about other more important things. The longer she thought about the whole situation, the more furious she became, finally erupting. "Just what do you think gives you the right to lie to me. I was beginning to think you were different, but you're just like every other man I know." Her face was beginning to turn an angry shade of red.

Trying to calm her down, Garrett opened his mouth, but she cut him off before he had a chance to say anything. "There's no need to try to explain, more than likely all you'll spout is more lies anyhow. I should have known better than to trust a man, in a way your just like my pa. He always told lies to my moth—" She was silenced in mid-sentence, Garrett had grabbed her, holding her tight against his rock hard body. She squirmed, but the iron bands that were holding her, never loosened. She was stuck!

Leaning close to her ear, Garrett spoke. "Never, and I mean never, compare me to your father. Do you understand, or do I need to draw you a picture?" She wasn't struggling now, but he wasn't going to take any chances. He still had an iron grip on the little wildcat.

"If you will calm down long enough, I can explain, in detail, the whole story." Shifting her weight in his arms, he looked at her face. "Can I let you go now?" he asked. When she nodded her head, he continued. "Are you ready to calm down and listen to me?" Again, she nodded her head. He relaxed his hold, slowly lowering her to the ground. Knowing that it wasn't going to be this easy, he braced himself for anything.

Spinning around to stand toe to toe, just as soon as her feet hit solid ground, Charlie was ready to fight. "Don't you ever grab me again, you low down skunk! The next time you try that, you'll be plenty sorry." She stomped off, eyes spitting fire, in the direction of the buggy. Her mind was in a whirl, never in her entire life had she ever been so mad. She had a good mind to just shoot him, then realized her gun was back in the hotel room. Why in tarnation had she ever let Mrs. Pruitt talk her into wearing this damn dress, it was beyond her. One thing was for sure, it would damn sure never happen again.

Stunned, that was the only word to describe what Garrett was feeling. How in the world had everything gotten so blown out of shape. One minute everything had been perfect, the next minute it had all gone to hell in a hand-basket. As hard as he tried, he couldn't keep the grin off his face, she sure was something when she was angry. After they were married, he would never know what to expect. One thing was for sure, it wouldn't be a typical marriage. Hearing a commotion over around the buggy, he looked just in time to see Charlie trying to climb into the buggy seat.

He sauntered over to the buggy, the closer he got, the louder the curses became. She was having a devil of a time trying to lift her leg high enough to step up. He stopped just a few steps behind her.

"Charlie," he said softly, "Please stop trying to run away from me. Just listen and I can explain everything." He waited, thinking she would whirl around a tear a strip out of his hide, but she didn't, in fact, she never moved at all. He moved closer, touching her shoulders with his hands, still she didn't acknowledge his presence.

He began talking in a calm voice. "I didn't advertise that I had been a marshall for several reasons. I didn't retire by choice, but I've never regretted it. I had to take care of Maddie, after our parents were killed. I was all she had left, she would go crazy the few times that I had to leave her to go on assignment, before I turned in my badge. That's why we came here, trying to start over. I wasn't trying to be dishonest with you, I'd never do that. Please believe me." Her body had been stiff, but Garrett felt her relax just a little. Taking that as a good sign, he hurried on. "You have become one of the most important things in my life. I'm telling you right now, and please believe me, I'll always take care of you, no matter what."

Maybe he was telling the truth, thinking back, she really never asked about his background. She just assumed he was a greenhorn. Besides, how in the hell was she supposed to think straight with his arms wrapped tight around her body, it felt so good. Twisting in his arms, she lifted her face. "Maybe I flew off the handle a little to quick. I'm sorry." She buried her face in the rough fabric of his shirt, inhaling the scent of his body. He smelled of leather and sunshine. Time passed slowly as the couple held each other, not willing to let go.

Suddenly Charlie pulled away. "You said you had several reasons for turning in your badge, but you only gave me one. What was the other reason?"

Garrett could tell by the look on her face, she wasn't going to take no for an answer.

Dropping his arms, he guided her over to sit under a tall tree. "Somehow I knew you were going to ask me that. It's kind of a long story." They settled down under the shade of the branches. "As I said before, our parents died about three years ago. They were killed in a stage holdup. I was still a Marshall back then, Maddie was little more than a baby, she wasn't along with them on the stage, some friends of my parents were watching her." He paused, it was very difficult to talk about his parents' death. "After the holdup, the sheriff finally got a telegram to me, but I didn't make it back in time for the funerals. About two weeks after the robbery, I started tracking the men that did it. There were four men all together." He picked up her hand, tracing the palm with his fingers, searching for the right words. "To make a long story short, I brought all four back, only two of them were dead, the other two were shot up, but they lived. The judge sent them to prison for life. Two of those men have two brothers that have been looking for me ever since."

Charlie felt so ashamed, she never should have doubted Garrett. "I'm sorry that I ever doubted you," she said, laying the palm of her hand on the side of Garrett's rough cheek.

He considered not telling her the rest, but he had promised to be honest with her. "There's something else you should know. I think maybe your father has contacted the men that are looking for me. Their names are Gilkey, Brett and Chad Gilkey. But I don't want you to worry, this could be for the best. If they find me, maybe we can get this mess cleared up."

"Why would my pa have contacted those two men?" "He's afraid he's going to have to give up part of his ranch. I have a legitimate claim on it. He owed my father and mother a large sum of money, which he never paid back."

Charlie looked puzzled. "I know that, but what does that have to do with…what did you say their names was…the Giddy brothers?" she asked.

"The Gilkey brothers," Garrett answered patiently. "Think about it. It's simple, if something were to happen to me, then the ranch would be his, or so he thinks."

It was a good thing Charlie was sitting down, as the color left her face. Her pa was trying to have Garrett killed. "You and Maddie have got to leave, get away from here quick." She had crawled to her feet, pulling on Garrett's hand, trying to get him off the ground. "You have to get away from those men and my pa."

Tugging on her hand, he pulled her down on his lap. "Calm down wildcat, I'm not going anywhere." She started to open her mouth to argue, but he silenced her with his finger, and it worked.

"Sit still and listen. I have an idea." He hoped to keep her on his lap for a little while, it sure felt good. "I don't run from trouble, besides, if I ran it wouldn't take them long to catch up to us. I've already talked to Jack and Mrs. Pruitt, they're willing to take Maddie if something should happen to me." She started to protest, but he held up his finger, silencing her again. "Remember, you promised to hear me out." She remained silent. "The only thing that worried me was the two beautiful women in my life. Maddie is taken care of, I know that Jack and Mrs. Pruitt will take good care of her. That only leaves you. So I've decided, if it's OK with you, we should get married while we're here in Santa Fe. That way, you'll legally be entitled to the ranch and all my possessions."

She had been content to listen, but her patience snapped. "Got it all figured out have you. What if I'm not willin' to go along with your hair-brained scheme. My pa is very dangerous, I don't think you understand just what I'm talkin' about." Her whole body was trembling, she had to make him understand. "Don't you understand, I've waited my whole life for you. I don't want to lose you now." Her eyes filled with tears.

"Sweetheart, please don't cry. Nothing is going to happen to me, I promise." He gathered her close in his arms, she fit against his body perfect. The limbs overhead was swaying in the breeze, making patterns on the ground. But the couple sitting beneath it didn't notice. They were in a world of their own, a world filled with love.

Garrett shifted Charlie on his lap. He wanted to stretch out beside her, let his hands roam over her body. God! She was perfect, every dip and curve of her body drove him wild. Starting at her shapely hip, his fingers scorched a path to her breast. "Charlie, we have to get married soon. I don't think that I can wait much longer, you're driving me wild."

Through the fog in her mind, Charlie realized Garrett had spoken to her, but couldn't comprehend his words. "Did you say someth—?" The question was cut short by her moan of pleasure, Garrett was cupping her sensitive breast with his large hand. She arched her back, giving him better access to her body.

He was going to burst any minute, never in his adult life had he ever wanted a woman this bad. She had somehow worked her way into his heart like no other woman. "I said, we have to stop this. I want to wait until you're my wife." At that moment, she rolled her head exposing the smooth skin of her neck. He could see the pulse beating at the base of her neck. And all he could think about was placing his lips to the throbbing spot, he had to, just one time. When he touched his lips to the sensitive area, all clear thinking went out the window.

"We have to stop this, I don't want to dishonor you this way. I want everything to be perfect for you." At the same time he was nibbling a path up her neck. Her skin tasted like the sweetest nectar. His hands found the tiny row of buttons on the back of her dress. It would be so easy to slip them free. But he had to wait, he wanted her to be his wife when they made love for the first time.

Charlie felt like she was floating. She had never experienced feelings like this before. Garrett's hands were all over her body, leaving a path of pure ecstasy. His body was pressed tight against her, it was honed to perfection. Everywhere she touched him, she could feel muscles contract. His fingers were toying with the buttons that ran down the back of her dress. She didn't know what would happen next, but she wasn't afraid. She ran her fingers through his thick hair, loving the feel of it. Suddenly he stiffened, pulling away. She wrapped her arms around his neck, wanting to keep him close. But he had different ideas.

"Charlie, we have to stop this now." He was pulling away from her, trying to put some distance between them.

Thinking that she had done something wrong, she started apologizing. "I'm sorry, I just don't know much about bein' a female. But if you'll give me some time, I'm sure I can learn," she said, lowering her head, looking at the ground.

"What do you mean, 'you don't know much about being a female' ? Sweetheart if you were any more female, I couldn't stand it," he said.

"Why did you want us to stop then?"

Garrett looked at her with his mouth hanging wide open. She really didn't have a clue. "Didn't you hear a word that I said to you a few minutes ago?"

Not giving her time to respond, he rushed on. "I want to make love to you for the first time as man and wife, in a real bed, with sheets and a soft mattress. Not out here in the middle of nowhere, in the grass and dirt. You're too good for that Charlie. I only want to give you the best." After finishing his explanation, he kissed her on the nose, not trusting himself to kiss her any place else.

"I thought I did something wrong when I was touching you. I didn't know if you liked it or not." The way she was looking at him with those dark eyes, almost unnerved him.

Taking her hand in his, he placed it over the front of his jeans. "Does that feel like you did anything wrong?" he asked, waiting for an answer.

She felt the huge bulge, moving under her hand. She finally realized why, her face turned dark red, but the embarrassment didn't last long. "If I agree to marry you, can we start where we left off?" she asked, a mischievous look dancing across her face.

"Sweetheart, after we're married, we can start anywhere you want to."

She pulled him toward the buggy, as fast as she could. "What are we standin' around talkin' for. Lets get back to Santa Fe and find us a preacher. I want to get married tonight, if we can." she said.

He followed her to the buggy. She sure was going to be a handful, but at least he wouldn't have to buy any larger pants.

Chapter Twenty-four

The rest of the day passed very quickly. Garrett had made arrangements for a small wedding at the church, and it was almost time to meet the preacher and his wife for the ceremony. He was all thumbs trying to make a knot in his string tie. He just couldn't believe that in less than an hour, Charlie was going to be his wife. A slow grin spread across his face as he thought about the night to come. He sure hoped he didn't disappoint her. He wanted everything to be perfect for her. Just being with her was all he wanted, well, maybe not all he wanted. Oh! What a night it was going to be. Whistling a tune, he turned from the mirror, finally satisfied with his tie.

There was a knock at the door before Jack poked his head inside. "You just about ready to go?" he asked. Not waiting for a reply, he stepped into the room, closing the door behind him. "Garrett," he said nervously, "I need to talk to you, I promise it won't take long." Jack walked closer to the younger man.

"What do you need to talk to me about? I'm kind of in a hurry. Can it wait until a little later?" Like tomorrow, Garrett thought. He stepped around Jack to get his coat, not wanting to be late for his own wedding.

"No, this can't wait. If you'd stand still for a minute, I'll say what I come to say, then we can go on to the church."

The tone of voice Jack used stopped Garrett in his tracks. "Is there something wrong? Has Charlie changed her mind about marrying me?" He was starting to panic.

Running out of patience, Jack held up his hand. "Please be still for just a minute, and sit down, you're making me nervous." Actually he was already nervous, but he was getting worse. "I don't know how to say this other that straight out. I want you to promise me one thing."

"What's that?"

"Will you please promise to take good care of Charlie, not just now, but for the rest of her life? Bea and I can't help worrying about that girl, she's a very special person, just like her mother was." Jack was looking closely at him. "That's all you have to do, promise me that you'll take care of her. But before you do, I want you to understand that I'll always hold you to that promise."

Garrett looked at Jack, not believing what he was hearing. Before answering Jack, he tried to find the right words to describe his feelings for Charlie, but words just weren't enough. He had to make Jack understand. "Jack, you and Bea can rest assured that as long as I'm able to draw a breath, I'll take good care of her. You're right, she's a very special person and I'm very lucky to have her for my wife. I'll always protect her and cherish her for as long as I'm able." He waited for Jack's decision.

"I knew you would son, I just had to make sure, that's all." Throwing his arm around Garrett's shoulder, he grinned. "We better get ourselves over to that church. The prettiest gal in Santa Fe will be there in a little bit, we don't want to keep her waiting." As they started for the door, Jack laughed. "Besides, she might just hunt us down with a gun, and that would be just plain embarrassin'." Both men laughed as they walked down the hallway, neither one of them had any intention of being late.

A fish out of water, that's exactly what she felt like. Why in the world had she let Garrett talk her into getting married in a church, let alone another new dress. The one she wore to the picnic was bad enough, but this one was even tighter, and showed more of her...what had Mrs. Pruitt called it...assets, whatever the hell that was. The only thing she wanted to do was marry Garrett and be done with it. Might as well make the best of the situation, she thought.

Twirling around in the middle of the room, thinking this was going to be the best day of her life. A look of sadness crossed her glowing features, if only her mother could be here today. Her mother would have liked Garrett, she just knew it. Stopping, she looked toward the ceiling, saying a quick prayer, hoping her mother could hear her. But somehow her mother knew that this was her wedding day. She had a feeling her mother was with her all the time.

The door to her room burst open. She wiped the tears out of her eyes before turning toward the door. She laughed out loud when Mrs. Pruitt rushed in, and she was in a hurry, a big hurry, and both little girls were hot on her heels.

"Charlie," Mrs. Pruitt shouted, "Are you ready to go yet? The menfolk just walked down the stairs, they're on their way to the church. The twins are going to meet us there." She was bustling around the room so fast, she looked like a tumbleweed caught in a windstorm.

Charlie was still standing in the same spot. Maddie and Taylor had climbed up on the bed, watching all the activity in the room. Maddie whispered into Taylor's ear. Taylor was listening very intently, her face bright with excitement. Taylor nodded her head when Maddie finished whispering, then Taylor turned to Charlie. "When you marry Garret, does that mean Maddie and me will be almost sisters?" Taylor asked. Both little girls sat on the edge of the bed, waiting for an answer.

Charlie watched them both, tears of happiness shining in her eyes. "No," she said. "You won't be almost sisters, you'll be sisters."

The little girls squealed in delight.

Mrs. Pruitt cut the celebration short. "I said we've got to shake a leg. If we don't get over to the church, you two won't be sisters. Now lets hurry." She had Maddie and Taylor on their feet, inspecting their dresses and hair ribbons. When she finished, she turned to Charlie. "Come here child and let me make sure your dress and hair are straight." Charlie walked over to Mrs. Pruitt, stopping in front of her. Mrs. Pruitt looked into Charlie's dark eyes, pride showing on her face. "Your mother would have been so proud of you today. You're beautiful, you look just like her."

Charlie's eyes were filled with tears. Before she could say anything to Mrs. Pruitt, Taylor said the most wonderful thing. "I think she looks just like one of the princess' in the book that Austin reads to us." Then she looked at Maddie. "Ain't that right Maddie?" she asked.

Nodding her head up and down, Maddie finally answered. "Yep, she does. And we're not the only one that thinks that she looks like a princess." She folded her hands behind her back, then continued. "Garrett told me you are the most beautiful woman in the whole wide world. And that he is always going to treat you like a princess."

Charlie was stunned, Garrett actually thought she was the most beautiful woman in the world. That couldn't be right, she was just plain old Charlie.

Mrs. Pruitt placed her hand under Charlie's elbow. "Come on, we've got to leave now. There's a buggy waiting downstairs to take us all to the church." She motioned with her free hand for the little girls to follow. The little group stepped out into the hallway. The door was closed softly, and they descended the stairs.

Adjusting his tie for the tenth time, Garrett looked at his pocket watch. It was almost time for the ceremony to begin, and Charlie wasn't here, maybe she had changed her mind. He could feel the fear rising in his body, he was on the verge of panicking. Looking around the small church, he imagined Charlie walking toward him, eager to become his bride, he hoped. He must have had a stupid look on his face, because Tristen and Austin started laughing. Realizing what they were laughing at, he looked around a little sheepishly. Before he could say something to the boys sitting in the front pew, he heard a buggy stop in front of the church.

Jack had been standing at the bottom of the steps, waiting on the women to arrive. When the buggy stopped, he helped all four ladies down. After the buggy pulled away, he held out both arms. Mrs. Pruitt and Charlie each accepted an elbow, Maddie and Taylor walked in front of the three adults.

Leaning close to Charlie, Jack spoke to her quietly. "Charlie girl, you're one of the most beautiful women that I've ever seen. Almost as beautiful as Mrs. Pruitt here."

The older woman turned beet red. "Would you hush up you old coot. This is Charlie and Garrett's special day." Mrs. Pruitt gave him a swat on the arm, loving every minute of his teasing.

Charlie was quiet, as they moved closer to the church. The closer they got, the more nervous she became. But watching the older couple at her side, it was obvious they were deeply in love with each other, it somehow seemed to relax her. Then she suddenly realized that they always seemed to make her feel better about herself, just like parents would treat their own child. The last thought made her smile and hug Jack's arm tighter.

"I want to thank you both for all the things you've done for me and my brothers and sister. I'll always think of both of you as my parents, if that's all right with you."

Mrs. Pruitt couldn't speak at all, she dabbed at her eyes with a little lace hanky. Jack cleared his throat several times before speaking. "Little girl, I think I speak for both of us. You can always count on us with anything you need, and we'd be proud if you wanted to think of us as your parents. Wouldn't we Bea?"

The emotion was still too strong for Mrs. Pruitt to speak, she simply nodded her head in agreement.

Not giving Charlie or Mrs. Pruitt time to start crying, Jack ushered them up the steps of the church. "We've got to get you inside Charlie girl, before that young man of yours wears a hole in the floor. I swear he's paced a good ten miles in the last thirty minutes or so. Come on, lets go put him out of his misery." All three adults were laughing as they reached the top of the steps, Maddie and Taylor was waiting for them. They all entered the church together.

Garrett was talking to the preacher, Eli Snow. He heard the door open, his breath caught in his throat at the sight. Entering the church was the most beautiful vision he had ever seen. His sister Maddie, and Taylor was walking side by side, Mrs. Pruitt was walking behind them. They all looked lovely. But his attention was drawn back to the door, it looked like an angel floating down from heaven. When the angel came through the door, she had Jack by her side. Garrett's heart started beating wildly, turning to Preacher Snow. "I think the ceremony is about to begin," he said.

Mrs. Pruitt and the girls had reached the pew where Austin and Tristen were waiting. The boys slid over, making room for them. They all turned to see what had grabbed Garrett's attention.

"Is that really our sister?" Tristen whispered to Austin.

Not saying anything at first, Austin finally answered. "Well, I guess it must be, she's supposed to marry Garret today. But it sure don't look at all like her. That lady is beautiful."

"You boys be quiet now, do you hear me? That most certainly is your sister. Now, show a little respect." Mrs. Pruitt finished scolding them, then turned to watch Charlie and Jack walk down the aisle. They made their way slowly, Jack beaming with pride, Charlie's face was bright with excitement. Mrs. Pruitt glanced at Garrett, just to see his expression. It was a look of smoldering passion. She could tell by the look in his eyes that he truly loved and cared for Charlie. She was so happy for them.

Garrett watched the couple walking down the aisle. His eyes were drawn to Charlie's. How he loved her. The closer they got, the harder his heart pounded in his chest. They stopped beside Garrett. Jack looked over Charlie's head and nodded at Garrett, then placed Charlie's hand in Garrett's hand. Garrett felt instant fire shoot through his hand and up his arm. This was going to be some kind of marriage, he thought with a sly grin.

The preacher motioned for them both to move to the front of the church, by the altar. They were instructed to face each other, holding hands. Later neither one of them remembered much about the ceremony. After their vows had been repeated, which seemed like an eternity, they were pronounced man and wife. The only words that Garrett could comprehend were 'you may kiss your bride', and that he understood.

Taking Charlie in his arms, he lowered his mouth to hers. It was a simple kiss, but it robbed them both of their breath. He raised his head, looking at her face. "I'll cherish you for the rest of my life, Mrs. Steele," he whispered softly.

Everything had happened in such a blur, Charlie was slightly disoriented. But when Garrett wrapped his arms around her, it seemed time stood still. Then he kissed her. He whispered soft words into her ear, after hearing the words, she couldn't stop the smile that appeared on her face. "Is that a promise Mr. Steele?" she asked with a heart-stopping smile. "Because as you know, I'll probably need a lot of lookin' after."

They turned to face the back of the church. The preacher's voice announcing to the world. "Let me introduce to you, Mr. and Mrs. Garrett Steele," he said in a booming voice.

As the newly married couple stepped away from the altar, their family surrounded them. There was a lot of laughing and hugging going on. When the congratulations had all been said, the new little family walked out together. They were all going to eat a celebration meal at the restaurant in the hotel.

Charlie started walking away with the others, but strong hands pulled her back. "Don't run off so fast Mrs. Steele. I was kind of hoping you'd walk along with your new husband." He pulled her soft body up next to his much harder one, and she fit perfectly.

"You don't ever have to worry about me going anywhere without you. I think I've loved you from the first minute I clapped eyes on you," she said, snuggling closer into his embrace.

Garrett pulled back away from her. "Was that when you called me a greenhorn, or slow?" he asked.

She punched him lightly on the arm. "Well, you are somewhat of a greenhorn around the ranch," she said.

A look of pure fire came into his eyes. "Maybe in the cow department, but not in the loving department," he whispered. The sound of his low, deep voice was sending shivers up her arms. He grasped her elbow. "Come on, we need to catch up with the others. There's plenty of time for everything else tonight," he said.

The newly married couple hurried out the door, both of them counting the hours until nightfall.

Chapter Twenty-five

It was late afternoon and James was returning from the north line shack. He had been talking to Brett and Chad Gilkey. They were becoming a little restless, in fact James was too. They had discussed a number of things, mainly how to dispose of Garrett Steele. The thought of getting rid of Steele brought great pleasure to James. He liked the ideas the Gilkeys had come up with. They hated Steele almost as much as he did, almost.

Stopping his horse in front of the barn, he motioned for one of the hands to take his horse. "Take him and cool him out real good," he said. He removed his gloves, watching the ranch hand lead his horse into the cool interior of the barn.

James looked around for Pete, he needed to speak to him. He called out to the ranch hand. "Where the hell is Pete at this afternoon?"

The young man stopped, looking over the horse's back. "Him and John went in to Broken Tongue, it's their night off," he called back. He waited to see if James had any more questions. He knew he was free to go when James turned his back.

Something better happen pretty soon, James thought. What in the hell could they be doing for so long in Santa Fe. He was growing very impatient. Thinking back, he should have taken care of his stepbrother, Ben, years ago. If he had, none of this would be happening right now. His thoughts returned to Ben Steele, actually Ben's wife, Diane. What a sight she had been, always so prim and proper, nothing at all like the whore he had married. He wondered if Ben had ever worried about Diane being unfaithful to him. Probably not, she was a real lady.

By this time he had reached the back steps, he climbed them, and entered the dark kitchen. He was really beginning to enjoy all the peace and quiet. Walking down the hall he looked around at all his possessions. He had a grand home. When all of this was over with, and he was rid of that damn nosy housekeeper, maybe he would find a woman to cook and clean, and share his bed. After entering his office, he sat down in his chair, and propped his booted feet up on his desk. His mind was racing. It wouldn't be long now, he could feel it in his bones.

The sound of a horse pounding into the yard jerked him back to the present. He jumped up, looking out the window. He discovered it was Gimpy, riding hard. Good! Maybe he had some good news. Rubbing his hands together in anticipation, he waited.

Sliding to a halt, dust billowing around him, Gimpy dismounted before the horse came to a complete stop. The boss was sure going to be pissed at the news. He almost dreaded telling him. He didn't knock at the front door, he just walked on in. When he reached the office door, it was open, James was standing by the windows.

"Have you heard something? Have they started back to the ranch yet? If they have, I need to go tell Brett and Chad." James' eyes had taken on an evil glow.

"I've got news boss. But I don't think it's what you've been expectin'." Gimpy shifted from one foot to he other, not wanting to look James in the eye.

Walking back over to his desk, James pounded his fists down hard. "Are you going to tell me or keep me in suspense? You better make it quick, you stupid bastard." He was angry!

One of these days, I'm going to tell him where to get off, Gimpy thought, but not today. "I got a telegram from my contact in Santa Fe. It seems that late this afternoon, Steele and that bitch daughter of yours went and got married." He waited to see if James was going to explode. When he didn't, he continued with the news. "My contact also says, that Steele has been sendin' a bunch of telegrams to Tucson, and he's been gettin' a bunch back in the past two days. But he couldn't find out what was in the telegrams, or who had sent them."

James was quiet, too quiet. Of all the things that they could have done, this was just about the worst one. Suddenly, as he replayed the events in his mind, maybe it wasn't so bad after all. He would just have to have the Gilkeys dispose of Charlie also, that way all her property would go to him, as her next of kin of course. Handing Gimpy a cigar, he struck a match, first holding it to his own cigar, then lighting Gimpy's. "You know what, that little bit of information wasn't near as upsetting as I first thought," he said. He tilted his head back, blowing smoke high into the air, waiting.

"What do you mean by that boss?" Gimpy asked, eyeing him nervously, still waiting for the real explosion.

"It's simple. I'll just have the Gilkey brothers take care of them both, at the same time. Sort of like killing two birds with one stone," he said. "After supper, we'll head back up to the line shack, and let 'em know what's going on." James shook his head, thinking about killing them both at the same time, it was going to be well worth the cost.

The celebration meal was in full swing, everyone was enjoying it. The children were laughing, and the adults had smiles from ear to ear. Charlie, never one to get overly nervous, couldn't hardly eat a thing. She toyed with her food, pushing it from one side of her plate to the other. All she could think about was the night to come. It made her feel hot and cold all over, at the same time. She glanced up at Garrett, catching him looking at her. Her face flamed.

He had been watching her closely. And what he saw made him grin, the little wildcat was thinking about tonight. He had to keep his mind clear of those kind of images, if not, he would sure as hell embarrass himself. He could already feel his pants getting tighter.

"Charlie, you better eat your supper." Waiting until he had her full attention, then he continued with a wicked grin on his handsome features. "Your going to need all the energy you can get tonight."

The last statement made the heat flood her face. She quickly turned to look at Mrs. Pruitt and Jack. They were both grinning like fools. Garrett was trying to embarrass her, two could play that game, she thought. Turning toward him, she answered innocently. "I don't know what you're talkin' about Garrett, sleeping with Mrs. Pruitt tonight won't take any more energy than it did last night."

The grin disappeared from Garrett's face quickly. Everyone at the table was roaring with laughter. Jack was wiping the tears from his eyes, and Mrs. Pruitt was shaking like a bowl of jelly. Charlie sat with her hands folded in her lap, her eyes just daring Garrett to say something else. God! How he loved her.

After everyone settled down, Garrett reached for Charlie's hand. His larger hand dwarfing her smaller one. He brought it to his lips, lightly kissing each knuckle. He spoke to her very softly. "From this day forward, we will always be together, day and night. I don't want to ever be apart from you. Do you understand?"

"Yes."

The magic spell was broken when Mrs. Pruitt cleared her throat. "Charlie, if you're done with your dinner, we need to go on upstairs and move some of your belongings. Earlier this afternoon, Jack and I rented the honeymoon suite for you and Garrett, it's down at the end of the hallway."

Both men stood, helping the ladies from their seats. Tristen and Austin, who had been quiet all evening, helped the younger girls with their chairs.

Garrett didn't want to let Charlie go. He leaned over, placing a light kiss on her inviting mouth. It was heaven on earth. He whispered in her ear. "I hope that will hold you until later sweetheart."

She simply nodded, standing on her toes, whispering in Garrett's ear. "I just want you to know, I always give as good as I get." Then she was gone in a flurry of lace and satin.

He stood there, watching her disappear up the stairs with Mrs. Pruitt. Maddie and Taylor were skipping along behind them, happy as larks. He shook his head in amazement, she sure was something else.

He returned to the table. Jack and the boys were having some sort of discussion. They were arguing over something. "What's going on?" he asked. He sat back down, waiting for an answer.

"The boys just wanted to know if they could go back over to the livery stable and spend the night," Jack said, eyeing Austin and Tristen.

"What's the problem with that?" Garrett asked.

After a moment of hesitation, Tristen finally spoke up. "Jack was telling us, that we needed to start asking you for permission, since you're the head of the family now." Both boys looked down at the table, waiting for the noose to tighten around their necks.

"Look boys, I don't want to be your boss. I just want to be your friend. You guys are almost grown. I don't want to treat you like a couple of small children." He paused a minute, looking at Jack for support. The older man nodded his head in agreement.

"I don't want to change a thing. You guys can continue to ask Jack and Mrs. Pruitt for permission to do things, I just want you to know, I'm here to help you boys, any way I can." Garrett watched both boys, searching for a reaction. Tristen answered first. "It's not that we don't like you. It's just that Jack and Mrs. Pruitt have taken care of us for so long, it's hard for us to explain—" He stopped, trying to find the right words.

Austin, who had been listening, started talking where his twin left off. "What my brother is trying to say...is... we've never had anybody to care about us as much as Jack and Mrs. Pruitt. Well, Charlie does, but she really don't count, because she's our sister and all. It's going to take some getting used to, that's all." Both boys sat there, looking at Garrett, their eyes telling the story.

"If Jack doesn't mind you going over to the livery, it's all right with me." Garrett grinned when two sets of eyes, exactly alike, turned toward Jack, pleading.

"Go on you scamps, get out of here," Jack said gruffly. His eyes followed the boys as they hurried through the dining room doors. "I want to thank you for the way you handled that situation. They really are good boys, just never had anybody to take care of them."

"That's all going to change. I plan on being around for a long time. When I promised to take care of Charlie, that also meant her brothers and sister to." Garrett was quiet for a minute, watching the older man. "I want you to know that I would be honored if you would stay on and help me take care of them, and everything else."

"Have you forgotten about James? You act like everything is perfectly fine. I just hope you're not under estimatin' him."

"As I've said before, I can handle the likes of James McCuan. But there is something I want to tell you," he said. "That telegram that came today was from my attorney. Everything is in order, if anything should happen to me, my share of the ranch goes to Charlie, it's airtight. The only thing I want you to promise me, is, that you'll stay on and help her run the ranch, make sure her and the kids are taken care of."

"You know I'd do that anyhow. Or, at least you should," Jack said agitated.

Garrett smiled. "I just had to make sure, for Charlie's sake." He started digging in the pocket of his new trousers, the ones he had bought for the wedding, until he found a small slip of paper. Handing it over to Jack, he explained. "There's two names on that paper. If something goes wrong, and you need help, don't hesitate to contact both of them. You can find them in Tucson. Just tell them." He hesitated for a moment, then blurted it out. "Tell them that Cold Steele needs them to come quick, they'll know what you mean."

Jack was dumbfounded. His brain slowly started to work again. "Are you tryin' to tell me boy, that you're Cold Steele?"

"Well maybe."

"Sonofabitch, Charlie girl went and married a legend." His face split into a wide grin. "Why didn't you tell me before? I feel like a complete fool tryin' to warn you against the likes of James McCuan. An idiot is more like it. Why the hell didn't you tell me?"

"I told you. I'm trying to make a fresh start. I wanted to leave that old life behind, but it keeps catching up to me." Before Jack could ask any more questions, Garrett changed the subject. "Do you think Mrs. Pruitt and Charlie have everything moved into the honeymoon suite?" he asked, wiggling his eyebrows.

"I don't know, but lets go find out." Jack slapped Garrett on the shoulder as they left the dining room. Both men were to busy discussing Garrett's legend status to notice the man watching them through the window of the hotel. Things were calm now, but there was unexpected trouble brewing in the near future.

Chapter Twenty-six

Twirling around in front of the full-length mirror one more time, which didn't help, Charlie started to fret. The nightgown that Mrs. Pruitt had picked out for her was fairly modest, it just showed some of her legs, well actually a lot of her legs. She wondered if Garrett would think it was too daring. After spinning in front of the mirror one last time, a frown creased her face. She felt like a calf on a sale block.

All afternoon she had looked forward to spending some time alone with Garrett, now she was a nervous wreck. The only thing she knew about the physical side of marriage, was what she had picked up around the bunkhouse, and that wasn't saying much.

Walking over to the edge of the high bed, she sat down, waiting for Garrett to come to their room. She suddenly realized that she should have told Mrs. Pruitt the truth, admitted to the older woman that she knew nothing about men. But no, that would have been too easy, she had to act like she knew everything already. She sure hoped Garrett knew more than she did, if not, they were going to be in one hell of a mess.

When Garrett and Jack reached the top of the stairs, they saw Mrs. Pruitt and the girls heading down the hallway. Garrett noticed right away that Charlie wasn't with them.

"Evenin' ladies, it's kind of late for single females to be out taking a stroll. You know, you really should have a man with you," Jack said, winking at Garrett.

Taylor tilted her head back. "You know we ain't takin' no stroll. We're walking in the hallway with Mrs. Pruitt. We just left Charlie back there in the honey suite, and boy, she sure was pretty. You should have seen her go—" Her sentence was interrupted, Maddie had nudged her hard.

Noticing the glare that his sister was giving Taylor, Garrett thought he had better intervene. "Maddie are you happy?" Garrett asked, hoping to keep the peace between the two little girls, because Taylor had let the cat out of the bag about Charlie.

As she walked by Taylor, Maddie couldn't help herself, she had to give Taylor one last menacing look. "Yes Garrett. I'm very happy, and I'm so glad you married Charlie, now we have a real family again, even though some of us have very big mouths." The last remark received an angry look from

Taylor.

Picking Maddie up in his strong arms, Garrett hugged her close. "Maddie, Taylor didn't tell any secrets. I've known for a while that Charlie is beautiful. Please, I don't want you two girls mad at each other." He nuzzled her neck, loving her little girl smell. "Is Charlie's gown really beautiful?" he asked, whispering into Maddie's ear. The little girl giggled, nodding her head against his shoulder.

Placing Maddie back down on the carpet, he motioned for Taylor. He picked her up, holding her tight in his arms. He kissed her on the cheek, loving the sound of her laughter. "Is your sister really beautiful?" he asked in a low voice.

"You know I'd never lie to you. She's about near perfect."

Garrett eyed the little fireball in his arms. She reminded him so much of his wife. Lord help him, he would be gray headed in a matter of months.

"Come on girls, it's time for bed." Mrs. Pruitt was trying to herd them toward their hotel room. "Come on Jack, you can help me get these ragmuffins ready for bed," she said, looking back over her shoulder.

Jack extended his hand. "Congratulations son, you got yourself one fine woman, and a pretty nice ready made family."

Shaking hands, Garrett added. "With you and Mrs. Pruitt, I'd say I have a perfect ready made family."

"You better get yourself on down the hall boy. And don't worry about the girls, we'll watch after them real good."

As he walked past the open hotel door, he heard Maddie and Taylor telling Mrs. Pruitt good night. He felt good, so good, he started whistling, life was just starting to look up. Glancing down he noticed other things were starting to look up to. He started walking a little faster, he had to see Charlie.

Whistling, she heard someone whistling, sounded like they were coming closer. She held her breath, realizing the whistling had stopped right in front of her door. It was so quiet in the room, she could hear her own heart beating.

Someone knocked on the door, it echoed so loud it startled her. What in the world was she going to do. Before she had time to come up with a plan, there was another knock at the door. She stood rooted to the spot, just like her feet were nailed to the floor. A voice penetrated the fog in her brain, it almost sounded like Garrett. Listening real close, she remembered that she had been waiting for him to come their room. Again she heard the deep voice on the other side of the door, this time there was no mistake, it was Garrett. Looking around the room, she realized it wouldn't do any good to hide, he'd find her for sure.

That was strange, no answer. He was going to try one more time, then he was going in whether she liked it or not. "Charlie, it's me Garrett. Can I come in now?" That had been stupid, of course she knew it was him, who else would she be waiting for on her wedding night. He placed his ear next to the door, listening for movement, nothing.

Moving a little closer, he leaned harder against the door, hoping to hear her, still nothing. Where could she be? Letting his mind wander, he didn't hear the doorknob rattle until it was too late.

The door was jerked open, causing him to lose his balance and fall. He didn't slow down until hit the floor with a loud thump. Looking up, thinking he had hit his head harder than he thought. He saw an angel standing over him, yards and yards of white lace floating around her heavenly body. Once his gaze drifted past her fantastic body, he focused on her face, funny, she looked exactly like Charlie…it was Charlie. He raised up on one elbow, trying to get a better look at her. She was breathtaking.

Looking down at her new husband, she chuckled. "Well greenhorn, I guess you need walkin' lessons, just like you need ridin' lessons." She leaned over to help him to his feet, not realizing the view that she was giving him. And he wasn't about to complain, in fact, he just might have to fall more often.

"You didn't have to jerk the door open," he complained.

"How was I supposed to know you was leanin' against it. Most people stand up outside the door, not lay against it." She eyed him, thinking he sure was acting strange. Maybe she wasn't the only one a little nervous.

He walked over and put his hands on her shoulders. "I don't want to discuss my habits right now. I've got the prettiest woman in Santa Fe here in the room with me, and she just so happens to be my new bride. I think we've got better things to do, don't you?"

Swallowing hard, Charlie blurted out. "Garrett, I've got to be honest with you. I don't know much about what comes next. I mean, between a husband and wife. I'm just a little bit scared. I don't want to disappoint you." She looked away, fearing she would find disgust in Garrett's eyes.

The little wildcat was afraid. His heart melted, if possible, he loved her even more. He rubbed his finger lightly over her cheek. "You could never disappoint me. We'll go slow, I'll teach you. You just do what comes natural, that's all." He placed a gentle kiss on her full lips. He gathered her tighter against his body, deepening the kiss. He pulled back, looking down at her, seeing the desire in her eyes.

"We've got entirely too many clothes on. We can start with your wrapper," he whispered. He slid her arms out of the silky garment, letting it slide to the floor. His eyes darkened with desire when he saw the outline of her generous breasts clear in the candlelight.

She didn't know what was happening to her body. She wanted to be closer to Garrett. Slowly, shyly, she unbuttoned his shirt, letting it fall open to reveal his muscle-hardened chest. She placed her hands on his chest, loving the feel of his bare skin. But she didn't know what to do next. He said to do whatever comes natural, so she touched her lips to his chest, causing him to shiver from head to toe. She liked the fact that she could make him shiver, maybe this wasn't going to be too hard after all, she thought with a mischievous smile.

If she kept that sweet, little tongue on his chest much longer, lesson one was going to be over before it really got started. Stepping back out of her reach, he had to slow her down. Besides, he wanted to see more of her, all of her in the candlelight. Taking the small straps of her gown, he moved them down her arms. As the scrap of lace, her gown, moved lower, his anticipation grew, among other things.

"I want to see all of you sweetheart. Is that all right with you?" He watched her face closely, watching for her reaction. He didn't notice that he had been holding his breath, until she nodded her head in agreement. "If you want me to stop at any time, just tell me. I promise I'll stop, even if it kills me." God, how he hoped she didn't ask him to stop.

The gown slipped to the floor. Charlie could feel her face heating up. She tried to cover herself with her hands, but he pulled them away. Knowing that her body was far from perfect. "I know I'm bigger than most women. My belly is fat, and my...well hell, most of me is fat all over," she said quietly. She turned her back, reaching for her wrapper, trying to cover up. Hearing a sharp intake of breath, she turned and expected to see pure disgust on Garrett's face, instead she saw anger.

"Who gave you those marks on your back? Don't even think about lying to me. If you try to, I'll go ask Jack and Mrs. Pruitt right now." There was sparks shooting from his gray eyes. He moved closer, placing gentle hands on her back, rubbing up and down along her spine. "Please tell me Charlie," he said, in a much calmer voice.

"My pa did it," she whispered.

Cursing softly, Garrett sat down in a chair, pulling her down on his lap. "The next time I get a chance, I'm going to give that bastard a taste of his own medicine." She started to protest, but he held his fingers to her lips. "I want you to listen to me for a minute. First of all, we're not going to let your father ruin our wedding night. I'll take care of him soon enough," he said, placing a kiss on the end of her nose. "The next thing I want to get straight, is you. Your not fat by any means, I happen to like everything about your body. You have beautiful breasts. Do you know what would make them even more gorgeous?" He waited for her to answer, but she only shook her head. "I'll tell you then. Our child nursing, that's what would make them even more beautiful. Don't you agree?"

A child of her own, she had always dreamed of a family. But she had always known it would take a miracle for that to happen. Looking into her husband's gray eyes, she suddenly realized that miracle could very well happen now.

"I've always dreamed of a family of my own. But you do understand that I'm going to take care of my brothers and sister. I don't want them anywhere around Pa."

"You know I don't mind, I think the world of your brothers and sister. Besides, I'm going to take care of my sister as well." His hands were beginning to roam the hills and valleys of her body, making her feel lightheaded with desire. "But I was also hoping to have a child of my own. I hope our first one is a sassy little girl, just like her mother."

His hands stopped at the scars on her back, it was all he could do not to get mad all over again. Slowly he caressed every inch of her lovely back.

Feeling bold, she placed her lips to his. There was always a jolt of pure electricity that coursed through their bodies when they touched, and it was no different this time. "Garrett, I love you with all my heart." She kissed him again, leaning against his strong body. His hands were all over her. She felt like she was on fire!

"I love you to," he whispered against her soft lips. He trailed hot kisses down her throat, stopping at each sensitive spot, taking care not to leave any out. When his head moved between her breasts, her breath caught deep in her throat. He continued his downward search, tasting every inch of her skin. When his mouth closed over her nipple, she almost jumped off his lap, only the tight hold he had on her prevented her from moving.

"Take it easy wildcat. Don't you like that? I know I do."

Not able to speak, she nodded her head. He chuckled against her plump breast, then continued on his quest. Not wanting the other nipple to feel left out, he shifted his attentions. He was delighted to find out both were equally sensitive.

She was trying to think straight. She had to ask him a question. "Garrett, please stop. I need to ask you something."

STOP! That's all he heard. Pulling away from her, he groaned, this couldn't possibly be happening. "What did you say sweetheart?" He hoped it was just a temporary setback.

"I said, I need to ask you a question."

"Well go ahead, ask away."

"What exactly does it mean to 'dip your worm'?" she asked, waiting patiently for an answer.

He tried to keep a straight face, but it was hard. "It would be easier to show you than try to explain it to you. Afterwards, if you have any more questions, I'll try to answer them in detail."

"I trust you Garrett, but you have to promise, if I don't completely understand, you'll tell me everything you know about it."

"Cross my heart and hope to die," he said, crossing his chest with his finger. He picked her up and carried her to bed, lowering her gently down to the soft mattress. He removed his trousers and stretched out beside her, more than willing to start her first lesson.

Much later, they lay in the center of the big bed, arms and legs entwined. Garrett was stroking her hair. "Do you have any questions Mrs. Steele?" he asked.

"Not a one," she replied sleepily. Her body went limp as she fell into a deep, relaxing sleep.

He grinned in the darkness, she sure had turned out to be a little wildcat, in bed and out. His expression changed when his hand touched the little scars on her back. Soon, very soon, James McCuan would pay for his cruelty. His eyelids was getting heavy, he was worn to a frazzle. Pulling his exhausted bride closer, he finally let sleep claim him.

Chapter Twenty-seven

Her pillow just wasn't right, it was hard, and it was also moving. Her head snapped up, she found herself staring at the most handsome face she had ever seen. And her pillow, her husband's chest, wasn't half bad either. Then the memories of the night before came flooding back. Just thinking about it embarrassed her. But the things they had done were wonderful.

Garrett had been watching her through half closed eyes. The minute she had moved, he had become alert. Sleeping with someone was going to take some getting used to. He saw the heat flood her face and shoulders, probably thinking about last night, it had been the best night of his entire life. She was more than he had ever imagined in a wife. That delectable body would drive a man completely out of his mind, but what a way to go, he thought. His hand rubbed the small of her back, slowly making its way down to her full hip.

Looking at his face, Charlie discovered that he was awake. His hand was getting close to unknown territory, but it felt good. She had to get a handle on things, before they got out of hand. She popped up out of bed, which wasn't a very good idea, because the quilt slipped, revealing one plump breast.

"You don't have to stare at me like I'm a prized heifer or something," she snapped. She continued to look for her wrapper, which had been discarded rather hastily the night before. She finally found it under the bed. She slipped both arms into the sleeves, and tightened the belt around her waist.

Folding his hands behind his head, he watched his bride scramble around the room, looking for the rest of her nightclothes. They were scattered all around the room. He groaned low in his throat when she bent over to look under a chair, her lush bottom sticking up, the light fabric of her wrapper stretched tight. He could feel his blood starting to heat up. He wrapped a sheet around his waist, climbed out of bed, and swaggered toward her.

"You need to get your clothes on. It's probably a good half hour past dawn." She had straightened up, holding her gown in front of her like a shield.

"I'm not ready to get my clothes on yet. I want you to come back to bed with me. We need a little more rest." He continued walking slowly toward her, a wicked gleam in his eye.

"If you wanted more rest, you should have got some more shut eye last night."

Stopping in front of her, he looked down. "Sweetheart, how could I rest last night when I had a gorgeous woman in bed with me? He gathered her up close, loving the feel of silk over her body. "And," he paused, placing a kiss on the side of her throat, "I really don't have rest on my mind now. Come on back to bed and let me love you again."

Charlie knew it was sinful. But she wanted to go back to bed with her husband for just a while longer. "What will Jack and Mrs. Pruitt think?" Leaning closer, she could feel the strength of her husband's body, the unleashed power, it felt wonderful.

"They won't think a thing, this is what newlyweds are supposed to do. Besides, when everything settles down, I'm going to take you on a real honeymoon." He let go of the sheet that was wrapped around his lower body. He wanted to feel every inch of her. The sheet slipped to the floor. He was standing naked in the middle of the room.

Pulling away from him, she looked at the sheet puddled on the floor at their feet. She let her hands roam over his bare chest, then around to his muscular back, loving the feel of his strong body. Biting her lower lip between her teeth, she made the decision, letting her hands roam lower, lightly massaging his naked buttocks. She grinned, hearing his sharp intake of breath. She continued her assault on his flesh.

Sweeping her into his arms, he carried her back to their bed. "Now, you little wildcat, it's my turn to torment you." After he had settled her on the bed, she held her arms open wide, welcoming him.

A couple of hours later, Garrett closed the door to their room softly, going in search of Jack. He had to talk to him right away. Before starting down the stairs, he checked his pistol. He hated having to wear a gun again, but he had to protect his family.

When he reached the bottom of the stairs, he started to ask the clerk at the desk about Jack. But before he reached the desk, Maddie came running through the door. He turned just as the little girl launched herself at him, trusting him to catch her.

"Where have you been Garrett? Mrs. Pruitt said to let you and Charlie sleep late this morning. You two must have really been tired to sleep this long," Maddie said, hugging Garrett's neck.

He winked at Mrs. Pruitt, who had just walked in the door. "We sure was. In fact, Charlie is still sleeping. She's turning into a regular lazy bones." He looked over the little girl's head, noticing Mrs. Pruitt blushing to the roots of her hair. "What have you been up to this morning?"

Maddie held on to her brother's neck, not willing to let go. "We've been shopping, and we had breakfast in the dining room. Tristen and Austin are down at the livery stable with Jack, and Taylor is sitting out front on a bench, watching the horses on the street."

"If Taylor is out front, then what are you doing here?"

Maddie looked back at Mrs. Pruitt, then down at the floor. "We had an argument this morning, just a little one." She held up her thumb and forefinger to indicate the severity of the trouble.

Mrs. Pruitt had been quiet, listening to the conversation between brother and sister. "We were on our way to find you Garrett. I was hoping you and Charlie could settle the disagreement between the girls."

Garrett studied his sister closely, noticing the pinched looked on her face. "Maddie, what's this argument about? Tell me, and maybe I can help you both work it out. Charlie and I want all of us to be happy. Now, what's the problem?"

"Go ahead child, tell him what's bothering you," Mrs. Pruitt said.

"Taylor said, that since you and Charlie got married, that you would be having your own babies, and that you probably wouldn't want us anymore." The tears were running down her baby soft cheeks.

Glancing at Mrs. Pruitt, with a questioning look, Garrett rubbed Maddie's back, trying to comfort her. The deep sobs tearing a hole in his heart.

"It was Austin and Tristen. They told Taylor, and she told Maddie and they've been fussin' ever since," Mrs. Pruitt said.

"Please go tell Taylor to come in here. I want to tell them both at the same time, then I'll deal with the boys."

"You won't have to deal with the boys. Jack is taking care of them right now. They're not down at the livery, probably out behind it, taking their punishment." The older woman turned and hurried out the front door, glad that the argument would soon be over.

Carrying Maddie into the sitting room, Garrett sat down on the settee, waiting for Mrs. Pruitt to return with Taylor. He held his sister on his lap. He could feel her nervousness, her small body was tense.

Feeling Charlie's presence, he looked up. There in the doorway she stood, her back straight, her head high, and a wonderful glow on her beautiful face. She has the look of a well-loved woman, he thought.

Charlie entered the sitting room to find her husband holding his little sister on his lap. What a wonderful father he would make. She touched her stomach with her hand, hoping that they had created a new life last night. She floated, not walked, over to the settee. Looking down at Garrett and Maddie, a huge lump formed in her throat. She had grown to love both of these individuals very much, and it had happened so fast, it scared her.

"What's going on this morning?" she asked.

Garrett patted the empty space beside him. "Please have a seat. We've got big trouble this morning," he said. He tilted his head to indicate the little girl sitting on his lap. "It seems Maddie and Taylor have some concerns about the two of us getting married."

Charlie looked around the room. "Where's Taylor at?" she asked.

"Mrs. Pruitt went to get her. They should be back any minute."

Raising Maddie up off his chest, he looked directly at her. "Do you want to tell her what's going on, or would you like me to explain?"

"You can," the little girl mumbled, not looking at Charlie.

Just about that time, Mrs. Pruitt entered with Taylor in tow. "I almost had to drag her in here." They stopped just inside the doorway. "Look there Taylor, Charlie has finally made it down."

Taylor raised her head from Mrs. Pruitt's skirt, looking around the room for Charlie. When she spotted her, she headed straight for her older sister's lap. She climbed on her lap, trying not to touch Maddie, who was sitting on Garrett's lap. Both little girls started wiggling around, trying to put some space between them, which was really hard because both adults were sitting very close.

"What's going on?" Charlie asked, trying to hold the wiggling child still.

"Well it seems that the girls think that we're going to forget all about them, if we have a baby of our own," Garrett said, watching both little girls. "I was just getting ready to try to explain to them, that they couldn't be more wrong."

At the mention of new babies, Taylor sniffed loud. Her eyes starting to water up. Maddie on the other hand looked sullen, unwilling to loosen her hold on Garrett's neck.

Charlie was stunned. How could the girls even possibly think they would be forgotten. Three words, Tristen and Austin. She couldn't wait to get her hands on those two. They were always upsetting Taylor, and now they had two little girls to antagonize. And the rascals hadn't wasted any time.

Babies! With love shining in his eyes, Garrett thought of the previous night. He watched as Charlie shifted Taylor on her lap. He tried to imagine her belly swollen with his child. He hoped he didn't have to wait long. But first, they had to get things ironed out between the two small girls sitting on their laps.

"Listen girls, one day soon we hope to have children of our own. But that doesn't mean that we will think any less of you. Charlie and I have plenty of room in our hearts, and we have a lot of love to share." He hugged his sister close, and gently squeezed Taylor's arm.

He raised his eyes, looking directly at Charlie, searching for some help with his explanation. Instead he found himself staring into the darkest, warmest eyes he had ever seen. It seemed like they had taken on a special glow. He could feel himself starting to react, and that was not a good thing, because his sister was sitting on his lap, and Mrs. Pruitt was standing just inside the door. He began to squirm.

Stifling a giggle, Charlie noticed Garrett looking a little uncomfortable. He shifted Maddie on his lap. Thinking about the reason for his discomfort, she couldn't keep the grin from her face. Suddenly, she realized he was waiting for her to say something.

She looked at Taylor. "You know we have always stuck together, and you should know that we always will. The only difference now is that we have Garrett and Maddie as part of our family," she paused, giving Taylor time to think about everything. She hesitated before continuing. "The only thing that will change, when me and Garrett have children, if we have children, will be the size of our family. That's all."

Both adults waited, hoping their first family crisis was over. Taylor was the first one to break the silence. "Will you both promise Maddie and me that you'll always take care of us as long as we need you?"

"Yes," Garrett and Charlie replied at the same time.

Maddie slid down from her perch on Garrett's lap, standing in front of Taylor. "Can we be friends and sisters again?" she asked.

It didn't take long for Taylor to answer her. "I'm not mad anymore if you're not." She climbed down from Charlie's lap, grabbing Maddie's hand. "I don't like it very much when we're mad at each other, it's not any fun."

Mrs. Pruitt had been listening intently, she relaxed when she sensed the conflict between the girls had ended. "Come with me girls, we can go for a walk around town. Maybe even stop over at the mercantile for some candy," she said.

Holding hands tight, Maddie and Taylor skipped over to Mrs. Pruitt. They stopped, looking back over their shoulders. "We love you both very much," Maddie said. Taylor was quiet, she just nodded her head in agreement. They turned, hurrying after Mrs. Pruitt, not wanting to be left behind.

After Mrs. Pruitt and the girls had left the room, Charlie turned to Garrett. "Did the twins have anything to do with the girls being upset?" she asked. She

ALONG COMES A LEGEND

knew the answer before she had asked the questions, but she needed to know for sure.

"I believe they did. But Mrs. Pruitt informed me that Jack is handling the situation down at the livery stable, right now."

"If I know Jack, they're not at the livery, they're out behind the livery stable. Been there a time or two myself." Charlie's eyes took on a far away look, remembering parts of her childhood. She had some fond memories of her childhood, although she had more bad ones than good ones.

Sliding closer on the settee, Garrett scooped her up on his lap. He held her tight, letting her feel the evidence of his desire. He nibbled her soft neck, working his way down, loving the feel of her soft skin.

She couldn't think straight, his mouth and hands were all over her body. Weaving her hands through his thick hair, she pulled him closer, inhaling his scent. She felt his hot breath on the tops of her exposed breasts. Looking down, she discovered several buttons had been undone. Things were beginning to get out of hand quick, but she loved the way he made her feel.

A noise at the door pulled her back to reality. It was someone laughing. It was Jack's voice. Trying to pull away from Garrett, she managed to shift her weight, losing her balance. Her elbow slammed into Garrett's aroused groin. She knew what she had done when a deep groan was torn from his lips. This was bad, real bad.

One minute ecstasy, the next excruciating pain. The little wildcat had almost torn off the family jewels, and she was still wiggling around like a worm in hot ashes. Hearing a deep male voice booming with laughter, he twisted on the small settee. Seeing Jack doubled over, holding his stomach didn't help his mood.

Grabbing Charlie around the waist, pulling her back upright, Garrett whispered loudly in her ear. "Would you please hold still. You busted me in the jewels and every time you wiggle, it takes my breath away." She stopped almost instantly. "I'll say one thing for you wildcat, you sure know how to cool a man's ardor."

With fire spitting from her eyes, she turned on him. "If you hadn't been tryin' to... what's the word I'm lookin' for...say-duce me in broad open daylight, none of this would have happened." She had managed to get off his lap by this time. But she was far from done with him. "The next time you pull a stunt like this, I might just take a notion to shoot you." She turned around, stomping past Jack, heading for the stairs.

"You sure made her mad," Jack said with a loud snort.

"Me! Everything was just fine until you showed up," Garrett replied hotly, pulling at the front on his trousers. He was trying to create a little extra room for his sore jewels.

"I tell you one thing boy. You're certainly going to have your hands full with her over the next fifty years or so." Jack was still busy wiping the tears from his face. "And," he continued, "I can't even imagine what your young'uns are going to be like."

"Hell, if they're anything like their mother, they'll be impossible to control."

Both men got a laugh out of the last statement. Each man considering the idea of trying to control Charlie or her children. That would be like trying to hold back a river.

After the humor passed, Garrett asked Jack about the twins. "Did you find out why the twins said those things to Maddie and Taylor?"

"They were just being boys. They like to torment the girls just a little. Bea doesn't understand what it's like to be that age, when you're half way between being a man and a boy, it's a difficult time," Jack said. "The best thing to do, is just forget about it. Tell the womenfolk it's all been taken care of."

"I agree," Garrett said.

After a moment, Garrett spoke quietly to Jack. "I was on my way to find you this morning. I've been thinking, I'm going to go ahead and send a telegram to my friends, Dallas and Christian, ask them to come to the Circle Bar M." He paused, thinking about his next statement carefully. "I just don't want to take any chances with my new family. They mean the world to me, you and Mrs. Pruitt included." He waited for the older man to absorb the information he had just given him.

"I guess this means it's time to start heading for home."

"We can't put it off forever. Besides, the sooner we get home the sooner we'll find out what McCuan has been up to. I'll tell everyone over dinner tonight. We'll pull out sometime tomorrow afternoon. By that time, I'll know when to expect Christian and Dallas from Tucson." Garrett wished he could be as confident as he sounded, but he had a bad feeling about the whole situation. At least his mind would be at ease, just knowing his friends would be around to help take care of his family.

Jack slapped Garrett on the back, bringing him back to the present. "Come on son, we'll go start rounding up supplies for the trip back. We might even have to buy a new wagon for all the new doo-dads the womenfolk have bought."

As Garrett and Jack walked out the front door, they didn't notice the desk clerk writing a note on a piece of paper. When both men had disappeared down the street, the clerk headed straight for the telegraph office.

Chapter Twenty-eight

The two horses and their riders moved along slowly in the moonlight. The night was very still, the only sound that could be heard was the horses hooves striking an occasional rock along the path. Both riders were silent. They appeared to be in no hurry to reach their destination.

After climbing a small rise, the riders pulled their animals to a stop. They sat looking out over the ranch house below. When they saw no movement around the house, they continued to move forward. They descended the small hill, staying in the shadow of the trees. Moving along the tree line, they guided their animals with amazing accuracy. Both animals seemed to be at complete ease with their rider's demands. When the pair reached the trees closest to the main house, they stopped, still alert, watching everything going on around them. They were very cautious. When they were certain everything was quiet, they moved on toward the house.

James was in his office, looking over some of the ranch ledgers. He was completely engrossed with the books. He never noticed the shadow that crossed the window of his office.

The figures looked real good. The ranch had made a big profit in the last year. That put a huge smile on his face. He picked up one of his expensive cigars, clipped the end, and struck a match, holding it to the end of his cigar until the tip glowed red. Then he leaned back in his chair, thinking about the events of the past few weeks. If only, he thought, that bastard Steele hadn't showed up, he would be sitting on easy street about now. He wasn't going to let anything distract him right now. First, he was going to finish this fine cigar, second, he might just ride to town and find him a nice willing— He stopped in mid-thought when his office door swung open. The cigar, which he had been smoking, was forgotten. Because standing before him were the Gilkey brothers, Chad and Brett, and they didn't look none to happy.

The two brothers entered the room, both looking like they had been chasing the devil. Chad was the first one to speak. "We've been hole up in that shack, and you've been down here enjoyin' the finer things in life. We want to know what in the hell is goin' on." That was probably the most words either one of them had ever spoken at one time.

James, after regaining his composure, took a deep drag from his cigar, thinking about his answer. "Gimpy and I was going to ride out first thing in the morning. We found out that Steele and the rest of his little party are going to start home some time tomorrow afternoon." He watched the two brothers digest the information. He picked up the whiskey bottle, pouring three drinks. He wasn't afraid of anything, but he decided these two scared the hell out of him.

"Would you like a drink of some fine whiskey?" He lifted the two glasses, waiting to see if they were interested. It didn't take long to find out the answer. They were already taking the glasses from him. They drained both glasses with one gulp, then waited for him to pour more, which he did.

"How long will it take them to get back home?" Brett asked between drinks.

"I really don't know. Normally about four days, but our contacts in Santa Fe says they've been buying a lot of supplies, so they may be moving a little slower than usual."

After emptying their glasses several more times, the Gilkeys announced they were leaving, heading back to the line shack. Both brothers stood and walked to the door. Brett walked out first, waiting in the hallway. Chad was following closely behind him, but before leaving James' office, he turned. "I'm only going to tell you once, you better not be foolin' with us. We don't take kindly to that sort of treatment, from nobody." Then he followed his brother out of the house.

James hadn't noticed that he was sweating until he felt it run down the sides of his face. He swiped at the moisture, hating the feeling that had caused it. One thing was for sure, he was glad they were on his side. It wouldn't be long now, he could feel it down deep in his bones.

The wagon rolled along smoothly. The return trip was taking longer, but it seemed none of them were in a hurry to get back to the Circle Bar M, least of all Charlie. With each passing mile, she seemed to become more withdrawn. She always got this same feeling every time she had to return to the ranch.

Garrett had been riding along, beside his wife. She seemed deep in thought, all the color had left her face, he knew she was dreading going home. Guiding his horse closer, he picked up her hand, bringing it to his lips. Their eyes locked, and just for a minute all their troubles vanished.

"A penny for your thoughts," Garrett said, a twinkle shining in his eyes.

"Trust me greenhorn, they're not worth a penny."

"I'm interested in everything about you," Garrett whispered. He was undressing her with his eyes, and caressing her with his voice.

Looking back at the wagon, Charlie wished for about the hundredth time today, that they were alone. "I wish we could find a private spot, you know where we could be by ourselves." Her eyes had taken on a dreamy look.

Stopping his horse, Garrett twisted in the saddle, waving back at Jack, who was driving the wagon.

Jack waved his hat in the air, signaling that he understood.

"Come on," Garrett said, as he wheeled his horse around. "We've got some time to kill. We can find us a nice quiet spot. We can join up with the others later."

For the first time in her life, she just sat there with her mouth hanging wide open. A movement out of the corner of her eye got her attention, it was Jack and Mrs. Pruitt motioning for her to follow Garrett. Knowing a good thing when she saw it, she spurred her horse, following Garrett across the land.

Jack guided the horses across the field with experienced hands. Never asking more of the team than they could provide. They had traveled a short distance before Mrs. Pruitt finally spoke. "I sure hope their happiness lasts. I hope they realize that we'll be back at the ranch by tomorrow afternoon."

"I'm sure they know that Bea, that's why they took off today," Jack said, still looking at the trail ahead of them.

After a while, Jack looked behind the wagon, making sure the twins were following on their horses. He hoped everything worked out for all of them. Shifting the reins to one hand, he patted Mrs. Pruitt's leg. "Don't worry Bea, everything will be all right, I promise." They continued slowly across the land, neither adult bothering to talk, both of them worried.

Garrett and Charlie raced their horses across the wide open space. The wind slashing their faces. It felt wonderful. They came to a small cluster of trees, about two miles away from the wagon. Pulling his horse to a stop, Garrett motioned for Charlie to follow him.

The entered the small grove of trees. It was a perfect spot.

Slipping down from his horse, Garrett moved next to Charlie's horse. Grasping her around the waist, he lowered her to the ground, letting her body rub his. When her feet touched the ground, he shoved her hat back, letting it fall to the ground, her short hair swaying in the breeze. Cupping her full bottom, he pulled her close to his instant arousal. He loved the feel of her against him. He opened a few buttons on her blouse, then lowered his lips to her creamy skin. Her skin was so soft, it drove him wild.

Rolling her head back, Charlie wanted to feel Garrett's lips on her skin. Running her fingers through his thick hair, she pulled him closer. When his hands started to roam over her bottom, her knees almost buckled, she moaned low in her throat. Her knees did buckle when his lips touched the smooth skin on her shoulder. She would have fallen if his strong arms hadn't been anchored around her shapely body.

"Garrett, please, I can't wait. I've got to have all of you," she moaned breathlessly.

He chuckled against the smooth skin on her throat. "Don't be in such a hurry wildcat. We've got all afternoon." Then his mouth continued its assault on her exposed skin.

Pulling back, she looked into his dark, gray eyes. "We can go slower later, right now I'm going to die if I have to wait much longer," she said, licking his full lips with the tip of her tongue.

"I'm always willing to help a lady in distress. Especially when that lady happens to be my wife," he murmured.

They hurriedly stripped their clothing off, neither one of them wanting to waste one precious moment. They would worry about the rest of the world later, much later. They had more pressing matter to attend to right now. And attend to them they did, until they both fell into an exhausted slumber, still holding on to each other tightly. Thoughts of what tomorrow would bring pushed to the back of their minds.

Chapter Twenty-nine

In about two hours, they would be home, Garrett thought. He felt like a huge weight had been lifted from his shoulders. They had been traveling for about a week. They had all been alert, expecting trouble, and it had taken a toll on them.

Garrett was riding slightly ahead, watching for any signs of impending trouble. He was glad they were this close to home. He had had a chance to talk to Jack last night after supper, in fact, they had talked into the early hours of the morning. He had told Jack when to expect Dallas and Christian, his friends from Tucson. They would be here in a about ten more days.

Hearing a horse coming up behind him, Garrett stopped and turned, his hand moving closer to the gun on his hip. When he recognized the rider, he relaxed. It was Jack.

"Just thought I'd come out and ride with you for a while, keep you comp'ny," Jack said.

Garrett was sitting slumped in the saddle, his arms propped on the saddle horn. "Tell me the truth. What's the matter?" He watched the other man, waiting for an answer.

Twisting in the saddle, Jack looked back at the slow moving wagon. "To tell you the truth, the womenfolk are about near to drive me crazy. The closer we get to home, the harder they are to get along with." The exasperated look on the older man's face made Garrett laugh. "Well, it's nice to know I'm not the only one feeling that way. Charlie almost bit my head off this morning when I told her it was almost time to leave."

"What's so unusual about that? She's pretty well always just a might touchy," he said. After thinking about what he had said for a minute, he added. "She's just a little high strung, that's all."

That last statement sent both men into rounds of laughter. They both knew she was more than high strung, she was down right ornery at times.

"Jack, there is something else I need to talk to you about. Christian and Dallas, you'll be kind of surprised when you see them. They're pretty young, but don't let their appearance fool you. They can be cold blooded when they have to be. I'd trust them with my life, and the lives of my family." He paused, thinking about his friends, they were very loyal and trustworthy. "And," he continued, "They can be pretty ornery to. We better keep them away from my bride, because I think they'll get along too good."

The older man chuckled. "You know I'm just goin' on. I love that girl like she was my own. She's turned out better than most, considerin' her up-bringing." Jack watched the young man, looking for signs of regret. He saw nothing in his eyes, except love. "Do you know what's really bothering her?" Jack asked.

"I didn't know anything was bothering her," Garrett replied.

Jack looked back at the wagon, a smile appeared on his weathered face. Both ladies were sitting close together on the high seat. His smile faded. "It's her pa. She's worried that he'll do something to hurt you or one of the children." He tugged his hat down low over his eyes, covering most of his face. "Bea told me that Charlie has just about worried herself sick over it."

"What the hell do you mean? I've told her several times that I can take care of myself. I suppose she has no confidence in me at all." He sat there, thinking. "I'm going to ride down there and set her straight on a few things. Maybe, just maybe, she'll understand then."

"Understand what?"

"That I'm plenty capable of taking care of her rotten father." Wheeling his horse around in the direction of the wagon, he left Jack sitting with his mouth gathering dust.

Sitting atop the high seat, Charlie looked out over the field. The countryside was beautiful. Things would be perfect if they didn't have to go back to the ranch. She wished they could keep right on going, never looking back. She was jolted back to the present when the wagon hit a deep hole, causing it to rock violently from side to side. She had to grab hold of the seat to maintain her balance.

"I sure didn't see that hole," Mrs. Pruitt said when the wagon stopped rocking. "Just about shook my teeth loose."

Charlie didn't answer, her eyes were on the horse and rider moving toward the wagon. She would never get tired of watching him, her husband. Realizing Mrs. Pruitt was saying something she turned. "I'm sorry. Did you say something?" she asked.

"No child, I was just talking to these two knot-heads pullin' the wagon." Mrs. Pruitt pulled the team to a stop, waiting for Garrett to reach the wagon.

Seeing his wife perched up on the wagon seat, some of his anger disappeared. He wasn't really mad at her, just that sonofabitching father of hers. He would like to get a hold of that bastard one of these days.

When he reached the side of the wagon where Charlie was sitting, he stopped. "How are you ladies? It's good to be almost home, isn't it?" He had taken his hat off, hanging it on the saddle horn.

"Come on Charlie, take a short ride with me." He waited for her to make up her mind. "Just step off the wagon and climb on in front of me." He jammed his hat back down on his head, and moved his horse closer to the wagon.

"I'd rather ride my own horse," she answered hesitantly, eyeing the small space in front of Garrett.

Garrett looked up at her, then glanced over at Jack, who had just ridden up. "Oh come on and ride with me. It will be fun for us to ride double. You can ride up front, I'll scoot back." He kicked his feet out of the stirrups, sliding back in the saddle, making room for her.

Charlie started to protest, then changed her mind, deciding to go with him. Lifting her foot over the wagon, she backed out onto the wheel, then started to lower herself down to Garrett's horse. Everything went just fine. She shimmied into the saddle, it was a tight squeeze, but it was worth it, the feel of her husband's strong body wrapped around her was intoxicating.

Then disaster struck!

A bird circled overhead, the shadow crossed the horse's path, spooking him. Garrett, who was busy trying to find a comfortable place on the back of the saddle, wasn't ready for the unexpected movement of his horse. Off balance, Garrett slid further back on the horse's rump, startling the animal even more. Then all hell broke loose. The horse started crow hopping, trying to get his head down.

Charlie was stuck like glue in the saddle, fighting for control over the spooked animal.

Garrett on the other hand, was not so lucky. He had managed to stay with the animal for the first few hops, but that last big twist the animal had taken sent him straight into the air, with no place to go, but down.

After regaining control of the nervous horse, which had taken several yards, Charlie discovered that Garrett was no longer behind her. Looking back over her shoulder, it didn't take long to find him. He was sprawled flat of his back, a huge cloud of dust was fogging around him, and he wasn't moving. She had to reach him, find out if he had been hurt.

He was trying to force air into his lungs. They felt like they were going to explode. He couldn't move, the world seemed to be standing still. Then the face of an angel appeared, a dirt smeared angel, but an angel all the same. She was peering down at him, possibly talking to him, but he couldn't hear a word she was saying.

Suddenly rough hands rolled him onto his side. Those same hands were beating on his back, trying to force air into his oxygen starved lungs. The pain in his chest started to ease up a little as his lungs started to expand. The world started moving again, and he realized the angel was cursing a blue streak.

"Damn you, take a breath, you have to breathe, get some air back into your lungs." She paused, taking a deep breath, then continued to beat on his back. "You scared the livin' shit right out of me."

With his senses returning, he knew it was Charlie beating on his back. He tried to push her hands away. "You can stop beating me have to death...I just got...the wind knocked out ...of me. I'm breathing now." He managed to sit up, his arms resting on his knees. "Scared me to...for a minute," he rasped.

"Scared you! What do you think it did to me? I thought you had gone and got yourself killed." She was hot! "Of all the hair-brained things to do, go and get yourself bucked off the back of your own horse."

"What do you mean? I didn't do anything, it was you that was trying to distract me, twisting in the saddle like you were. Hell, you know I can't think straight when you do that," he bellowed. He had gotten back on his feet, brushing the dust from his clothing.

"Me!" she yelled, moving closer to Garrett, standing toe to toe with him. "What do you mean, twistin'? I was just tryin' to get down in the saddle, that's all." She moved a little closer, fire burning in her eyes. "I think you should learn how to ride a horse just a little better, greenhorn. That's twice I've seen you flat of your back, in the dirt."

"Greenhorn. If you call me that one more time, I'm going to turn you over my knee and paddle your behind." He was stepping forward, forcing her to take small steps backwards. "And just for the record, I've had a little help coming loose from the saddle, both times. Now, I don't want to hear any more about it, got that." He had stopped when he had backed her up against the wagon. He noticed Jack, Mrs. Pruitt, and all the children were watching the fireworks, with amused smiles. They made no move to separate the feuding newlyweds.

"I've got two questions," Charlie said. "The first one is...why did you want me to go for a ride with you? Did you have a specific reason or what?"

He looked a little sheepish, then admitted. "I wanted to reassure you that I could take care of myself. I don't want you worrying about me. I can handle myself." He waited for her laughter, but it never came. Her eyes had taken on a very soft, warm glow.

Charlie fell in love all over again. The expression he had on his face melted her heart. He had been worried about her. But she decided to make him squirm for a little while longer. "You really looked able to handle any situation a minute ago, you remember don't you, when you were lying flat on your back."

There were times when Garrett was really going to have to work at this marriage thing, and this was one of them. "I can't help being so much in love with you that I can't think straight, you have that kind of effect on me sweetheart." He moved closer, pulling her luscious body against him. He lowered his mouth to hers, tasting the sweetness of her lips.

After the kiss ended, he lifted his head, looking into her glowing eyes. "You said you had two questions, but you only asked me one. What was the other one?"

She looked up at him with a mischievous twinkle in her eyes. "I was just going to ask you what army was going to help you?"

"Help me what?"

"Paddle my behind. You sure can't do it by yourself," she said cockily.

Laughter erupted from the wagon, everybody was roaring. Garrett just shook his head. Thankful for the miracle that had given him a woman like Charlie.

James was waiting, watching through the window of his office. Pete Jackson had ridden in about five minutes ago with the news. The wagon was about fifteen minutes away from the ranch. He had decided to steer clear of all of them for a few days, let them get settled into some sort of routine, maybe let their guard down, then his men would strike.

He watched the activity around the barns and corrals. He loved this ranch, every square inch. He had worked hard, making it into the operation it was today, and he wasn't going to share it with anybody.

About twenty minutes later, the time had passed before he realized it, the sound of several horses and a wagon interrupted his thoughts. It was them. They had returned from Santa Fe. Stepping back away from the window, he watched them closely through the lace curtains. They had pulled the wagon up close to the house, it was full of supplies. Everybody started carrying supplies, even his two worthless sons.

His attention was drawn to Charlie. She had just stepped up on the porch, her face glowing with happiness. She looked just like her mother, the unfaithful bitch. But soon she would be sorry for disobeying him. Tomorrow he would send Gimpy out to the line shack. The Gilkeys would be glad to find out the news, everybody was becoming impatient.

Chapter Thirty

It had been a week since their return from Santa Fe, and it was a nasty day outside, strong thunderstorms and heavy rain pounded the whole area. Charlie was sitting in the kitchen, watching the rain through the window. Garrett had asked her to stay close to the house. She had argued at first, but after a few leisure hours of persuasion, she finally agreed.

Everything had gone pretty smooth since the return to the ranch. After the new living arrangements had been made, the girls were allowed in all parts of the house now, things had settled down. Charlie had been fearful, thinking her pa would have an absolute fit, but so far he hadn't even spoken to them. He left the house early in the morning, and didn't return until late in the evening. Then he went straight to his office, not bothering to come out until everyone was in bed. The bad thing was, Charlie couldn't make up her mind what was worse, her pa yelling all the time, or not talking at all. She decided both situations made her nervous.

A loud bang rattled the window panes, lightning had struck very close. Charlie jumped back from the window. She knew the dangers of lightning, especially for men and horses working around cattle.

"Did you see where that lightning hit?" Mrs. Pruitt asked, as she hurried into the kitchen. "I wished the men would get back to the house. I don't like for them to be out in weather like this any longer than they have to." She walked over to the window, peering through the heavy rains and wind.

"I'm going to go and change my clothes, put some old pants on. Then I'm going down to the barn and see if they've come back yet." Not giving Mrs. Pruitt time to object, Charlie rushed out of the kitchen. She climbed the stairs, entering the bedroom that she shared with Garrett. She blushed when she glanced at the neatly made bed, thinking about how wrinkled the sheets had been this morning. Garrett had laughed when she hurried and straightened the rumpled bed, before Mrs. Pruitt saw it. Trying not to think about the night before, she hurried and changed clothes, and left the room.

When she reached the edge of the kitchen door, Mrs. Pruitt was waiting, with a disapproving look on her face. "You know you promised Garrett that you'd stay close to the house. He's not going to like it one bit, you going down to the barn by yourself. And, I can't really blame him." Mrs. Pruitt was blocking the back door, and she was waiting for Charlie to back down.

"I'm just going down to have a look around, that's all. Besides, what Garrett don't know won't hurt him." Charlie made a move toward the door, then stopped. "I promise not to tell him if you don't."

The stern look on Mrs. Pruitt's face faded, replaced by a shy smile. "I'm not trying to tell you what to do Charlie, it's just that you have to remember, one of these days you might have more than just yourself to think about, that's all." Mrs. Pruitt cradled her lower stomach with both hands.

Charlie looked at Mrs. Pruitt with a funny look on her face. She knew her stomach was a little plump, but Mrs. Pruitt didn't have to remind her. Then it dawned on her, a baby, Mrs. Pruitt had been referring to a baby. Color flooded her face. "I think it's a little soon for that to be happenin'," she murmured.

"Not unless I miss my guess about that husband of yours. He doesn't strike me as the meek kind, and he's been whistling a tune every morning on his way to the breakfast table," Mrs. Pruitt said, enjoying the embarrassment on the younger woman's face. She never thought she would see that special glow on Charlie's face, but she already had her suspicions.

Taking her hat and slicker from the rack, Charlie slipped her arms into her coat and slapped her old battered hat down tight. She opened the back door. "I won't be gone long, just going to check things out." She stepped out and was quickly swallowed up by the raging storm.

Mrs. Pruitt stood at the back door, watching the storm engulf Charlie. She rubbed her hands together, wishing the men would get back, this weather was making her a little jumpy.

Entering the barn, the first thing Charlie noticed was the animals. The noise was loud from the storm, but the animals were all content, the horses were standing with their heads down, picking through the bedding on the floor. She walked farther into the barn. A noise at the far end of the barn startled her. She moved ahead slowly, peeking around the corner of the last stall, what she found made her made her laugh.

It was Tristen and Austin. They were sound asleep, and snoring so loud that you could hear them over the storm outside. They looked so young, all the worry lines that normally surrounded their mouth was gone, maybe soon their worries would be over with, or at least most of them.

She stepped past the twins, walking to the back of the barn. She saw the heavy run-off in the field, it looked like a small river. Someone needed to check on the cattle behind the barn, if the creek flooded down there, they might loose some cattle. It was real bad to flood down there. It didn't take her long to make up her mind. She would ride down there and make sure the creek hadn't flooded yet, it wouldn't take long. Nobody would even know she was gone.

A short while later, her horse ready, she swung into the saddle, and galloped toward the swollen creek.

Rousing up from sleep, Tristen rubbed the sleep from his eyes. He had heard a horse, thinking it might be Garrett and Jack, he stumbled to his feet. He could barely make out the shape of a horse and rider in the blowing sheets of rain, but there was no mistake, it was Charlie. Garrett was going to be mad as a wet hen.

After waking his brother, both boys ran to the house, knowing Mrs. Pruitt would know exactly what to do. They sprinted to the house, not seeing the two horses tied to the rail beside the kitchen. Just as they were about to open the kitchen door, it swung open, and standing in the doorway was Garrett, and he didn't look none to happy.

Garrett had been standing at the kitchen window, holding a steaming cup of coffee. He had been watching the barn for any sign of movement. When he saw both boys running to the house, his heart almost stopped. He knew without a doubt it had to be Charlie. Striding over to the door, he threw it open. Both boys seemed reluctant to look him in the eye.

"What's she up to now?" When neither boy said anything, he tried again. "I know she's up to something, so you might as well tell me now."

Standing in the doorway, dripping wet, the twins looked over at Jack, who nodded. Tristen was the first one to start talking. "Well," he said, pausing for a minute, "She rode out of the barn about five minutes ago." He looked down at the toe of his muddy boot, not daring to look up at Garrett.

She rode out of the barn, which was impossible. He had been watching the front door for the last twenty minutes or so. You fool! She probably rode out the back way. "Did she go out the back doors?"

"Yes," both boys said quietly.

A million thoughts passed through Garrett's head. He had to find her, he and Jack had made a discovery up in the north pasture. There was some things going on around here that he didn't understand. He turned back to the boys. "Why did you let her ride out? You should have tried to stop her."

"We were asleep," Austin said, a look of pure anguish on his young features.

It suddenly dawned on Garrett just how young and innocent these two boys were. "Don't worry, I'll find her and bring her back home." He turned to Jack as he gathered up his rain gear. "You stay here and keep an eye on things. Don't let anybody near the house, shoot first and ask questions later. Don't take any chances."

When Garrett closed the door, Mrs. Pruitt turned, walking into Jack's waiting arms. "I sure hope she'll be OK. That girl can get into more trouble than ten outlaws," she said, laying her head against his chest, drawing on his inner strength.

"Don't worry none Bea, Garrett will see to our Charlie girl," Jack said. It was a good thing Mrs. Pruitt couldn't see the worry in his eyes.

Garrett was furious, and worried sick. He had told her to stay close to home. But had she listened. Hell no! The first chance she got, she took off. And to make matters worse, the weather was terrible outside, and the rain water was running down his back, soaking him. He looked up at the heavy clouds, wishing the rain would let up, but there was no chance of that happening.

It didn't take him long to pick up her trail behind the barn. He set out after her, he really was going to paddle her behind this time.

Charlie climbed back in the saddle, soaked to the bone. She sure was glad she came down to check on the creek. She had found a cow and her calf huddled under some trees, next to the rising water. After trying to drive the cow to a safe location, she discovered that the calf was stuck in the mud. They probably both would have been swept away in the flood water, if she hadn't found them.

Looking up at the sky, she noticed the clouds were still heavy with rain, it didn't look like it was going to quit anytime soon. She needed to get back to the ranch, Garrett would be home soon, and he'd be furious if she wasn't back. When she turned her horse, she was startled to find two scraggly looking men blocking her path. Reaching for her pistol, she realized that she had left it at home, after all she had kind a sneaked out of the house. This could be bad, real bad.

"Is there something I can help you with?" Charlie asked, looking back and forth at both men.

Chad and Brett Gilkey couldn't believe their luck. They had been wondering how they were going to get their hands on the girl. They had been watching the ranch from a distance, and suddenly she just rode off, all alone.

Chad walked his horse around behind her, boxing her in. They had her blocked in between them. "As a matter of fact there is something you can do for my brother and me. You see, it's been a real long time since we had ourselves a woman," Chad said, looking over at his brother Brett for confirmation. "And from the looks of you, there's plenty for both of us."

Brett smiled, a look of pure lust on his ugly face. "Yes sir, it's been a hell of a long time for both of us. After we both bed you, then we'll finish what we come here for." He moved his horse closer, crowding Charlie even more.

She had to get away. She looked around for the best possible escape route, noticing that she was blocked in. She was in trouble. "What did you come here for?" she asked, trying to stall, she needed time to think.

"To kill you," both men said in unison. They both started moving closer with their horses, reading her mind. They knew she was going to run. But they were ready for her.

If only she had listened to Garrett, then she wouldn't be in this predicament right now. He was going to be mad when, and if, he found her body. But she wasn't ready to give up just yet.

"If you get any closer, I'm goin' to have to hurt you, and I'd rather not." She was busy looking for an opening between the two horses. The rain was coming down in blinding sheets, visibility was just a few feet, but she knew the area like the back of her hand. She spurred her horse, trying to squeeze through the outlaw's horses, and she was almost out in the clear, when an iron hand grabbed her horse's reins, causing her horse to throw his head back, hitting her hard on the chin. The pain was immediate, the taste of blood on her tongue. She was momentarily dazed. Her head was spinning so bad, she didn't hear the approach of other horses, until she heard more masculine voices.

Oh great! Just what I need, more men to deal with. But the words being exchanged surprised her. She managed to get a look at the newcomers. She was shocked, they weren't men, there were little more than boys. She groaned as another wave of pain shot through her head. She slid down to the muddy ground. The last words she heard was threats being issued from the two young strangers.

"Hey there gents, I don't think the lady wants your attention," said the smaller of the two young strangers. He had a smile on his face, but his hand never left the vicinity of his gun. He looked over at his partner, motioning towards Charlie, who had slid off her horse and was lying in the mud.

The two scraggly looking men who had jumped Charlie, was getting ready to reach for their guns. They weren't going to give the McCuan bitch up without a fight. Just before all hell broke loose, a horse pounded over the hill, running hard, the rider leaning low, and he was coming right at them. The odds were getting worse, deciding to pick a better day to get even with the woman on the ground, the Gilkeys spun their horses away from the oncoming rider. The hard blowing rain hid their departure, it seemed like they had vanished into thin air.

The second stranger had reached Charlie. He had dismounted and was kneeling beside her. He pushed the wet limp hair from her face, seeing a darkening bruise on her chin. She had taken a pretty good lick, knocked her clean out. Before the younger man could lift Charlie off the wet ground, there was a shout from the rider bearing down on them, he looked like Lucifer himself.

"You better not touch a hair on her head, you sonofabitch," the rider shouted, pulling his blowing horse to a stop.

"Garrett, is that you?" asked the man still sitting atop his horse. "Man, if I hadn't of recognized you, you'd have scared the livin' hell right out of me."

Stopping dead in his tracks, Garrett stared at the man sitting on the horse, then smiled. "Dallas, I sure am glad to see you. What the hell took you two so long?" That was when he remembered Charlie. He saw Christian kneeling down beside her. She was lying so still.

Walking on wooden legs to her side, he dropped down in the mud beside her, afraid of what he was going to find. "Christian, what happened to her?" he asked, his eyes never leaving the bedraggled woman.

Christian had a funny look on his face, he had never seen Garrett act like this before, not even when his parents had been killed. "I think she's going to be fine, just took a pretty good shot to the chin. I don't think there's anything to worry about." He noticed Garrett had been holding his breath, waiting for the news. He wondered who this woman was, she looked kind of like an orphan. Maybe Garret was responsible for her. He was always taking on some lost cause. Just look at him and Dallas.

Dallas dismounted, trying to get a better look at the woman that had Garrett tied up in knots. "Who is she? Do you know her Garrett?"

Looking down at his mud-speckled wife, he grinned. "I sure do boys, this is my wife Charlie." The love he had for her was plain in his gray eyes. "And I'm only going to tell you once, she's a handful, but I love her with all my heart."

Dallas opened his mouth, but was interrupted by a female voice.

"If you love me so much, why ain't you got me up off this wet ground yet? I'm about to freeze to death in case you haven't noticed." She rubbed her chin, wincing when she found the deep bruise. "That old jackass about broke my jaw when he smacked me with his head."

Garrett stood, pulling her to her feet. He wrapped her tight in his embrace, thanking God that Christian and Dallas had come along when they did. "If you had listened to me, you wouldn't be all wet and cold right now," he said, not being able to resist gouging her just a little.

"I know, and I'm real sorry. I should have listened to you, but I was worried about the creek flooding." She snuggled deeper into his strong arms, feeling very protected. They were lost in their own world, until someone cleared their throat.

Turning Charlie around, Garrett introduced her to his friends. "Charlie, I'd like you to meet two of my friends. This is Dallas Murray," he said, pointing to the smaller man. "And this fellow over here is Christian Candlis. They've come to help me with your father."

Charlie looked at both young men. "It's very nice to meet you. Garrett has talked a lot about both of you, but I was expecting older men," she said. After those last words were out of her mouth, she blushed beet red.

Dallas burst out laughing, Christian on the other hand, never cracked a smile. "Miss Charlie, that's what everybody always tells us," Dallas said. He pointed to Christian. "It always bothers Chris here, I mean when somebody tells us that. But it don't bother me none. Nope, not a bit." He swung into the saddle, waiting for the others to follow his lead. When they didn't, he became a little fidgety. "I know you'd have to be a fish to enjoy this weather, and I know I ain't no fish. I want to find a good warm dry establishment. Maybe even get some hot food."

Garrett helped Charlie mount her horse, then climbed on his horse. As they rode by Christian and Dallas, Garrett looked over at Christian and winked. "I see he still talks as much as always. Has he talked all the way from Tucson?"

Christian grunted. "Hell yes! He damn near talked my leg off. I had to threaten to shoot him twice." He stopped beside Dallas, glaring at him through the rain. "You go ahead Marshall, we'll watch your back trail."

Dallas leaned over close to Christian. "Did you ever think you'd see Cold Steele acting like a besotted husband?" he whispered.

"Nope, I surely didn't. Especially not with a sharp tongued female like that. Why, she called her horse a jackass, wasn't his fault that he hit her."

The wind was howling and the rain was still coming down by the buckets, but as they passed by, Charlie heard Garrett's friends whispering. She heard them say something about Cold Steele. They couldn't possibly know him, he was practically a legend.

Not giving it another thought, she followed her husband back to the ranch.

There was a lone rider sitting deep in the trees, watching the little drama. He had cursed when he saw the Gilkeys cut and run, maybe they weren't as good as everybody thought.

At that moment a bolt of lightning hit, identifying the hidden rider. It was James McCuan.

After watching the group of riders leave, he turned his horse, heading for Broken Tongue. He had to find out who the two cowboys were that had helped Steele. When he found out who they were, he would make them pay. Pulling his collar tighter around his neck, he sure would be glad to get to town. The Rusted Bucket was calling him. He'd take care of everything later, after relaxing a little. There was no need to get in any hurry now.

Chapter Thirty-one

It was a short ride back to the ranch, but a miserable one for Charlie. She was shivering from shock because it wasn't cold outside, just very wet. The closer they got to home, the harder her teeth chattered. She was coming apart at the seams.

Garrett was riding close to Charlie. He was watching her, when he saw her teeth chattering violently, he knew she was starting to go into shock. He sure wished he had a hold of the Gilkeys or James McCuan right now. He hadn't seen the faces of Charlie's attackers, but he knew it was them, the Gilkeys. He and Jack had found tracks all around the ranch. They had been made by horses other than those on the Circle Bar M. In fact, they were probably hiding right now, watching, waiting for another chance to strike again. Gritting his teeth, he promised himself that they would have to work for the next opportunity, it wouldn't be handed to them.

The four riders moved along in silence.

When the ranch yard came into view, Garrett looked at Charlie. "We'll stop at the house first, you need to go on in and get some dry clothes on. You'll feel much better then," he said.

She turned toward him, her eyes glazed with shock. "I'm sorry Garrett. I should have listened to you." Her eyes were no longer glowing, her spirit was gone.

Reaching out to pat the back of her cold, damp hands. "It's all right. I promised I wouldn't ever let anybody hurt you again, and that's exactly what I mean to do. Cross my heart and hope to die." He made the motion across his rain soaked chest, making her smile a little.

Before Garrett had dismounted, the front door was thrown open, and Mrs. Pruitt came barreling out, her arms flapping like a bird. "Oh, I just knew Garrett would find you." She came down the steps, not even noticing the rain soaking her skirt. She didn't stop until she had reached Charlie's horse. "Come on child, you need to be inside. You need dry clothing on and a nice warm bath." Her eyes found the large bruise on Charlie's chin, but she didn't mention it. As soon as Charlie was on the ground, Mrs. Pruitt hustled her toward the house.

By this time, Jack and all the children were standing on the front porch. Tristen and Austin appeared to be extremely happy to see their sister in one piece. Taylor and Maddie stood behind Jack, looking at the two strangers that rode up with Garrett and Charlie.

Mrs. Pruitt had dragged Charlie off her horse, leaving in such a rush, that Garrett didn't have time to introduce Dallas and Christian. Garrett looked up at Jack, who had read his mind, and grinned. Garrett had learned from his first meeting with Mrs. Pruitt, that you didn't try to get between her and one of the children, even though one of them was your wife.

"Jack, I'd like for you to meet Dallas Murray and Christian Candlis." He turned toward the two young men waiting behind him. "Boys, this is Jack Winsloe, and he's a good man. We can trust him."

Jack tipped his hat. "Nice to meet you fellows. I've heard a lot about you two." Looking at the two young guns, who didn't seem much older than the twins, Jack thought Garrett wasn't exaggerating when he had said they looked young. They looked like boys at first glance, except for the haunted look in their eyes.

"We'll talk later, right now we need to head down to the barn and see to our horses," Garrett said. It was Saturday night, so most of the hands would be gone to town, especially with the weather as nasty as it was.

"If you'll hold up a minute, I'll walk down there with you Garrett. That way we can talk. I have some questions I'd like to ask you," Jack replied.

Turning around to Christian and Dallas, Garrett pointed to the barn. "You two can go ahead and put your horses in the barn. You'll find everything you'll need to take care of 'em. There's plenty of feed in the bins. Help yourselves. I'll be down there in a minute. I want to wait for Jack." The rain had slacked up some, but it was still coming down pretty steady.

Christian simply nodded, and headed toward the barn. Dallas stopped his horse next to Garrett, the rain running in rivulets down his face. "Garrett, I just wanted to tell you. Me and Christian are real glad to be with you again. You've got yourself a nice little set up here, and we aim to make sure it stays that way." For a long time neither man spoke, a quiet understanding passing between them.

Finally, Dallas grinned. "I better check on Christian, he might have found somebody to shoot by now. I have to keep a close eye on him, sort of keep him out of trouble."

Garrett stood there, shaking his head, watching Dallas trying to catch up to Christian. He sure was glad they had showed up when they did. He didn't even want to think about what would have happened if they hadn't.

When Mrs. Pruitt entered the house with Charlie, they never slowed down until they reached Charlie's upstairs bedroom. Wrapping a thick, soft towel around Charlie's head, Mrs. Pruitt rubbed briskly, trying to soak up the water from her short dark curls. "We have to get you out of these wet clothes before you catch your death." Mrs. Pruitt was in a whirl, she was talking a mile a minute, shouting orders downstairs to the twins. She wanted warm water up here and she wanted it now.

After the wet clothes had been stripped off, Charlie felt better almost instantly. But she didn't want to spoil Mrs. Pruitt's fun.

"Let me look at that bruise on your face. It's going to look like a rainbow in a few days."

"It'll be all right, I've had plenty of bruises before. And, I'm sure this one won't be the last." Charlie sat down on the soft bed, wanting nothing more than to crawl between the covers and go to sleep. A knock sounded on the door, Tristen and Austin stepped through the door, each one carrying two steaming buckets of water, for the bath tub Mrs. Pruitt had dragged into the bedroom.

Sitting up straight, Charlie watched the steam rising from the buckets. It looked so good, she decided maybe she did need a good long soak. "Boys, that water looks so good. I can't hardly wait to try it."

The twins mumbled some sort of reply, but she didn't hear it. She really didn't care what they had said, she just wanted to get in that hot water.

Mrs. Pruitt started to close the door after the boys, when two small hands appeared on the edge of the door. It was Taylor. She stuck her head around the door, searching for Charlie. "Charlie, Maddie and me was wonderin' if we could come in and sit while you took your bath. We won't asturb you, we'll be real quiet." The little girl waited, holding her breath.

Looking at Mrs. Pruitt, who was shaking with laughter, Charlie nodded her head. "I would like it very much if you two girls kept me company during my bath."

Taylor smiled, turning to Maddie. "She said she would like it very much if we kept her company. See, I told you she was a nice sister," she whispered loudly.

The door swung open, both little girls skipped in, huge smiles on their faces. They walked over to the high bed, climbed up and dangled their feet over the side. It wasn't long until they were chattering like two birds.

"Since you have such fine company, I'm going downstairs and start supper. I'm sure everybody will have big appetites after the kind of day we've had." Mrs. Pruitt pulled the door closed. She stood in the hallway for a short period of time, listening to the sweet voices that had become so dear to her.

The horses had been stripped of their saddles and gear, and dried with feed sacks. Now they were busy munching on grain and hay.

Garrett and Jack were sitting on a bench, talking to Dallas and Christian. The two younger men were pacing up and down the hallway of the barn. They were absorbing all the information that Garrett and Jack were giving them.

Dallas was always the one full of questions. Christian always listened, hardly ever speaking.

"So, do you think it was Chad and Brett Gilkey that grabbed your wife?" Christian asked.

Garrett was surprised, he wasn't used to Christian voicing his opinion. He looked at Christian funny, trying to figure out what was going on.

Christian halfway smiled, noticing the strange look of Garrett's face. "If you rode with this fountain of information," he said, pointing to Dallas, "As much as I have, some of it's bound to rub off."

Everybody laughed, except Dallas. He was looking like his feelings had been stepped on, which made them all laugh harder.

"I'm not positive," Garrett replied. "You and Dallas were closer to them than I was. It was raining so hard, you could barely see your hand in front of your face." He kicked the dirt with the toe of his boot, wishing he had gotten closer.

Dallas squatted down beside Jack, a stem of hay hanging from his mouth. "It's been at least a year, maybe even a year and a half since we clapped eyes on them ugly buggers. Their beards and hair was so long, it mostly covered their whole face." He was quiet, replaying the scene over in his mind, searching for something that had been overlooked.

"Now that you mention it, it did kind of favor them. They had their hats pulled down low, hid the rest of their faces. But I did notice the spurs. One of them had on an odd looking pair of spurs," Christian supplied. He had always been one for details. "The rowels were shaped like an oval, not round like most spurs, they had very few points. They were just odd looking."

"That was Chad Gilkey," Garrett said, in a low, dangerous voice. "His brother wore an identical pair. Somehow, McCuan has located them, probably offered to pay them to get rid of me."

"And Charlie, don't forget Charlie," Jack said, "We're not going to be able to trust many men on this ranch. Most of them are loyal to McCuan.

Especially that weasel Jones. He's the biggest threat of all. He tells everything he knows to McCuan."

All eyes turned toward Garrett.

"The best thing we can do, is hunt the Gilkeys down. Don't wait for them to hit us again here at the ranch. They won't be expecting us to come looking for them. But that's exactly what we're going to do."

"What are we going to do about McCuan?" Jack asked, looking directly at Garrett.

"First things first. We'll take care of the Gilkeys first, then we'll worry about McCuan." Garrett stood, brushing the dirt and mud from his pants. "Right now, I think we should go on up to the house and get something to eat. Besides, I want to check on Charlie."

Not waiting for any more questions, Garrett turned away. He ran toward the kitchen. Dallas was right behind him, he was always first in line for food. Jack and Christian followed at a slower pace.

None of the men leaving the barn saw the man standing in the shadows.

Pete Jackson had heard every word. He had been hiding, listening to their plans. Now he had to find the boss and tell him what was going on. He caught his horse from the corral, saddled him and headed for town.

James and Gimpy were sitting at the back of the Rusted Bucket. They had been drinking steady for the past hour. James was in a hell of a mood. He was totally pissed off at the Gilkeys. They had had that bitch daughter of his, in their hands, and just rode off. He got mad every time he thought about it.

"They had her, all they had to do was shoot her and ride away," James grumbled. "But hell no! They just let her go, pretty as you please." He lifted his glass, not stopping until it was empty.

"What the hell was they thinkin' boss? You told 'em to get to Steele anyway they could." Gimpy popped the cork from the bottle of whiskey on the table, refilling both glasses. "I know what I would have done, I'd a blowed her head off'n her shoulders." He reared back, laughing so hard, he got choked.

James looked at his foreman, the man was totally ignorant, but he liked him. "Maybe I'll just give you the chance to do something about it Gimpy." That got the other man's attention real fast. "Have you found out any more information about Steele's attorney?"

"Not much. Just that his name is William Reynolds. He's been their family attorney for years. Everyone says he's untouchable."

The saloon doors opened, a man entered, looking around the room. He was definitely looking for something or someone in particular. Gimpy looked at the newcomer, instantly recognizing him. "Hey boss, look over there. Ain't that Pete Jackson? He's supposed to be at the ranch tonight. It's his night to watch after the place."

James twisted in his chair, waving a hand at Pete, calling out. "Over her Pete." He watched the ranch hand approach the table. He could tell by the look on his face, that he had information.

"Hey boss," Pete said. He turned, nodding to Gimpy. "Gimpy." He looked at the bottle of whiskey on the table like a drowning man would a boat. "Do you mind if I have a drink?"

"No help yourself." James watched him take a swig from the bottle. "Did you have a certain reason for coming to town tonight? Because I remember telling you to stay at the ranch."

Pete swallowed hard. "Yes sir, I know you did. But I got some information that I think you'll want to hear. There was two new fellers that showed up today. They look like they know their way around the business end of a gun." He paused, taking another swig of whiskey. "Anyhow," he continued, "I heard them all talking, Steele, Jack and them two new fellers. They're going to hunt some guys down that attacked Charlie. I believe they called them the Gilleys or something like that. I heard 'em say it with my own two ears." He pulled out a chair and sat down.

James couldn't believe what he was hearing, if they went on the hunt of the Gilkeys, that could work to his advantage, but he had to find out about the two young guns. "Do you know the names of the new men that arrived today?"

"No sir, I don't. But if you give me a little more time, I'm sure I can find out for you."

Tossing some coins down on the table, James looked at Pete. "Go get yourself some supper, then go back to the ranch. Be sure and listen for any helpful information, then report it to me. Got that?"

"I sure do boss." He scooped the money off the table and headed for the only restaurant in town.

Gimpy set his glass down on the table. "I guess you want me to ride out and warn the Gilkeys." He had already stood up, getting ready to leave.

Shaking his head, James laughed. "There's no need in that. They're both big boys, I'm sure they can take care of themselves. Besides, if Steele and those other bastards are concentrating on the Gilkeys, that will give us a

163

chance to surprise them."

Both men sat back and propped their feet up on the table. This was going to be more fun than either one of them had ever imagined.

Chapter Thirty-two

A few days after the run in with the Gilkeys, the atmosphere at the ranch had gotten better. The appearance of Christian and Dallas had worked wonders. They went out of their way trying to make everybody laugh, and they loved Garrett like a big brother. They would follow him to the end of the earth. But they never let their guard down, they were always alert for any sign of trouble. Today was no different.

Everyone was going about their everyday activities. Several of the more dependable ranch hands had started asking Jack for advice, and the older man was enjoying every minute of it. James had always pushed him to the side, but he was turning out to be a pretty good foreman, and the men liked to work for him. Jack and the men had left early that morning, checking on cattle after the recent storm, it would probably take most of the day.

Christian, Dallas and the twins were mending fences down by the corral. They stayed pretty close to the house during the day while Jack was gone. But they managed to stay busy and they always had time to spare for Austin and Tristen, and the twins thought they could walk on water. The twins were beginning to strut around, just like the two young guns.

Garrett was standing in the barn, grooming his horse, watching the twins pester each other. He chuckled to himself, thinking how much they had changed. They were starting to act like their older sister. God help him.

He had been riding all morning, searching for any clue that would help him find out where the Gilkeys were hiding. He knew they had to be close, but so far nothing had turned up.

A movement in the back of the barn caught his eye. It was Pete Jackson, and he wasn't alone. He was talking to someone, but the other person was hidden from view. Garrett stepped around his horse, patting him on the rump before walking into the shadow of the stalls. He moved quietly to the end of the barn. He finally got a glimpse of the person Pete was talking to. It was James McCuan. They were talking softly, and Pete kept looking around. He seemed nervous about something. They were definitely up to no good.

Before Garrett could get close enough to hear what was being said, James left, riding away from the barn. Pete stood, twisting his hat in his hands, watching him leave. Whatever they had been talking about sure had made Pete a little edgy.

Garrett was just getting ready to follow Pete, find out where he was headed, when Mrs. Pruitt rang the bell at the back door, signaling that lunch was on the table. Unable to make up his mind, he decided to talk to Christian and Dallas right after lunch, that way they could keep an eye on Pete this afternoon. He could talk to Jack later tonight, right now he wanted to see Charlie.

He took enough time to put his horse in the stall, and hurried toward the house.

The kitchen was full of activity when Garrett opened the door. He noticed that everybody had already gotten there, except Jack and himself. He grinned when he saw Christian and Dallas all slicked up. They were actually helping Mrs. Pruitt get the table ready. So much for the deadliest guns in the territory. All they had on their minds right now was filling their stomachs.

He felt a shiver run down his spine, somebody was watching him. Looking across the room, he found Charlie staring at him, with a smoldering look in her eye. Hanging his hat on the coat rack, he made his way across the busy room, stopping in front of his beautiful wife. Lunch just might have to wait.

She had been standing in the doorway, watching Mrs. Pruitt, when the kitchen door opened, and he stepped in. As always, he took her breath away. Her eyes followed him, aware of the power in his large frame. She was mesmerized by the ripple of muscles under his tight fitting shirt, remembering what those hard bulges and dips felt like under her seeking hands. Jerking her eyes up, she realized he was watching her with such intensity, that it made her face heat up with pleasure. Then she smiled, as he sauntered toward her, his motion smooth and fluid, like an animal on the prowl.

"How about a kiss pretty lady?" He stopped mere inches from her, causing her heart to jump to life in her chest. Not waiting for a reply, he lowered his mouth to hers with a soft gentle kiss. She was in heaven.

When they heard whistles coming from the other part of the room, they broke apart. The flames of desire had been lowered, but not completely extinguished.

Charlie pulled away from Garrett, playfully slapping his chest. "Geez, can't you control yourself? We're right here in front of God and everybody," she whispered, just loud enough for everyone in the room to hear. That started everybody laughing again.

Garrett couldn't keep his eyes off the gentle sway of her full hips. It was torture, pure and simple.

After everyone was seated around the table, the noise was so loud you couldn't hardly hear yourself think. The silverware was clanking on empty plates, the children were chattering and laughing, and the adults were talking, just in a more sedate manner. Yes, things were very different now at meal time.

Mrs. Pruitt was busy trying to keep all the bowls on the table full, which was almost impossible, because Dallas and Christian was always hungry. Dallas noticed that Mrs. Pruitt was still filling bowls and glasses. He grabbed his napkin, wiping his mouth as he stood up, then started helping Mrs. Pruitt. "Here," he said, taking the heavy pitcher of milk from her. "Let me help you with that." He walked around the table filling all the children's milk glasses. He motioned for her to have a seat. "You go ahead and sit down here and have a bite to eat. This is a fine lunch you fixed for us. But you need to get some before it's all gone."

Mrs. Pruitt was amazed. She sat down in the chair he pulled out for her. "Thank you very much," she said.

Garrett watched Dallas fill all the glasses with milk. After a minute he leaned back and laughed. "Dallas, keep that sort of thing up, and one of these days you'll make some little gal a fine husband. You'll be able to set the table and cook her supper." He looked at Dallas, a twinkle of mischief in his eyes.

Christian was the first one that started laughing, pretty soon everybody was laughing, except Dallas. He was becoming more angry by the minute. He had just opened his mouth, going to give Garrett a piece of his mind, when a little voice at the table stopped him.

"I'm going to marry him, in a few years of course. And he'll make me a fine husband." All eyes turned to the voice. It was Taylor. She was sitting quietly, her eyes shining as she looked at Dallas. "Now," she continued, "I don't want to hear anymore about it. I've made up my mind." She picked up her silverware and started eating again.

Dallas stopped, almost dropping the pitcher of milk. He looked at Taylor sitting at the table. He didn't know what to say for once in his life. He just looked at her with a blank expression as he dropped down in an empty chair.

Garrett looked across the table where Dallas had plopped down in a chair. He had a stunned look on his face. Sitting back in his chair, folding his hands across his stomach, Garrett laughed, thinking Dallas didn't stand a chance, because Taylor was just like her big sister. He glanced down the length of the table, his eyes finding Charlie. She sure was something else. He winked at her when she looked up and found him staring at her, she ducked her head, trying to hide the look of desire. He would be glad when nightfall got here. He was ready to go to bed.

Mrs. Pruitt watched the growing family. She was amazed how fast things could change. Just a few short weeks ago the children were sullen and quiet, now they laughed and chattered all the time. It truly was a miracle. The one thing that would have made the situation perfect, would have been if their mother, Audree, could see them now. She would have been so proud of them, especially Charlie. She only hoped all this new found happiness would last.

Jack and three ranch hands were out looking for cows that the storm had scattered. They had looked all over the fields and thickets, where cows like to hide, and they were beginning to get tired, and they were all ready to start for home.

Pulling his horse to a stop under a sprawling tree, Jack looked out over the pasture. He would have given anything to have had a place like this when he was younger, but now it was too late. He was an old man, but Garrett had asked him to stay on, sort of help get things lined out. He had agreed, and that was good enough for him now.

He was just about to tell the other men to start for home when an idea struck him. The north pasture had a line shack, and nobody ever went up there this time of year. He didn't even know if Garrett knew it was there. He'd bet his last dollar that was where the Gilkeys were hiding.

He motioned for one of the hands to come over. It was Jigger O'Reilly. He waited for Jigger to get there.

Jigger stopped his horse beside Jack. "Need something Jack?" he asked. He was always willing to help out with anything.

"I just wanted to talk to you for a minute. You and the boys start on home with the cattle. I've got one more thing left to do, then I'll be right behind you fellows." Jack turned his horse away from Jigger and started north.

Jack stopped before he had gone too far. "Tell Garrett that I won't be long," he said, kicking his horse into a slow gallop, never looking back.

Jigger sat there scratching his head. He sure hoped Jack wasn't about to bite off more than he could chew. Oh well, he better tell the boys that they could head for home.

When Jack reached a small wooded area, about half a mile from the line shack, he stopped and surveyed the area. He could see the shack plain from where he was at. And sure enough, there was smoke curling from the small chimney. He waited, wanting to be sure it was them. It could be anybody up there.

About twenty minutes later, the door opened and a short, stocky man walked out, he had a thick, dirty beard that covered most of his face. He stopped at the edge of the shack with his back turned toward Jack.

Jack knew it was one of the Gilkeys. Garrett had given him a brief description, but he wished he could get a little closer, and get a better look at the man, but it was just to dangerous. He continued watching.

When the man turned around, he didn't go back into the shack immediately. He walked over to the small pen beside the shack. Inside were two horses standing in the far corner. They had their heads down, with their rumps turned his way. But there was no doubt about it, they were dark bays, and that was what the two men had been riding the other day.

With the adrenaline surging through his veins, Jack mounted his horse and rode hard for home. The sooner Garrett found out about this, the better. He was in such a hurry to get back to the ranch, he didn't notice the set of fresh tracks veering off deeper into the woods.

Gimpy wiped the sweat from his forehead. He had almost ran right smack into Jack. He wasn't expecting anyone to be around the old shack, and he hadn't been paying real close attention. He had just managed to get behind some big trees when Jack flew by. It was a good thing the older man had been in such a hurry, or he would have seen the tracks for sure.

Riding out from the cover of the trees, Gimpy decided to head back to town. He needed to tell James what was going on. He knew the boss would want to know that the Gilkeys location had been discovered.

Chapter Thirty-three

The following morning, James and Gimpy was riding toward the Circle Bar M. James needed to talk to Pete Jackson, find out what had went on last night. According to Gimpy, old Jack had found where the Gilkeys were hiding. Now the plan was to sit back and let Steele and his buddies fight it out with the outlaws.

"Boss, are you sure that's what the telegram said?" Gimpy asked for the third time, in about five minutes.

James was not at all happy this morning, and he was losing patience fast. "Look! The answer is still the same. You've asked me that very same question three times now. Are you hard hearing?" he yelled. How in the hell could anybody be that damn stupid, James thought. "Now listen close, because I'm only going to tell you one more time. My lawyer says that the contract that Steele has is iron clad. He's been in touch with Steele's attorney, and he's not willing to bend. He's completely unwilling to negotiate." By this time both men had stopped their horses.

Pushing his hat back on his head, concentration showing on his face. "Does this mean there's nothin' we can do about this whole sit-u-ation?" Gimpy asked.

"Oh, we're going to do something about it all right. We're going to sit back and let them tangle with the Gilkey boys. Then we'll start were they left off. Kind of like catching them with their pants down. Because to tell you the truth, I don't think we'd stand a chance against them in a fair fight." James had a strange look in his eye. He had the look of a madman.

Gimpy sat there, trying to digest the information that James had just given him. He still had a few things that he didn't quite understand. "Boss," he said. "How are we going to make sure the ranch goes back to you?"

James looked at Gimpy, with deadly intent in his eyes. "That's simple," he growled. "We leave no survivors. We'll claim it was the Gilkeys that shot their way in and killed my whole family." He spurred his horse to a gallop, laughing as he rode away.

Gimpy was right behind him.

The ranch was buzzing with activity. Well actually the kitchen. Garrett, Jack, Christian, and Dallas was sitting at the table. They were looking over a map that Jack had drawn. They were planning their attack on the line shack. Garrett knew the Gilkeys were very dangerous. He didn't want to take any unnecessary risks. They were going over every possible detail. They were going after the outlaws later that very afternoon.

Charlie and Mrs. Pruitt was outside. They were hanging laundry on the clothesline. It was a beautiful day.

Charlie was a bit pre-occupied. Her mind was on last night. It had been wonderful! There was no words that could describe the feelings that Garrett could invoke within her, with a single touch. But it was all over too soon.

She had lain awake the rest of the night, worrying about what was going to happen when the men went after the outlaws. She wished that the morning had stayed away just a little longer. But dawn came right on time. She just wished it was all over.

Mrs. Pruitt stopped hanging clothes on the line. She looked at Charlie and smiled. "Don't worry child, they'll be all right. That Garrett, he's a smart one." After a moment, she turned away and started hanging wet clothes again.

Hearing laughter, Charlie turned toward the sound. The girls, Maddie and Taylor, was playing on an old rope swing that Christian and Dallas had made for them the night before. They were having the time of their lives.

Charlie was drawn back to the present when Mrs. Pruitt asked her a question. She had been daydreaming. "I'm sorry, what was that you said Mrs. Pruitt?" she asked.

"I asked you, if you could get that other basket of laundry over by the tub, this basket is almost empty." Mrs. Pruitt never turned around, she had her back to Charlie.

"Sure," Charlie mumbled. She placed her hand against her forehead, all of a sudden not feeling to well. It seemed like Mrs. Pruitt was talking to her from a long distance, but she was standing just a few feet away. She walked over to the laundry basket, bending over to pick it up. The next thing she remembered was the ground moving under her feet. Then nothing, the whole world went dark.

Mrs. Pruitt heard a noise behind her, but thought nothing of it at first. She assumed it was one of the girls playing on the swing. She turned around, thinking she better check on them, then froze when she saw Charlie sprawled in the dirt, not moving at all. Dropping the wet clothes, she started running and yelling at the same time.

"Garrett, Jack, come quick. It's Charlie, something's happened to Charlie." She dropped down on the ground when she reached Charlie's side.

She lifted her head onto her lap, brushing the damp hair away from her pale face. She looked up at the back door, just as it was pushed open, so hard it barely stayed on the hinges. Garrett flew out, never touching the steps. He hit the ground at a dead run. The other men right behind him.

A cold sweat broke out on Garrett's forehead when he saw Charlie lying in the dirt. He had to get to her. Over his shoulder he called to the other men. "Get the girls inside the house until we figure out what's going on." He never looked back.

By the time he reached Mrs. Pruitt, he was a total wreck. A thousand things had passed through his mind. None of them good.

"What's wrong with her?" He was down on his knees, afraid to look to close, afraid of what he might find. "Is she alive?" he asked, waiting for Mrs. Pruitt to answer.

"Yes, but we need to get her in the house, out of this hot sun."

Not waiting to be told twice, Garrett slipped his arms under his wife, lifting her against his chest, and walked quickly to the house. He passed Jack on the way, not slowing down one bit. When he stepped up to the back door, Tristen was waiting to open it.

"What's wrong with my sister?" Tristen asked. He held the door open wide as Garrett entered the house.

"I don't know son." As he carried her through the kitchen, he could hear the girls crying, asking about Charlie. And Jack, bless his heart, trying to comfort them.

When he reached the bottom of the stairs, he turned, waiting for Mrs. Pruitt. She was right behind him with some towels and fresh water. He bounded up the stairs, taking two at a time. As he was waiting for Mrs. Pruitt to get to the top, he nuzzled Charlie's neck with his cheek, silently willing her to be all right. She had to be.

"Charlie, can you hear me sweetheart? Please wake up, tell me what's wrong, please." He felt her body move slightly. Hope surged to life in him.

She felt like she was in a heavy fog. She couldn't see a thing. One thing she did know, she knew Garrett was close by, she could feel him, but she had to get out of this fog before he left her. She struggled harder, trying to reach the light. She called out to him, hoping he would hear her. "Garrett, please help me," she said, her voice the slightest whisper.

Mrs. Pruitt had reached the top of the stairs. Her face was red from exertion. She swung the bedroom door open wide. "Bring her in here Garrett, we need to get her clothes loosened up." She was pulling the quilts back on the bed.

Garrett carried Charlie over to the bed and gently, as if she were delicate as glass, laid her down on their bed. He stepped back looking down at his precious wife, noticing that her face was starting to regain some color. She didn't resemble a ghost any longer, that was a good sign, he thought.

Dipping a towel in the cool water, Mrs. Pruitt wiped Charlie's face. Relief showed on her aging face when Charlie started to come around. "I think she's going to be all right. I was worried there for a minute, I thought she might have gotten hit harder than we thought the other day." She continued bathing Charlie's face with a damp towel.

She was confused. She wasn't sure where she was at. Then she opened her eyes, and looked around. The first thing she saw was Garrett. He looked kind of anxious, maybe even a little worried. "Garrett, where am I?" She turned her head to find Mrs. Pruitt with a wet towel in her hand, that explained the cool feeling on her forehead. But she couldn't remember a thing.

"You're in our bedroom," Garrett said softly, laying a large, gentle hand on her cheek. "How are you feeling now?"

What a strange question. "I'm feeling just fine," she said. She looked around, still a bit confused. "How did I get back to our room? The last thing I remember was, me helping Mrs. Pruitt hang laundry, and let me tell you, that's not one of my favorite chores." All this extra attention was making her nervous.

"I carried you up here. Don't you remember fainting in the yard? You scared us all half to death." He looked across the bed at Mrs. Pruitt, concern lining his handsome features. It surprised him to find that Mrs. Pruitt didn't seem overly concerned at all, in fact, she was smiling.

Not believing a word of it, Charlie turned to Mrs. Pruitt for confirmation. "Is that really what happened?"

"Yes child, that's exactly what happened."

Feeling a little embarrassed, she turned to Garrett. "From now on, just leave me where I fall. Don't you know that you'll hurt your back trying to carry me up the stairs." She paused trying to catch her breath. She was still a little unsteady. "Or at least get somebody to help you." She sat up a little straighter, but dizziness forced her to relax against the pillows at her back.

Mrs. Pruitt smiled, then turned to Garrett. "Why don't you go on downstairs and tell the others that she's going to be OK. And while you're gone, I'll help her get into a nightgown, so she can rest better." She stood up and walked around the bed when she saw that Garrett wasn't moving. "Come on now. Just as soon as I've got her comfortable, I'll let you know."

"Are you sure she's going to be all right?" He was looking down at his wife, she was reclining against the mound of pillows, her eyes closed.

"I'm positive."

He walked to the door, opened it, and disappeared down the hallway.

Charlie opened her eyes when Mrs. Pruitt sat down on the edge of the bed. "Did I really faint?" she asked.

"Yes."

"Well hells bells, Garrett must be stronger than even what I thought. I would have never thought he could have carried me." Charlie closed her eyes as another round of dizziness assaulted her. "Do you think I have a concussion of somethin'? I kind of felt like this that time that big buckskin stomped me. I felt awful for a long time after that."

Mrs. Pruitt smiled tenderly. "Could be, but I don't think so," she said softly.

"What do you think is wrong with me? If I don't have a concussion, then maybe it's a serious affliction." Charlie wrinkled her face. "I read about that very thing in a book once, it's an awful ailment."

Taking Charlie's work roughened hand, Mrs. Pruitt patted it between her older, wrinkled hands. "Charlie, you don't have some terrible ailment." The older woman was talking softly, tears were shining in her eyes. "You're going to have a baby. Garrett's baby."

Charlie looked up at Mrs. Pruitt. "Are you sure?" she asked, stunned. It was a dream come true, she had always hoped for a family all her own. But her pa always said it was something that would never happen. Because no man would ever look at a cow like her. "A baby," she whispered.

"I'm positive. You and Garrett have been married close to six weeks now, plenty of time to conceive a child." Mrs. Pruitt gathered Charlie up in her arms, hugging her close. "Oh child, your mother would have been so proud of you. And she would have liked Garrett to." She pulled back, looking Charlie in the eye. "And you've got to promise me that you'll start taking better care of yourself. No more horseback riding for a while."

The emotions was too thick in Charlie's throat, so she simply nodded.

"When are you going to tell the proud papa?"

"I can't tell him right now. He's got too much to worry about as it is. But I promise that I'll tell him just as soon as all the trouble is over with." She tugged on her nightgown and snuggled down under the quilts, falling asleep almost immediately.

Jack and Garrett were sitting at the kitchen table. Christian and Dallas was outside playing with the girls.

The two men at the table had a steaming cup of coffee in front of them. The map of the north pasture had been rolled up and put away for the time being. Charlie was the main concern now.

Jack was the first to see Mrs. Pruitt entering the kitchen. He jumped up from his chair. "How's Charlie girl? Is she going to be all right?"

"She's sound asleep right now," Mrs. Pruitt said, walking into the kitchen. "I think maybe she just got a little overheated when we were hanging clothes." She sat down at the table, in the chair that Jack had pulled out for her.

Jack looked a bit perplexed. "Did you say that she got overheated?" he asked. That didn't seem right, he had seen her work cattle in the blazing heat of summer and never complain a bit. In fact, she usually worked harder than the rest of the hands, Gimpy was always pushing her. So, just how in the hell could she get too hot hanging clothes on the line. He was going to get to the bottom of this.

"Can I go up and see her?" Garrett asked, setting his coffee cup down, "We'll be leaving in a few hours, and it might be a while before we get back."

"You can go on up, just try not to wake her. She needs to rest."

Garrett stood, walking out of the kitchen.

As soon as Garrett was gone, Jack turned to Mrs. Pruitt. "Now tell me, what's going on. I know she didn't get overheated hanging laundry out. I've worked with her for too many years. She's tougher than most men." He folded his arms across his chest, he wasn't going to budge until he found out the truth.

"I'll tell you, if you promise not to breath a word of it." She waited until he agreed.

"I promise."

Then she told him the good news.

"I'll be damned." He sat there with a stupid looking grin on his face. "I'll be damned," he repeated. Imagine, his Charlie girl going to have a baby. He felt like… like…a grandpa.

Later that day Charlie was up and feeling much better. She watched as Garrett, Dallas, and Christian rode away. Before Garrett had climbed into the saddle, he had kissed her, making her head spin. After they left the yard, she touched her stomach with a gentle pat, praying for Garrett's safe return.

It had been agreed upon, that Jack and the twins, stay and watch the ranch. But Garrett had left instructions with Jack, just in case something went wrong.

Jack was supposed to wire information to Tucson, to Garrett's attorney, and he'd know exactly what to do with it.

When the three riders reached the end of the ranch road, they all stopped, looking back in the direction of the house. They sat there for a minute, not bothering to say anything.

"The sooner we get started, the sooner we can get back and eat some of Mrs. Pruitt's apple pie," Dallas said. "She promised me this morning that she'd have one waiting for us."

They all laughed, then set about the task at hand, bringing in Chad and Brett Gilkey, no matter what.

James watched the three young men ride away. As soon as they were out of sight, he rode down to the bunkhouse. He immediately started assigning the cowboys with small jobs that would keep them away from the house the rest of the day.

After all the hands left, James decided to wait and see if Steele made it back alive. If he did, then he would have to come up with a different plan, but he already had one in mind. The hardest part now was waiting.

Chapter Thirty-four

Charlie, that's all Garrett could think about. He had to get his mind on his business. But all he could think about was Charlie. Something wasn't right. Charlie was tough as nails. What could have caused her to faint in the yard? A frown creased his forehead, Mrs. Pruitt could be wrong, maybe she had gotten hit harder than they all thought.

As soon as he got back from cleaning this mess up, he was going to take her to see a doctor. Even if he had to drag her the whole way, that thought brought a smile to his worried face.

Pulling his attention back to the present, he realized Christian seemed to be waiting for an answer. "I'm sorry. Did you say something?" he asked, trying to clear his thoughts.

Christian was staring straight ahead, acting like he was the only person within fifty miles. He turned in the saddle. "You're worried about her," he said. It was more of a statement than a question. He had always had the ability to sense what was wrong with people.

Garrett was amazed, he had forgotten Christian's ability to see down deep into a person's heart. "Yeah, I am. Something is not quite right about the story Mrs. Pruitt told." He was silent, looking ahead, but not really seeing anything. "Charlie's different, she's very special," he said, hesitating before continuing, "When I first met her, the attraction was instant, well on my part anyway. She actually threatened to shoot me," he chuckled.

By this time, Dallas had moved closer, not wanting to miss any of the details. All three riders moved as one. They appeared to be at complete ease traveling with each other.

"It's hard to explain," Garrett said after a while. He turned to Dallas grinning. "I walked around for a couple of weeks stiff as a fence post. I was miserable. Hell, I was on the verge of buying some bigger pants, before I embarrassed myself," he said, recalling his instant attraction to Charlie.

Dallas and Christian snickered as they rode along beside the legendary 'Cold Steele'. Both young guns picturing the ex-marshall all bent out of shape over a woman, especially one as rough around the edges as Charlie.

Garrett seemed to read their minds. He pushed his hat back on his head. "I know what you're both thinking," he said. "How could a woman like Charlie excite a man? Believe me, I've asked myself that same question at least a hundred times, maybe even more. But." He stopped thinking carefully about his next words. "When I was around her, or touched her, it just seemed right, like it was meant to be." He looked at Christian and Dallas. "I know that sounds kind of…hell not kind of…it does sound stupid, but that's the way it happened. And I'm telling you both right now, that I'm not one bit sorry."

The silence was almost unnerving, it was so still. The only sound that could be heard was the clicking of the horses hooves on an occasional rock that was scattered on top of the ground.

Christian finally broke the tension. "Well Marshall, if it makes you fell any better, me and Dallas here, we really like your new family, especially that beautiful wife of yours. She really is a special woman." He was a man of few words, and that was probably the most he had spoken at one time in his entire life.

"Besides," Dallas said grinning, "She'd have to be pretty special to put up with the likes of you. She's about near an angel as far as I'm concerned." Dallas guided his horse away from Garrett, laughing the whole time.

"We need to get our minds on the business at hand," Garrett said gruffly.

"Don't worry Marshall, she'll be all right," Christian said.

Garrett didn't reply, he just continued moving forward, heading for the unknown. But he sure hoped Christian was right about Charlie, he was really worried about her.

Leaning back, with the chair on two legs, Gimpy watched as James paced back and forth across the small kitchen. In a few hours things would be back to normal, he hoped. He was supposed to get a big bonus and a vacation, for helping James take care of Steele.

He had been trying to figure out just how he was going to spend his money, and where. At first, he thought he would just go to the Rusted Bucket, but now, he had decided on Tucson. He was going to meet up with his cousin Rowdy. They would have a humdinger of a time. He couldn't hardly wait.

Looking out the window, James noticed that there was still no sign of Jack, or anybody else around the main house. Pulling a chair back from the old battered table in the foreman's house, he dropped down wearily. He turned to Gimpy. "Do you have any coffee made? I sure could use a cup," he said. He looked around the kitchen. "Maybe even something stronger, if you have anything."

"I don't got no more whiskey boss. We drunk it all the last time we was here." Gimpy was getting everything ready to make coffee. Walking to the stove, he opened the door, stoking up the ashes a little. "It won't take long to make a pot of coffee. I'll have it made afore you know it."

"I'd like to know just where in the hell they're at right now. They should be getting real close to the line shack by now," James said, thinking out loud, hoping it would ease his mind. But it didn't, it only made him worry more.

When the coffee was done, Gimpy filled two cups, and set them down on the old table. After sliding a chair back, he sat down, and took a sip of the strong brew. "Maybe it won't be much longer. I'm sure we'll hear somethin' afore too much longer." He could tell by the look on James' face, that now was not the time to be asking any questions.

The line shack was about a half a mile away. Garrett was hunkered down in a small thicket, watching for any sign of the two outlaw brothers. So far, he had not seen any sign of them. He continued to wait.

A movement to his far right caught his eye. It was Dallas! He was signaling, and sure enough one of the brothers walked around the corner of the shack. Garrett picked up a small mirror, and flashed a message to Dallas and Christian. He wanted to wait until both brothers were out in the clear. They'd just have to sit tight and wait a little longer.

Charlie was as nervous as a long tail cat in a room full of rocking chairs. Jack and Mrs. Pruitt had tried to talk to her, get her mind off of Garrett, but it didn't work. The only thing that was going to put her mind at ease, would be when Garrett and the boys walked through the kitchen door. Then, and only then, would she calm down.

She walked to the kitchen door and started to open it to look around outside, hoping beyond all odds, that she would see Garrett riding into the yard, but Jack's voice stopped her.

"Garrett said we need to stay in the house until they get back. He didn't even want none of us close to the windows." Jack didn't tell her the reason. Garrett had been afraid someone might try to take a shot at them. He stood up from the table, and made his way to the back door. Reaching around Charlie, he made sure the curtains were pulled together.

Turning her back to Jack and Mrs. Pruitt, Charlie let the tears roll down her cheeks, she had fought them too long, there was no holding them back now. Her vision blurred, so much, that she couldn't tell who had wrapped their arms around her trembling body. And to tell the truth, she didn't care who it was. She leaned into the comforting embrace.

Seeing Charlie like this ripped a hole through her heart. Mrs. Pruitt gathered her in her arms, hugging her close. "It will be all right. Before long Garrett will come riding down that road, a big grin on his face, and two hungry lads following him," she whispered, holding Charlie tight in her arms. She stroked Charlie's back, rocking her back and forth.

Pulling back from Mrs. Pruitt's embrace, Charlie wiped her face. "Do you really think so? Or, are you just trying to make me feel better?" She pulled out of the older woman's reach. She studied Mrs. Pruitt's face, looking for an answer. When she didn't find the answer she was looking for, she turned to Jack. But all she found was understanding.

Her hands dropped to her slightly rounded stomach. It was impossible to tell that she was pregnant, but just the thought of Garrett's baby lying nestled under her heart, created a surge of hope. "He promised me he would be back, just as soon as he could. And he always keeps his promises," Charlie whispered.

Garrett wanted to stretch his legs out, work out the kinks, but he couldn't move. He had been sitting in the same position for about an hour, afraid to move. If the Gilkeys didn't stir before too much longer, they were going to have to go in after them.

He was just getting ready to signal Dallas and Christian, when the door of the shack opened. Chad walked out, followed closely be Brett. They had their gun belts on, but they didn't head for the horses. He could hear bits and pieces of their conversations, but not all of it. He wanted to get them away from their horses, cut off their escape route.

He signaled Christian, who was on the opposite side of the shack, then he waited. The outlaws were walking around to the side. It didn't take Garrett long to realize this was the opportunity he had been waiting for. He gave the signal to move in, but when he started inching forward, his muscles screamed in protest, they were slow to respond to his commands, but that didn't stop him. He had too much riding on the outcome of this venture.

"I'm getting too old for this business," he muttered. But that really wasn't the case. His heart was pounding, the adrenaline starting to flow. He was ready for a fight. He realized just how much he had missed this type of work. He was born to be a lawman.

Christian had worked his way up to the edge of the small pen, beside the shack. he inched his way forward, stopping by the side of the shack, waiting for Garrett and Dallas to get into position. This was going to be like taking candy from a baby, he thought with a grin. They were going to be back home eating pie before nightfall.

Garrett had almost reached the front door, when Chad Gilkey stepped out from behind the door. He had his gun pointed at Garrett's chest.

"Stop right there," he growled. He walked out farther away from the door, never taking his eyes off of Garrett's face. "We thought we could wait you out. But we got tired of waitin', decided to go ahead and give you a little bait," he laughed. "Must not have knowed there was a back way to this fine place," he said, pulling the hammer back on his pistol. "I climbed through the wind'r. Brett will be around here any minute. Then we're goin' to have to kill you." His eyes gleamed with hatred.

This was just great, he really must be getting old, walked right into an ambush. Charlie was going to be pissed at him. Hearing a slight scrapping noise, he cut his eyes around to the right. He let out a deep breathe, when he saw Dallas moving into position. But what had him worried was Brett, where in the hell could he be? He had to be close. He hoped Dallas and Christian knew where he was.

"You got anything to say lawman, before I send you to hell."

Focusing his attention on the outlaw standing before him, he forgot all about Brett. He had more important matters to attend to at the moment. "Yeah, if you're going to send me to hell, would you like for me to give your brothers any messages?" he asked. He was trying to keep Chad's attention, maybe give Dallas and Christian time to get behind him, and it worked.

"You sonofabitch," Chad yelled, "I was going to wait until Brett got here before I put a bullet in your head, but I just decided I can't wait no more." The scraggly outlaw raised his pistol, pointing it at Garrett's forehead. "I'll be sure and give your wife my regards later, when we visit—" Chad was caught off guard when Garrett rushed forward. As the two men were falling to the ground, the gun went off.

Garrett saw red! The filthy bastard had no right to talk about Charlie like that. Before he had time to think, he charged straight ahead, catching the outlaw vermin by surprise. They both fell to the ground. The gun went off when they bounced in the dirt. Garrett felt a sharp pain in his side, but it didn't slow him down. He was furious!

"You don't even have the right to speak my wife's name, you filthy bastard." He wrestled the gun away from Chad, throwing it several feet away. He started to slowly and methodically pound every inch of Chad Gilkey.

Christian had left his hiding place, when the first shot had been fired. He knew it would draw the other snake out of hiding, and sure enough, it worked. Leveling his gun, he waited at the corner of the shack, that was when he saw Dallas, over behind the water trough. But he didn't have time to plan his next move, because he heard the other outlaw, and he was in a hurry.

After hearing the shot, Brett came running from around the back of the shack, only to find himself staring down the barrel of a colt. And the man holding it didn't look none to friendly. The stranger's calm voice was deceiving. Brett raised his hands away from his pistol. He knew when the odds were stacked against him. He glanced at his brother, who seemed to be getting the worst end of the fight.

"If you know what's good for you, you'll keep them hands of yours away from that pistol in your belt," Christian said. "Come on over here Dallas, and help me tie this sonofabitch up."

When Dallas and Christian got Brett settled, trussed up like a Christmas turkey, they turned their attention to the two men fighting on the ground. It was a nasty fight.

"You think the Marshall needs any help?" Dallas asked.

"Nah," Christian replied, never taking his eyes off the fight. "He seems to be holding his own, that is for an old man." After that last remark, both men hooted with laughter. "Besides," Christian continued, "The Marshall knocked the scum out about five minutes ago." That sent both men into another round of howling.

Garrett finally came to his senses, realizing Chad was unconscious. He had no idea how long he had been that way, not really caring either. He straightened up, wincing at the pain in his side. Looking down, he saw that his shirt was torn. It must have been the bullet, it probably grazed his side. He had felt a sharp pain. But it seemed to be just a minor injury. Picking up his hat, he slapped it against his leg, trying to get the dust out of it. He pulled it low over his eyes, trying to hide part of the bruises on his face. His face felt like he had been kicked by a mule, one eye was already starting to swell.

"You two all right?"

"Yeah Marshall, we're just fine." Dallas was always the first one to answer. "You're the one that looks like you tangled with the south end of a north bound mule," he snorted.

"You know, for once you're right," Garrett chuckled, relief apparent on his battered face. "Come on, lets get these two on their horses and head for home."

That sounded good, home. He couldn't hardly wait to get home to Charlie.

The three men rounded up the outlaw's horses and belongings. Each man ready to go home for a different reason.

Chapter Thirty-five

"Hey boss! Better come here and have a look see," Gimpy said. He had been standing, looking out the window, up toward the main house. When James didn't answer, he called out again. "Boss, I'm tellin' you, you need to come here quick and see this," he said, not bothering to turn away from the window.

James' nerves had been stretched to the limit. When Gimpy hollered the second time, it was more than he could take. "One of these days I'm going to beat the livin' hell right out of you," he growled. Moving closer to the window, he saw the reason why Gimpy was so excited. It was Steele! And he was riding into the yard as pretty as you please. Then James saw the Gilkey brothers riding between the two young guns. They were behind Steele.

"This didn't work out like I had it planned. I thought those two I hired was better than that. I guess not."

Gimpy had been quiet since James spouted off. "What are we going to do now boss? We kind of figured on them two you hired to take care of all three of them fellers," he said, taking his life in his own hands. He cut his eyes around to watch the other man, almost afraid not to keep an eye on him.

"We're not going to do anything. We're just going to sit tight and plan our strategy. We can't get in a hurry." He had waited this long, now was not the time to get in a hurry. "I'll think of something."

The closer they got to the ranch, the faster Garrett wanted to travel. He had to stop himself from spurring his horse to a quicker pace, but he wanted to see Charlie, hold her in his arms, make sure she was all right.

A half mile from the ranch, Garrett called back to Dallas and Christian. "I'm going to ride ahead, make sure there are no surprises waiting for us." He let his horse have some rein, urging him to a faster pace. He couldn't wait to hold Charlie in his arms.

Charlie had decided to try to rest, while Garrett was gone. She went upstairs to rest on the bed, knowing it would be impossible to sleep. That was the last thing she remembered before dropping off to sleep.

She came awake with a start. Not knowing what had disturbed her rest, she lay still, trying to focus on the room. Something had scared her. She had been dreaming about Garrett and their child. It was such a wonderful dream. Garrett had been standing, holding a blanket wrapped bundle. A smile on his handsome face. He had been waiting for her to catch up, calling her name. But the faster she ran, the farther away he seemed. She was becoming frantic, trying to reach them. Before long, she could barely make out the shape of Garrett and their child, he appeared to be shouting something at her, but he was too far away.

That is where the dream ended. She woke up with a start. Something was not right, maybe it was a sign. She hurried off the bed, heading downstairs. That was when she heard the shout from the kitchen.

Garrett was home!

Stepping down from his horse, Garrett had just reached the bottom of the steps, when a bundle of energy came flying through the door, hitting him square in the chest. He lost his balance, staggering backwards. Everything was all right until his boot scrapped the corner of the flower bed, sending him sprawling in the dirt. Charlie was lying on top on him, smothering his face and neck with kisses.

"Whoa there sweetheart. I've been in the dirt more since I met you, than in my entire life." It was hard for him to concentrate with her raining kisses all over his face and neck. He was going to have to put a stop to this, before things got out of hand. "Take it easy wildcat, we need to get up off the ground. There will be plenty of time later for celebrating," he whispered in her ear.

"I'm just so happy your home. I've been worried sick about you and the boys. Oh my! I forgot all about Dallas and Christian." She searched his eyes until she found the answer. They were all right. She pulled back away from Garrett, that was when she noticed the blood on his side. She swayed, her face losing all color, then went limp against Garrett's strong body.

"Charlie, Charlie," Garrett said, panic rising within him. He scrambled up off the ground. "Charlie what's wrong? The first thing I'm going to do is take you to see a doctor."

At the mention of a doctor, Charlie came roaring back to life. "Take me to a doctor. What the hell for?" The color was back in her face, and she was ready to fight. "Just for your information greenhorn, I'm not the one that's leakin' blood all over the ground," she said, pointing to his side. It was sticky with oozing blood. "Take me to the doctor. Of all the crazy hair-brained ideas," she muttered.

God she was beautiful! He would never get tired of watching her for the next eighty years. And there would never be a dull moment. "It's just a scratch. Just barely caught my skin." He moved closer, wanting to pull her close to his side, and never let her go.

She was still trying to make up her mind, when Dallas and Christian rode into the yard, with the outlaw brothers between them. As usual Dallas was already talking.

Dallas tipped his hat to Mrs. Pruitt, who was standing just inside the kitchen door. "Did you happen to get that apple pie baked? I sure hope so. That's all I've had on my mind all day long." He rolled his eyes, making a face that looked like that of an angel, making everybody laugh.

He dismounted, leaving his horse with Christian, and walked closer to the back door. They wanted to keep the Gilkeys as far away from Charlie and the rest of the family as they could.

"If you're ready for that pie, I've got one baked just for you," Mrs. Pruitt said. She was standing at the edge of the back door, trying to keep Taylor and Maddie inside. She didn't want them to have any contact with the outlaws.

Dallas looked at Garrett, hopeful. "Do we have time to grab a bite to eat, before we take these boys to town?" he asked. He could already taste that apple pie. It would probably melt in your mouth.

He hated to leave again, but Garrett knew they needed to get to Broken Tongue with their prisoners. "You can eat later. Right now we need to get these two into town, so the sheriff can lock them up. Then I'm going to send a wire to Tucson, kind of let the sheriff there know what's going on." He almost laughed, because he didn't know which one had the worst expression, Charlie or Dallas.

Pulling Charlie closer, he placed a kiss in top of her head. "I won't be gone long. You'll hardly miss me." He placed a gentle kiss on her luscious mouth. "I promise," he whispered.

"Charlie girl," Jack said, stepping up beside her. "Are you sure those are the two that jumped you in the pasture the other day?" He looked mad enough to bite a nail in two with his teeth.

Raising her head from Garrett's shoulder, she glanced in the direction of the outlaws. "Yes, that's them." She turned her back, not wanting to see them ever again, knowing her pa had brought them here to harm Garrett.

"I've got an idea," Jack said. "Why don't I go along with the boys to take those two in. That way you can stay here with Charlie," he said, turning to Garrett.

"I don't know," Garrett said. "I would feel better if I rode along." He looked down into Charlie's dark eyes, seeing the disappointment surface.

After that it didn't take him long to make up his mind. "I guess that will be fine, besides I need some attention," he laughed, holding his injured side.

A short time later Jack, Dallas, and Christian rode away. They were on their way to Broken Tongue with the Gilkeys in tow. Dallas was in a hurry, he was afraid somebody would eat his pie. Before he left, he made Mrs. Pruitt promise to put his pie away.

When they rode off, Dallas was talking a mile a minute, Christian was threatening to shoot him, and Jack was shaking his head.

"Come on in the house and let me have a look at your side," Charlie said. She had been standing beside Garrett, watching Jack and the boys ride away. She had been so relieved when Garrett had agreed to stay home. "I love you," she said, looking up into Garrett's smoky gray eyes. "I was so afraid," she paused, taking a deep breath, before whispering, "That you wouldn't come home to me."

"There was no chance of that happening." He bent down to give her a quick kiss. "I told you that I always keep my promises. Cross my heart and hope to die," he said, making the motion across his broad chest. "Now lets go inside woman. I need some medical attention." They walked into the kitchen, arm in arm, both laughing like a couple of school children. Both unaware that they were being watched at that very moment.

James watched the little group ride away. He had to grit his teeth when he saw the display between that bitch daughter of his and that no good bastard, Steele. He was cursing his luck when an idea struck him. With Jack and those other two guns gone, that left only Steele. If he and Gimpy could catch him off guard, they could take him. It was worth a try.

Spinning away from the window, he called to Gimpy. "I've got an idea… make sure your gun is loaded. We're going after Steele." He sat down at the table. "We need to wait a little while, let them get all settled in, then we'll just walk in and gun that bastard down," he said, grinning.

"What about the rest of 'em in the house?" Gimpy asked.

"Kill them all." He paused to light a cigar, then he tilted his head back, blowing smoke up in the air. "With all the hands away from the ranch, that means no witnesses."

As usual, it took Gimpy a little longer to catch on to the plan. Then he laughed. "You know what boss, I think it just might work." As soon as James finished his cigar, they both checked their guns, then left the foreman's small house, walking straight toward the main house.

Chapter Thirty-six

Garrett was sitting at the table, his eyes following his lovely wife around the kitchen. She was busy gathering up supplies to treat the wound in his side. If he lived to be a hundred, he would never get tired of watching her. How could anyone think she was unattractive? Her face had an absolute glow about it. And as usual her temper was starting to flare up. She was something else.

Feeling a tug on his arm, Garrett turned his attention in that direction. It was Maddie. She was twisting her hands in the front of her dress, and she had tears shining in her eyes. He opened his arms, welcoming her into his embrace. "What's wrong sweet Maddie?" he asked. With the pad of his thumb, he wiped the tears from her soft cheek. "What's the tears for sweetheart?" He loosened his hold on her, shifting her in his arms, watching her tear stained face.

" I was…was afraid that you wouldn't come home—" She couldn't finish the sentence, the tears started flowing, choking her voice. Burying her face against his shirt, she cried harder, the sobs wracking her small body.

Holding her close, he tried to soothe her fears. "I told you that I'd always be here for you. And I always keep my promises," he whispered. He rocked his little sister, keeping her close to his body. "I promise that Charlie and I both, will always be here for you and Taylor, and the boys." Looking over the little girls ahead, his eyes locked with Charlie's. And what he saw in her eyes made his heart start thundering in his chest. There was no words to describe how he felt.

Standing beside Mrs. Pruitt, Charlie had her arms wrapped around Taylor's shoulders. She could hear the older woman sniffling, which caused her own eyes to tear up. A rush of emotion washed over her as she watched Garrett hold his little sister so tenderly. Her hands automatically dropped to her lower stomach, thinking about their unborn child. She smiled, thinking what a wonderful father he would be.

Charlie moved away from Taylor. "Mrs. Pruitt, why don't you take the girls to the living room. When I get Garrett all patched up, we'll meet you in there." She picked up her supplies, walking over to Garrett's side. "Maddie, would you mind if I take Garrett away from you, just for a little while. I've got to put some medicine on his side. But I promise it won't take long at all," she said, smiling down at the little girl.

Maddie straightened up on Garrett's lap, looking up into his eyes. "I bet it's going to burn. If you want me to, I'll stay and blow on it for you. That always seems to help me," she said, with serious look.

Garrett couldn't hardly keep from laughing, but she looked so serious he didn't. Instead he hugged her close. "No, you go ahead, go with Mrs. Pruitt and Taylor. If I need someone to blow on it, Charlie will do it," he said. He looked at his wife, fire burning in his gray eyes. "Won't you Charlie?" he asked, a mischievous smile dancing on his handsome face.

"Yes," she answered calmly, not bothering to look up. She could feel the heat scorching her cheeks. She was going to give him a piece of her mind just as soon as the girls were out of the room. When Maddie climbed down from her perch on Garrett's lap, Charlie gave him a sizzling look.

Mrs. Pruitt noticed the expression on Charlie's face, before leaving the kitchen. "Charlie, you be sure and behave yourself, and you know exactly what I mean. You don't need to be getting upset right now." She strolled out the kitchen door, but not before she saw the questioning look on Garrett's face. It was going to get interesting, she thought. She ushered the little girls out of the kitchen, leaving the young couple alone.

"You better get that shirt off so I can see your side. I need to get it doctored and get a bandage on it." She was trying to distract him. But it didn't work.

"What did she mean when she said that you didn't need to be upset right now? Is there something going on that I should know about?' He was starting to panic now, he knew she should have gone to the doctor after she was hit in the head. "Tell me. I have to know if something is wrong with you. I couldn't stand it, if something happened to you." He pulled her onto his lap, his arms tightening around her, pulling her close to his powerful body.

Seeing the fear on his face, Charlie tried to calm him down. "Garrett, there's nothing bad wrong with me. I don't need a doctor, at least not right away," she said with a shy smile. "I was going to tell you earlier, but I didn't want to worry you none." She laid her work roughened hand against his stubbly cheek, loving the feel of his unshaven face.

Turning his head, he kissed the palm of her hand. "Charlie, please tell me what's wrong with you. Whatever it is, we'll handle it together, no matter what," he whispered.

"Well greenhorn, you're right about one thing. We are going to have to handle this problem together. But the first part, I'm goin' to have to do it alone." She picked up his large hand, placing it on the slight swell of her stomach, a brilliant smile on her face. "You're going to be a father," she said, waiting until the news soaked through his foggy brain.

Garrett was shocked! He thought she said that she was having a baby. But that couldn't be right, could it. He didn't know anything about babies. But soon his fears vanished when he imagined a little girl with dark eyes strutting around the ranch, wearing boots and jeans.

"Are you sure?" he asked. He cradled her in his lap, his big hand resting on the small mound, where his child lay, right beneath her heart. "Maybe you should be resting." He stood up, still cradling his wife in his strong arms. "I'll take you upstairs."

She wrapped her arms around his neck. "I'll go upstairs, if you're willin' to come with me," she whispered, desire flashing in her eyes. They were both so engrossed in each other, neither one of them heard the back door open. The only sound they heard was a click, it was the sound of a pistol being cocked.

Garrett turned, pushing Charlie behind him in one smooth motion. He found himself staring down the barrel of a pistol, James McCuan's pistol. He had really gotten himself backed into a corner this time.

James and Gimpy was standing outside the kitchen, listening to the conversation going on inside. When they heard Mrs. Pruitt and the girls leave the room, they decided to make their move. Leaving Gimpy outside, keeping watch, James entered the back door. He found his daughter and Steele together. He stepped farther inside the kitchen, away from the back door. He aimed his pistol, pulling the hammer back. He wanted to be ready, Steele was legendary with a gun.

"I knew you were just like that bitch mother of yours, never did trust her," McCuan sneered. He never moved the pistol from Garrett's chest. "It doesn't matter now. In a few minutes you'll both be dead. Then I'm going to get rid of the rest of the family."

He had gone mad.

Garrett had to keep him talking. He was trying to distract him long enough to get Charlie out of harms way. "Why don't you and me step outside, settle this thing like men," Garrett said. He shifted his weight, inching over toward the doorway, keeping Charlie behind him, away from her pa.

Sweat was dripping down on James' forehead. He swiped at it with his free hand, keeping the gun steady, pointed at Garrett. "You must think I'm crazy. I know I don't stand a chance against the likes of you." He was out of control.

Charlie had been trying to peek around Garrett's broad back. She was trying to get a good look at her pa. He didn't even sound like himself. Garrett shifted his weight, allowing her to catch a brief glimpse of him. After seeing the look in his eyes she leaned close to Garrett, "Please be careful. He looks like the team has pulled away from the wagon." She looked up into Garrett's face, grinning just a little. She sure had a way with words.

"I see you back there daughter, hiding behind this miserable excuse of a man." He was starting to sweat profusely now. His face was turning dull red. "Did you know that you jumped in the sack with a real honest to goodness legend?" He stopped, waiting for a chance to get a clear shot at his daughter. "This here is the legendary U.S. Marshall Steele, or better known as Cold Steele," he growled.

"Charlie, don't believe everything you hear about me. Most of those stories are untrue." Garrett was whispering, just loud enough for Charlie's ears. "Watch my lead, when the time is right, I'm going to make a move. I want you to go through the door, then go straight to the living room. You and Mrs. Pruitt take the children and go upstairs, to our bedroom, and lock the door." He stopped, afraid McCuan would hear him. He waited, noticing that McCuan appeared to be unaware of his conversation with Charlie. "And don't unlock the door, unless it's Jack or me. One more thing, always remember that I love you and our child. Now get ready."

James had an evil smile on his face. His eyes were cold as ice. "I'm getting tired of this game. I think it's time to end it." He raised the pistol, aiming at Garrett's face, squeezing the trigger. Before his weapon fired, a shot from outside startled him, drawing his attention away from Garrett and Charlie for a short time. But a movement in their direction drew his attention back.

It was Steele! He was trying to escape. Without thinking, he lifted his gun and fired.

Garrett had been waiting for a good time to make his move. When the shot exploded outside, it distracted James just long enough for Garrett to push Charlie out of the way. Relief washed over him, just knowing she was out of the way. Now he had to deal with McCuan. He grabbed his gun, pulling it from his holster. Just as his gun cleared leather, the sound of a shot filled the kitchen.

The pain jolted his thigh instantly. It felt like a red hot poker being pushed into his leg. McCuan had shot him! Looking up, Garrett realized that McCuan's gun was still pointed at him. He saw McCuan squeeze the trigger. This time the bullet hit him square in the chest, knocking him backwards to the floor. When he lost consciousness, he knew the wound was bad, but his last clear thoughts were of Charlie and their unborn child.

Charlie was standing just a few feet away from the kitchen doorway. She listened to the shots being fired, praying that Garrett was all right. Deciding to take a peek she inched around the corner. She almost fainted when she saw Garrett lying on the floor in a pool of blood, her pa standing over him, getting ready to shoot him again. She had to do something.

Making up her mind, she walked out into the open doorway. Her eyes glued to the prone figure on the floor. She prayed again that he wasn't dead. Her pa's evil voice interrupted her thoughts.

"I'm glad you're here. Keeps me from having to hunt you down." He pointed to the figure on the floor. "He wasn't as tough as everybody said. In fact, it was almost too easy," he laughed, shoving Garrett with the toe of his boot. Pulling his gaze from Garrett, he fixed it on Charlie. Raising his gun. "I'm going to kill you with the first shot," he said, pulling the hammer back.

Charlie closed her eyes, waiting for the explosion and the pain that would follow being shot. She flinched when the sound echoed in the small room. She cracked one eye open when there was no pain. Relief made her knees weak when she saw her pa pitch forward, face down. He looked like he was dead.

When the shock started to wear off, she looked over at the open back door. It was her friend, Jigger O'Reilly. And he had a gun in his hand. He had saved her.

Jigger was the first one to recover from the events that had just taken place. "Miss Charlie, I rode back here as fast as I could when I realized that your pa had sent all of us out on piddly, little jobs. I knowed somethin' was up." He walked farther into the kitchen, stopping beside James. He motioned with his head toward the back of the house. "Don't worry none about that weasel foreman. I took care of him a little while ago," he said grinning. "He tried to pull a gun on me. Can you imagine that?"

Charlie nodded her head. She was unable to speak, tears were flowing down her cheeks. Turning back to Garrett's prone figure on the floor, she finally found her voice. "Please," she choked out, "Help me with Garrett. He's hurt real bad." By this time she was down on her knees beside him. Carefully lifting his head, begging him to wake up. But it didn't happen.

"There's a couple of boys outside, they rode back with me. Let me go and get 'em. Then we'll help take care of Garrett," he said, walking to the back door, calling for the others to come in and help. It didn't take long for the men to come into the kitchen. They were ready to help any way they could. When

Mrs. Pruitt entered the kitchen, she found the men standing, looking down at the two figures huddled on the kitchen floor. It was Charlie holding Garrett's head in her lap. A large pool of blood had puddled beneath Garrett on the floor. After seeing the amount of blood he had already lost, she knew they had to act fast. She started giving out orders faster than an army sergeant.

"Charlie move over out of the way. Let me in there and see how bad he's hurt." Not waiting for Charlie to move, Mrs. Pruitt scooted her over. She opened Garrett's shirt, finding a gaping, bloody hole high in his chest. The sight made her grimace, it was bad. "One of you boys hand me some on them clean dish cloths on the shelf, over there by the sink." She turned Garrett over, just enough to check and see if the bullet had gone all the way through him, soon discovering that it hadn't. It was still in there.

A handful of clean cloths were pressed into her hands. She folded them, making a thick padding, pressing it tight to the bullet wound. After a moment, she turned to Jigger. "Jigger, you better send one of the boys to town for the doctor. Have them see if they can find Jack, and send him home." She was busy wrapping a bandage around Garrett's chest, trying to get him ready for the men to move upstairs.

While Jigger was giving one of the ranch hands instructions, Mrs. Pruitt turned to Charlie. "Charlie, listen to me. We've got to get Garrett upstairs, and try to stop the bleeding. Do you think you can help me?"

When Charlie didn't answer, Mrs. Pruitt shook Charlie's shoulder. "You've got to keep your wits, going all to pieces now is not going to help Garrett.

By this time, Jigger and the other men were ready to move Garrett. Mrs. Pruitt had the bandage in place, the bleeding had slowed for the moment. Pulling Charlie to her feet, Mrs. Pruitt pushed her toward the hallway. "You go on up and get the bed ready. I'll follow the boys up. I'm going to bring some supplies and hot water up." She hugged Charlie close before sending her on her way. "Now go on."

Tears blurred her vision, but she knew the way by heart. She started climbing the stairs, but Tristen and Austin came running from the living room. Their eyes wide after seeing the blood smeared all over her clothes.

"What's going on? We thought we heard gun shots." Both boys were excited, talking at the same time.

After taking a deep breath, Charlie turned and looked at them. "Please boys, keep Taylor and Maddie in the living room. And please keep them busy." She looked down at the blood that covered her clothes. "Garrett has been hurt real bad, but don't tell the girls," she said. "Can you do that?"

"Yes," answered both boys. They wanted to ask if Garrett was going to be all right, but they could tell by the look on Charlie's face, that he wasn't.

Charlie walked away, slowly climbing the stairs. She had taken two steps when she stopped. "Boys, Pa is dead," she said, never turning around. She waited, when the twins didn't say anything, she began to climb the stairs again, trying to concentrate on putting one foot in front of the other.

When she reached the top of the stairs, she could hear Mrs. Pruitt's voice, giving orders to the men carrying Garrett.

Once again, she prayed that he would be all right.

Chapter Thirty-seven

About four hours later, everyone was still waiting in the living room. The doctor had arrived several hours ago. He was still in the room with Garrett. Things didn't look very good.

Mrs. Pruitt had gone up to help the doctor. She made Jack promise to watch after Charlie. Dallas and Christian had returned from Broken Tongue just a few minutes ago. They were still in the barn, they hadn't reached the house yet. But it wouldn't take them long.

Charlie was sitting beside Jack on the settee. Both of them were tense. The last few hours had seemed like a week, the waiting was almost more than either one of them could stand.

Jack looked over at Charlie. He noticed the purple shadows beneath her eyes. He had known her most of her life, but for the first time she looked fragile. Wrapping an arm around her shoulders, he pulled her close, trying to give her strength. "You know Charlie girl," he said quietly, "That Garrett, he's strong and he's a fighter. He has an awful lot to live for. He'll pull through." He rubbed her arm, amazed at how cold she seemed, because it was a warm evening. He was just about to get up and go find a blanket to wrap around her, when the front door burst open. It was Dallas and Christian.

When they arrived at the barn, there was a ranch hand waiting to take care of their horses. After they handed him the reins, Dallas and Christian ran to the house. They had to check on Garrett.

Dallas threw the door open so hard, it bounced against the inside wall of the house, making a loud noise that echoed through the house. Christian was right behind him.

"How is he? We got here as fast as we could," Dallas said.

For once, when Dallas quit talking, Christian began, "We tried to hurry that crackpot sheriff up, but he was not to cooperative. The guys down at the barn said the doctor was still here." They were both talking so fast, Jack couldn't answer them.

Finally Jack butted in and began to talk, still keeping an eye on Charlie. "The doc is still up there with him. Bea is up there to. We ain't heard nothing yet. Bea has been coming in and out, getting more supplies, but that's about it." He glanced over at Charlie, noticing the color had completely left her face. She looked like she'd seen a ghost.

"Did you get to see him at all?" Dallas asked. "Where was he hit?"

Jack shook his head. "Nah, when I got here they already had him upstairs. From what I understand, he took two shots. One to the leg, and the other one to the chest." He felt Charlie flinch. He looked over at her, tears were slipping down her pale cheeks. He gathered her up in his arms, rocking her back and forth like a child. "He'll be all right Charlie girl. Like I told you before, he's a tough one." He just wished he could believe his own words. He had seen the extent of Garrett's injuries when he had gone upstairs to help Bea, before the doctor had arrived. They were bad, life threatening in fact.

Unfolding from Jack's embrace, Charlie stood. "I'm going to the kitchen for some coffee, would any of you like some?" she asked. Her features were drawn, worry lines had formed around her eyes and mouth. She looked like she had aged in the last few hours.

All three men answered at one time. "No thanks."

They watched from their seat as Charlie left the room. Jack waited until he knew for sure she was in the kitchen, out of hearing distance. "It looks bad boys, he took that blast to the chest almost point blank. He's lost a lot of blood." Looking toward the kitchen, making sure Charlie was still in there, after seeing no sign of her, he continued. "When Bea came down a while ago, she said the doctor wasn't sure if he could stop the bleeding. I guess he's still tryin'."

"I knew something was going to happen. Everything went to damn easy. We should have known McCuan wouldn't give up that easy." Christian had stood up, now he was pacing around the living room, like a caged cat. He was lethal looking.

"None of us could have guessed what that bastard was up to. He was crazy, has been ever since I knowed him." Jack was still sitting, watching the top of the stairs, wishing they would hear something. "While Charlie is gone, I need to talk to you boys. She didn't need to hear this." He looked back toward the kitchen, wanting to make certain she was still in there. "A while back Garrett gave me a letter in case something happened to him. He wanted it wired to his attorney in Tucson. First thing in the morning I want one of you to ride to Broken Tongue and see that it gets sent." He lowered his head, not wanting to face the possibility that Garrett wouldn't make it.

"We'll both ride in. We need to see that McCuan's body gets to the sheriff's office," Christian said. He stopped in front of Jack, his hands resting on his hips. "As soon as we find out if Garrett's going to make it, we'll go out and take care of that bastard Jones." After he was done talking, he continued

196

to pace back and forth, too nervous to sit down.

"Where is Gimpy's body anyhow? I was just kind of wonderin' where Jigger and the boys put him." Jack was trying to keep both young guns calm, but so far it wasn't working.

Dallas, who had been unnaturally quiet, finally piped up. "The sonofabitch is layin' out back of the barn with all the other horse shit. That's exactly where he's at." He crossed his arms over his chest, a serious look on his face. "I'll tell you something else, the bastard better be glad he's already dead, or I'd really make him hurt."

All three men nodded in agreement. They were so deep in thought, they didn't hear Charlie enter the room. She was standing just inside the living room.

"I can tell you one damn thing, if Garrett dies—" That was as far as Christian got, he was brought up short by a startled gasp.

It was Charlie.

She rushed into the living room, dropping down beside Jack. "Have you heard something since I was out of the room?" She was frantic, pulling at Jack's vest. "You've got to tell me. I have to know what's happened to him." She was clawing at his clothes, her voice growing louder and more hysterical with every word.

Christian and Dallas hurried over to help Jack. They were at a loss, they had no idea how to deal with a hysterical female. And judging by the look on Jack's face, they weren't alone.

"Come on Charlie girl, get hold of yourself. We haven't heard anything yet, and you've got to think about the baby." He was trying to calm her down, keep her from injuring herself or the baby. He was so busy trying to comfort Charlie, he didn't see the startled expressions on Dallas and Christian's face at the mention of a baby, or the huge grins that soon followed.

The minute Jack mentioned the baby, Charlie immediately settled down. She went limp against his chest, deep sobs racking her body. All the fight was gone. Jack stroked her hair, whispering to her. Christian and Dallas sat down, one on each side of Jack and Charlie. They were also telling her to relax.

The somber little group was so pre-occupied that they didn't hear the bedroom door open upstairs, and they didn't see the doctor descending the stairs. He had a haggard look on his face.

When the doctor reached the bottom of the stairs, he headed directly to the living room. He needed a strong drink. He walked into the living room, and the first thing he saw was Charlie, surrounded by Jack and two other men.

"Excuse me," he said, "Jack, I need some whiskey if you've got any." He looked worn out.

Charlie shot up from Jack's lap when she heard the doctor's voice. She started asking questions immediately. "How is he? Is he going to be all right?" She ran across the room, her face very pale. "You have to tell me the truth," she begged. She looked like a feather would knock her over any minute.

The doctor held up his hand, trying to slow the questions down. When that didn't work, he tried a different approach. "Charlie, Charlie, listen to me," he said, holding on to her arms. He was afraid she was going to faint. "If you promise me that you'll calm down, I'll tell you what I can. But you have to promise me that you'll calm down. Mrs. Pruitt told me that you think you're expecting a baby." He was leading her back over to the settee. Christian and Dallas following, Jack had gone to get the whiskey.

After sitting down, Charlie looked at the doctor, pleading with her eyes. "I promise," she said, so soft it almost sounded like the wind.

Waiting for Jack, the doctor settled down beside Charlie. He looked over her drawn features, making a quick assessment. She looked tired.

When Jack returned, he had a bottle of whiskey and a glass. He filled the glass and handed it to the doctor. The doctor drained his glass in one big gulp, and waited for a refill. After the whiskey hit his stomach, you could see him relaxing, but the others were in no mood for whiskey, they wanted news about Garrett.

"Doc Jenkins, is the boy going to be all right," Jack asked, almost as impatient as Charlie. He had voiced the question that was on everybody's mind.

Doc Jenkins took another big swallow before answering. "He's bad, no doubt about it. The wound in his leg is pretty bad, the bullet nicked the femur bone. I don't know if there is any bone fragments or not. It's a possibility that there isn't any, I hope." He stopped, rubbing the back of his neck, it was more a nervous gesture than one of fatigue. "Right now, he's not strong enough to do surgery on his leg, if I have to. The main thing right this minute is the wound in his chest. He lost a lot a blood. The bullet appeared to have struck him point blank. I finally managed to locate the bullet, and one thing you can be thankful for, it didn't do a lot of internal damage. I mean, no major organs were injured. I can tell you one thing, he's tough. Most men would have already given up, but not that one," he said, pointing upstairs. He pulled out his pocket watch, glancing at the hands, then put it away. "I'm going to get a few hours sleep, then I'll check on him again," he said. He picked up the glass of whiskey, and started to walk away when Charlie's voice stopped him.

"Doc, when will we know if he's going to be all right? I mean what do we need to watch for?" She was still sitting down, truth be known she probably wasn't able to stand.

Noticing her ashen features, Doc Jenkins told her some of the details, but not all of them. "I'd say the next twenty-four to forty-eight hours will probably be the worst. We'll have to watch for fever and infection most of all." He watched her sway on the seat, fighting to stay upright. "Little lady, I want you to get something to eat, then get some rest. If his condition changes, you'll be the first one to know about it. Now you get some rest, that's an order." He turned to Jack, Dallas and Christian. "You men are going to be in charge of making sure she gets her rest." When Jack and the boys didn't acknowledge, Doc Jenkins blurted out. "Is that clear?"

"Yes Doc," Jack said, looking at Dallas and Christian.

Charlie had one more question. "Doc, is it OK if I go up and see him, just for a minute. Then I promise to go lie down and rest." She had already made up her mind, she was going up there whether he said it was all right or not, it didn't matter to her.

Recognizing the look of defiance, Doc Jenkins agreed. "You can go up, but just for a minute." He turned and walked away, looking for the spare bedrooms.

Before Charlie went upstairs, she turned to Jack. "Jack, will you come with me? For the first time in my life, I'm afraid of what I might find."

When he nodded, she waited for him. She was holding his arm tight walking up the stairs. Each step seemed like a mile. When they reached the top, she tapped on the door. She smiled when she heard Mrs. Pruitt's voice call out. When Jack pushed the door open, she soon realized that she was not prepared for Garrett's condition. He looked more dead than alive. It was not long before the room started spinning, but she didn't remember hitting the floor, because everything had gone black before she fell.

Chapter Thirty-eight

The first twenty-four hours were touch and go. Garrett's fever had soared during the night. Mrs. Pruitt stayed busy trying to care for all of Garrett's needs. Jack was busy with Charlie, and the twins were taking care of the girls.

Dallas and Christian had returned from Broken Tongue with a message from William Reynolds, Garrett's attorney. He was on his way to the Circle Bar M.

Mr. Reynolds had explained in a wire that he needed to be here, no matter what happened to Garrett. Besides, he was a very good friend of Garrett's. He would be leaving on the stage from Tucson that very afternoon. If he encountered no bad luck, he estimated that he should arrive within seven days.

At the moment, Charlie was resting. She had been awake a good part of the night, against the doctor's wishes. With each passing hour, when Garrett's condition didn't improve, Charlie started showing signs of fatigue. She was physically and mentally worn out.

The upstairs guest room was small, and sparsely furnished, and the bed was too hard. Charlie was tossing and turning, not able to find a comfortable spot. She missed Garrett. After flopping over on her back, she realized she wasn't going to be able to sleep until Garrett was beside her.

Garrett. Just thinking about him made her smile. Never had she imagined that she would find a man like him. There was one thing that was troubling her, it was this legend thing. Several times she had heard Garrett's name associated with legend, even her pa had mentioned something about it before he was killed. But for the life of her she couldn't figure it out.

Looking at the clock on the nightstand, she soon discovered that she had been tossing and turning for about two hours. Deciding to check on Garrett, she rose slowly from the bed. She'd learned not to move too fast, it made her dizzy. But Doc Jenkins had assured her that was a normal part of pregnancy.

She placed a gentle hand on her stomach, smiling, thinking about the life growing inside her body this very minute. It was going to be a boy, she just knew it. He was going to be the spitting image of his father.

Tears gathered on the corner of her eyes. What if Garrett didn't survive. Doc had warned her several times that his wounds were bad. How could she go on without him? He had promised never to leave her, and he always kept his promises. After taking a few minutes to freshen up, she cracked the door open, checking the hallway in both directions. When she didn't see any sign of Jack or Doc Jenkins, she opened the door wider, walking out into the hallway, there was no sign of movement. She turned in the direction of their bedroom, where Garrett was at. She was determined to sit with him a while.

When she reached the door to their room, she hesitated, standing in the hallway with her head against the door. She dreaded opening the door, seeing Garrett in bed, unmoving and so pale. But it was something she had to do. Taking a deep breath, she gathered her courage, opening the door slowly, peeking inside. She found Mrs. Pruitt sitting in a rocking chair, with a blanket pulled up around her shoulders, sound asleep. Trying not to wake her, Charlie walked slowly across the bedroom floor. She stopped on the opposite side of the bed, close to Garrett.

The smile vanished from her face when her gaze settled on Garrett. He looked so pale, his skin was translucent, except for the color in his sunken checks. His fever still hadn't broken. She walked closer to the bed, sitting gently on the edge. She touched his forehead with the back of her fingers, and what she discovered was unexpected. He was warm, but it felt like his fever had gone down.

She looked around the room, trying to find the wash bowl and towels. After locating them, she carried them around the bed, placing them on the floor by her feet. She carefully wrung all the excess water from the towels, then bathed Garrett's heated face, memorizing every plane and angle of his handsome features. After a few minutes, she noticed the cool water seemed to be helping, the color wasn't as high in his cheeks. Hope surged within her, she decided right then and there, that she would bath him night and day, if that's what it took, no matter what. She was so busy caring for Garrett, she didn't notice Mrs. Pruitt's approving smile. When the older woman began to speak softly, it startled her, causing her to shake the bed.

"He seems to like you attention," Mrs. Pruitt said. She had been watching Charlie for the past few minutes, glad that she had finally come in. Garrett had been restless, calling out for Charlie.

Charlie couldn't take her eyes off Garrett. When she moved the bed, she saw him make a face. "Did you see him wrinkle his nose just then? He acted like it hurt him, when I moved the bed." She scooted closer, watching Garrett closely, searching for any movement. When there was none, she looked at Mrs. Pruitt, a shattered look on her face. "I really did see him move a little," she said quietly.

Mrs. Pruitt stood, stretching, trying to work some of the stiffness from her bones. She had sat in the rocker far too long. "If you're going to be here for a little while, I'm going to slip downstairs and get a fresh cup of coffee. I won't be long."

After Mrs. Pruitt left, Charlie found herself alone with her husband. He looked terrible. She picked up the towel and continued to bath his face and chest. Hoping it would bring his fever down. She slid the cool, damp cloth over this skin. "Garrett, can you hear me?" she asked, willing him to wake up. "That's OK, you don't have to answer me, I know deep down that you can hear every word." She poured some fresh water in the wash bowl, dipping the cloth again. "There's a thousand things I wish I had told you. But I can tell you later. The main thing right now is that you get better. Do you hear me?" She swallowed hard, trying to keep the tears from choking her. "I wish Pa hadn't shot you, I wish he had shot me instead. You're the only good thing that's ever happened to me." The tears were flowing freely down her cheeks now, but she didn't care. Leaning over, she lowered her head to his shoulder, loving the feel of his body. She had been unable to rest before, but after curling up next to him, she dozed off to sleep.

Jerking awake, she thought she heard a masculine voice. She realized it was Garrett, he was awake. She pushed to a sitting position, not believing her eyes. He really was awake, and he was talking to her in a slow, slightly slurred voice. It sounded wonderful!

"I'm sorry, what did you say?" She scooted closer, trying to hear every word. She was so excited, she couldn't sit still.

His lips were so dry, they hurt. He licked them, trying to moisten them. "What's the matter…wildcat. Has your…hearing gone?" he asked, pausing every few words.

"Nothin' wrong with my hearin'. You're the one that peers to be under the weather." She didn't want to blink, afraid it was all a dream, and she would wake up. "You scared the livin' life out a me Garrett. Don't ever get yourself shot again. I don't think my heart can stand it." She still wasn't certain about it yet, it was beating like a drum at this very minute.

"I heard what you…said. Wishing it had…been you." He closed his eyes, concentrating on filling his lungs with oxygen. "Have you…forgotten about my… daughter?" He was watching her, his eyes slightly glassy. He was trying to focus.

"No I haven't. And it's goin' to be a boy, just like his pa."

"Well discuss our daughter later, right now I'm going to have to rest. I'm really tired." His eyes closed again, his breathing wasn't quite as labored as before. "One more thing. Crawl up here beside me. I promise to behave myself." A smile tugged at the corner of his mouth, knowing the only bedroom activity he could handle right now, was sleeping. But it sure didn't hurt to dream about it.

"Behave yourself my ass. You can hardly keep your eyes open." Pulling the quilts back, she slid into bed beside him. This was her most favorite place to be in the whole world. Right before sleep claimed her, she heard the bedroom door open, and small footsteps padding across the wooden floor. When she opened her eyes, she found herself staring at Maddie. She thought her heart was going to break in half, the little girl had been crying, in fact, she still was.

"What's the matter Maddie?" she asked softly, trying not to wake Garrett.

Inching closer, the little girl looked at Garrett. "Is my brother going to die? Because if he is, I'm going to be really mad." Her little body was shaking, she was trying so hard to be brave. "He said he would always be here for me. He prom...promised," she cried.

Before Charlie could respond, Garrett spoke softly. "I'm only going to tell you both one...more time. I'm not...going anywhere." He became quiet, he looked like he had dropped off to sleep. When nobody moved, he opened his eyes, looking at Maddie. "Maddie, climb up here in bed with me and Charlie. Then maybe we can all get some rest."

Not needing a second invitation, the little girl climbed in next to Charlie. She snuggled down deep under the covers. It wasn't long before sleep claimed all three of them.

That was how Mrs. Pruitt and Doc Jenkins found them later. After seeing the little family sleeping peacefully, Doc announced that Garrett would make a full recovery. But Mrs. Pruitt already knew that, because Garrett was Charlie's miracle.

They pulled the door closed, going downstairs to give everybody the good news.

Several weeks later, Charlie and Garrett was sitting in the front porch swing. Garrett was on his way to making a full recovery, and Charlie was well on her way to motherhood.

Garrett had grown lean from his injuries, on the other hand, Charlie was starting to grow a little more plump.

Garrett couldn't keep his eyes off his wife, she took his breath away.

"Greenhorn, do you think Mr. Reynolds has made it back to Tucson yet? He's been gone about five days now." She looked at her husband's profile, if she lived to be a hundred, she would never get tired of looking at him.

Garrett looked out over the land, it was all theirs now. The Circle Bar M had officially been transferred two weeks ago, after William Reynolds had arrived. Garrett had been glad to see him. It had been a long time since he had last seen him. He was like a second father. He had been there for Garrett and Maddie anytime they needed him. He had left about a week ago, but not before he was sure all the necessary paperwork had been completed for the transfer of the ranch. He had given Charlie and Garrett all the details of the arrangement between James McCuan and Benjamin Steele.

They had also learned several details about James, from William. He had never been a very sociable person. That was why he had moved to New Mexico Territory. But the past had eventually caught up with him, but with James gone, things had already changed for the better.

Wrapping his arm a little tighter around his wife, Garrett pulled her closer. Things couldn't be better he thought. The ranch was doing well. Most of the hands had stayed on, except a few that was loyal to McCuan, and Jack was the new foreman, and it looked like he and Mrs. Pruitt might soon be getting married. Dallas and Christian was planning on staying around, they liked being part of a family. But every now and then, Christian still threatened to shoot Dallas for talking too much. The twins, Tristen and Austin, were still following the young guns around, hanging on every word. And the girls, Maddie and Taylor, were inseparable.

Maddie wasn't afraid of Garrett leaving her anymore, and Taylor still insisted that she was going to marry Dallas, although he swore she was just a silly little girl. It would be worth watching over the next few years, Garrett thought with a grin.

Garrett pulled Charlie closer, placing his hand on her slightly swollen middle. He just knew the baby was going to be a little girl, just like her mother. He must have had a silly look on his face, because Charlie started laughing.

"What are you laughing about?" he asked.

"I just remembered something. I've been aimin' to ask you for the past few weeks about something I heard." She twisted in the swing, pulling away from him. "I keep hearin' Dallas and Christian talkin' about 'Cold Steele', the legendary Marshall. Do you happen to know him?" She had grown serious, and she was waiting for an answer.

He started laughing, thinking about her reaction when she found out the truth. "As a matter of fact I do, sweetheart." he whispered. "I might have forgotten to tell you that you married a legend. You see, I'm Cold Steele." The look on her face made him roar with laughter, it was priceless.

Charlie grinned after the initial shock passed. "You might me Cold Steele to everybody else, but you'll always be greenhorn to me." She smiled, rising from the swing, pulling him to his feet. "I think it's time for you and me to go upstairs and rest. I'll go along with you, make sure you follow the doctor's orders."

Garrett pulled her close. "We'll go upstairs, but I doubt we'll get much rest," he whispered. He lowered his mouth to hers. The fire that passed between them was instant, just like it always was. The only thing different, it seemed to be growing stronger. When he raised his head, they walked through the door, holding hands, whispering like two young lovers.

Their love was the kind that lasted a lifetime.

Epilogue
Ten Years Later

There was going to be a wedding. All the arrangements and final preparations had been made. Most of the people from town and the surrounding ranches had shown up, it was quite a social event.

Taylor had finally worn Dallas down.

Charlie watched Jack walking down the aisle between the row of benches, proudly escorting Taylor. Charlie couldn't believe that her sister was old enough to be getting married, but she was, and she had grown into a fine young woman.

As the ceremony began, Charlie's thoughts wandered. A lot had happened over the last ten years.

Jack had retired. He and Mrs. Pruitt, well Mrs. Winsloe, still lived on the ranch. They were family, besides they loved seeing the children running around the ranch. The twins, Tristen and Austin, had gone back east to study. Now they were very successful businessmen. They had started their own company. Christian had taken over the cattle operation, after Jack had retired, and he was spending a lot of time with a young lady from town. And Maddie was engaged to the neighbor's son. They were supposed to be married in a few months. Garrett had frowned at the idea of Maddie getting married. He said she was too young, but Charlie had convinced him differently.

Thinking about her husband always brought a smile to her face. She was sitting beside him right now, holding their youngest child, a boy named Jack. He was actually their fourth child. She had given birth to four children over the last ten years, and she was almost positive the fifth one was on the way. But she hadn't told Garrett yet.

She looked down the long bench, checking on her other children.

Their first child had been born about ten months after they were married. His name was Benjamin, after Garrett's father. He was the spitting image of Garrett, in actions and appearance. Two years later, she had given birth to twin daughters, Lora and Sara. They were just like their mother. They were pistols. And little Jack was two years old. He was a lot like his older brother.

Feeling a nudge in the ribs, she looked up at Garrett. "What put that smile on your face wildcat?" he asked, looking down at his wife. She was more beautiful now than ever. Four children had added a little more shape over the last ten years, but it only made her more appealing to him.

"I was just thinking what a fine family we have," she whispered.

"That we do wildcat. I sure hope that Taylor and Maddie find the same kind of love that we have." He was lost in the depths of her dark eyes, they were glowing with love.

She looked up at him shyly. "They will. Taylor and Maddie have found their own legends. And we both know that miracles happen every day, but especially when along comes a legend."

Garrett grasped her hand in his, bringing it to his lips, kissing the back of her hand. They listened to the rest of the ceremony, knowing that their love would only grow stronger.

Printed in the United States
16761LVS00004B/259